Debris

By L.M. Brown

Ink Smith Publishing

www.ink-smith.com

For my husband, Matias,

With all my love

"A haunting story about friendship, loss and family secrets. No easy answers here, but Brown makes you care about her people. A powerful book."

- Susan Breen, author of the *Maggie Dove* mystery series

"L.M. Brown gives a fresh new voice to family struggle and family loss with an edgy and mysterious story about broken connections and important bonds that can't be torn apart. Her setting is both eerie and inviting and her characters come to life in their search for answers about a past that hovers with dangerous discoveries about the present."

- Maria Flook, author of *Invisible Eden* and *Mothers and Lovers*

I love those spirits
that men stand off and point at,
or shudder and hood up their souls—
those ruined ones.

- Lola Ridge (1873)

Chapter One

From Eugene's house the sea was audible and across the garden's stone wall the dark surface lit by stars was still as glass. It had started to snow in the early hours of the morning while the family slept. Six-year-old Ines was the first to wake. She scrambled out of bed and down the narrow hall. It was still dark. Behind closed blinds the white dots of snow landed on the window and melted on touch. Ines did not see the snow. With her teddy in hand she was going straight for her brother's room. Her parent's door was open to let out the slit of darkness and maybe the sound of breathing if she thought to stand and listen. But she did not. Her brother's closed door beckoned and she clasped the handle and pushed. She tiptoed to his bed and said his name. The second time she voiced it she heard the familiar ruffle and his question, "Are you okay?"

Since she was a toddler, she'd gone to him at night. "Was it a nightmare?" he said when she pulled at his sheets. She nodded and clung to his hand in an attempt to pull herself up.

The bed was high with drawers at the base. Some mornings he'd sigh and say, "Do you want a story?" She would nod and in the dim half-light he'd share the tales he'd read. From him she'd heard about the Selkies and the Faeries. But on that final morning, when the snow dissolved on the window and the sea moved back and forth in a constant moan, Ines said she was scared. Andre told her there was nothing to be afraid of.

"How do you know?" Ines asked.

"Ines, go to sleep." She slid in beside him for the last time.

Their mother found them lying together. It was not only the affection that stilled Usao at the door, but the fact that her children looked like twins while they slept with their dark hair and sallow skin. When they were awake, Andre's brown eyes glinted with mischief and his body was a coiled wire. While Ines with her bright blue eyes and timidity liked to sit in corners and watch everything that was going on. She was a quiet child, who tiptoed around the house and could often be heard whispering to her dolls.

When Ines was born, their mother was so frightened that Andre would hurt her that for the first forty-eight hours at home she refused to get out of bed with Ines. Six-year-old Andre had waited patiently at the bedroom door to see his sister. He might have been kept away indefinitely if not for his father Eugene. Eugene was an imposing man, broad and tall, a CEO of a publishing and trade company he cut a daunting figure in his suit. He'd been concerned with his wife's refusal to rise, but after hearing Usao say. "No, Andre, she's too small," in a shaky fearful voice, he realized what she was doing.

He understood his wife's fears Usao had been an only child, she thought she should shield her daughter, but it incensed him too. "He's her brother. You don't need to protect her from him."

So Andre was allowed to climb up on the bed to his sister.

"Did you tell her about the faeries yet?" he said and Usao eased. She told him no, maybe he could tell her, so he did. Lying beside his baby sister, he whispered about the little people who lived under the hills.

Later, when Usao watched her children together, she'd often wonder if the hours she'd kept them apart had brought them closer.

****

The children slept late that morning. It was still snowing and the ground was covered by a white sheet by the time Eugene's sister, Michelle, and her children arrived later that day. Since Andre was born, every Sunday the two families had dinner together. Michelle was older than her brother Eugene by three years. Both had a stoic air of independence from being left orphans as young adults. Whenever his sister stepped into the room, Eugene's face softened and his shoulders eased. Usao had often joked that if he reached old age, he would still define himself as Michelle's younger brother. He'd never argued. Michelle was one of the only people he could relax completely with. His wife too, of course, but his love for her was so great that he never forgot himself in her presence. Usao heightened everything when she walked into the room. Beside her, he was still the lovesick teenage boy who'd waited for her arrival every summer.

"I don't like driving in the snow," Michelle said when she was taking her coat off in the hall. She wore her usual jeans and sweater. She'd worked as a secretary and helped put her brother through college, but she'd given up work eight years ago when Martha was born and had never worn a skirt since. Her two-year-old, Jamie, hugged her legs.

"I don't like driving period," Usao said, and Michelle laughed and said if it was Usao driving, they'd still be in Dublin.

Michelle called for Martha to wait for her brother and tutted about her daughter's ease at ignoring her. Martha was slender and quick on her feet and before Michelle could do anything Martha was through the kitchen door and out the back. Michelle picked Jamie up and followed her daughter. The kitchen window looked out onto the back garden, a long rectangular area of grass made shiny by the sprinkling of snow. A low stone wall marked its border and on the right corner was a Windmill Palm tree. Eugene had not believed that any could grow in the Irish climate, but Usao had been adamant. She was from a small town near Madrid called Guadalajara, which was surrounded by dry sandy hills and a few thin trees dotted here and there. It was the palm trees she missed the most. The tree had survived eight years and was growing strong.

2

Debris

Usao's black curly hair was tied back. The greasy apron did nothing to deter her loveliness. The smell of garlic and roast made Michelle take deep appreciating breaths as the two women looked out the back window at their children. Thirteen-year-old Andre was holding Ines' hand and nodding at something Martha was saying. Ines was frowning. Her little body leaned against Andre. He said something to her and her frown eased.

Michelle became aware of her brother's presence behind her when Jamie buried his head on her shoulder to hide. Jamie was a quiet two-year-old with fair hair. He was also Michelle's shadow. She could put him at the back door and tell him to go out and play but he would stay beside her with a disgruntled face that had often made them laugh.

"He's like an old man," Michelle's husband, Ron, liked to say.

Eugene said, "Ron didn't get finished then?"

Michelle groaned, "This doesn't feel right does it?" Ron was doing a job for the council, finishing kitchens for houses that were supposed to have been ready last week. He had to have the job done in two days. The children's shouts filtered through the open back door along with the cold and Michelle was raging that Ron had to miss a Sunday. Since the loss of their parents, Eugene and Michelle had not missed one Sunday together. Usao had been there from the beginning. A year before the accident she'd decided to go to college in Dublin. Ron had come into the fold within months of the accident. Before the children were born, the couples would spend the day in the city or take drives around the Wicklow Mountains. After the children they started to take turns cooking. Michelle liked it better now, with the warmth of the houses, the easy entry and gliding around rooms and the children running towards each other. Sundays enveloped her in warmth. It was like crawling under a warm duvet after an exhausting day. To have Ron missing left a draft and inability to fully relax. It annoyed her.

Usao gently touched Michelle's arm to ease her. In the months to come, Michelle would think of the brief touch and she would hate that it had not been appreciated fully. She'd yearn to stand in that kitchen again with her sister-in-law and brother, and have another chance to watch Usao's hand find the small of Eugene's back. He glanced at Usao with a smile and asked if there was anything that needed to be done. Usao shook her head and they watched each other for a moment. The two had a way of forgetting anyone else in the room for seconds at a time. Eugene turned away and Usao took a breath as if she'd been touched. Without Ron, this intimacy had irritated Michelle. But in the years to come she'd try and find the moment again and again.

Whenever Michelle thought of that day, no matter how painful it was to remember how they'd been in the kitchen; it was easier than looking outside and thinking of the children. Still she was revisited with

3

images of them. There would be flashes of Andre lifting Ines up, and twirling her around, and the three children digging through the thin layer of snow, looking for insects' maybe. Michelle hadn't thought to ask, she'd taken for granted their cheerful adventure. At one stage, Andre glanced towards the kitchen window. His face was open and smiling. He waved. Jamie was opening and closing kitchen drawers at that stage. Michelle told him to stop making such a racket. Usao laying the table said it was okay, it would be noisier in a few minutes once Eugene got the others inside. Michelle was too distracted to wave back to Andre. She didn't know that she should hold onto his happiness, that already it had started to ebb away. Usao lifted Jamie up and kissed his cheek. She laughed when Jamie looked towards his mother for escape. "He's a real Irish man," Usao said and they laughed.

Michelle put her son in the high chair. The kids came running inside and were hurdled towards the bathroom to wash their hands. Usao had her apron off and was standing by the sink. Grey light spilled from the window towards her. She seemed distracted as if she was thinking of something, and whatever it was brought a smile onto her face.

The following evening, when Michelle received the phone call from Bray, this image of Usao's lovely face would come back to her, and she'd wish she'd asked what Usao was smiling about.

****

On that fateful night, Eugene didn't look up from his papers when Usao told him she was going to the village. Work was busy, so she'd offered to drive for their Saturday night take-way a mile and a half away. Her son had asked to keep her company. Of that night, Ines remembers the crackle of paper under the crayons and the warmth of the fire, but there was no comfort in that memory. It is a prelude to the shrill sound of the phone and the strangeness in her father's voice. "Where?" She looked up from her picture. Sometimes she thinks the picture was one of the family, hands joined together, her father a distant figure in the background and her mother bigger than them all. Other times she believes it was the sun, round and yellow and blinding. Her father had risen by the time she looked up. He had started to shake. He dialed their neighbor's number. "Denise," he said, "There's been an accident, can you come?" His hands were trembling. Ines' mouth had dropped open, she might have cried if the surprise hadn't been so great. She saw the moment her father started to peel away. It was like watching something wither. When he went for the door, she said, "Daddy?"

He stopped to tell her that Denise would be here soon. Ines doesn't remember what happened in the interlude, if her father ran straight out and the banging door kept her stiff with fright or if he waited for Denise to arrive. In any case, Denise appeared at the door, just as Ines noticed her father's favorite pen had fallen onto the ground close to his chair. Denise, a small nervous woman in her forties, picked up Eugene's phone and after a moment, she said, "Michelle, Eugene told me to call."

****

Michelle and her husband Ron lived on the other side of Dublin in the house Michelle and Eugene had grown up in. Every summer the family used to take excursions to the sea. As children, taking the train from their housing estate with the constant bustle of neighbors to the beach was like going to a different world.

That night they made the journey in silence. Michelle kept replaying Denise's worried voice. "Eugene told me to call."

"What is it?" Michelle had asked, though her blood had already turned cold. She knew phone calls like this. "There's been an accident. He wants you to come out to Ines. I don't know anything more."

Michelle called Eugene on his car phone straight away.

"I don't know anything," he said.

Michelle wanted to ask who was in the car with Usao and who Eugene had spoken to. She wanted to know where he was going. If she could get the facts, maybe it would all make sense? But she couldn't say anything.

She didn't feel Ron's reassuring hand on her or hear the low droning of the radio when they were pulling into the house. The lights were on in the living room but there were no cars. Michelle started to tremble. She must have known under that dark sky with the streetlights distant and intermittent, and the sounds of the ocean gruff and cruel, that there would be no answers to this. Ines was still sitting on the floor in the study. When she saw Michelle at the door, she started to cry.

****

In the early hours, Eugene came into the house with Andre beside him. A wool blanket was wrapped around Andre and his face looked haggard and pale. Ines had refused to go to bed. She'd fallen asleep on the couch. Michelle had fallen asleep beside her with the lights still on. Ron must have gone to lie down in one of the rooms, though Michelle couldn't remember. In any case he wasn't present when Michelle saw her brother. His entry had been stealthy, the click of the front door quiet, the steps light. Eugene didn't want to wake anyone and have to speak about what happened. He wished with all his heart that he was alone, without his son and daughter or his sister. But Ines stirred and sat up.

"Daddy," she whispered and lurched off the couch. She managed to escape Michelle's feathery grasp.

"Daddy," Ines said again. He looked down at her as if he hadn't noticed her darting approach. Her dark hair was long and thick down her back, her eyes wide.

"Where's Mama?" Ines said.

Eugene's mouth moved, and Michelle remained immobile. Her body was bigger than the couch, gaining weight every second without Usao's appearance. "Mammy's gone," Eugene said and Ines started to cry. Michelle stood and said her brother's name, but he shook his head. Tears were running down his face. Andre was beside him, but they were no longer holding hands. The boy was like an animal trying to hide. His small body shook and trembled, as he leaned towards the man.

"Donde?" Ines shouted. Her father took her in his arms.

"Donde esta Mama?" Ines cried.

"Oh God," Eugene said. He looked as if he might fall and didn't fight when Michelle plucked Ines from his hands. There was brief resistance. Her skinny arms reaching for her father before she became engulfed in Michelle's warmth. She let her aunt hold her in an embrace Eugene hadn't been capable of. Andre, red eyed and pale refused to look Michelle in the eye. His head stayed close to his father's hip. Eugene's hand went to his son, but Michelle had the feeling that it was automatic gestures more than a need to hold him close, or maybe it was how she remembered it after Eugene tried to give Andre away.

"What's happened?" Ron said from the living room door and Eugene was unable to look at his brother-in-law. He was just another person Eugene wanted gone. They were crowding him and he had no idea why he wasn't pulling the place asunder and screaming for everyone to get the fuck away from him. On the journey home from the hospital he couldn't understand how his body refused to do what his heart wanted and he wasn't driving headlong into a tree, or into a ditch. Although his son was in the car with him, it seemed more than this, a natural inbuilt mechanism that he couldn't go against and hated.

Ron led them from that room. Without him they would have stood there all night, not knowing how to carry on. In the kitchen Ron made tea. He started to make sandwiches for the children and Michelle wanted to shout, "What are you doing?"

She wanted to grab the knife from his hands and throw it in the sink, "Don't act normal. This isn't normal."

But the children kept her quiet. Ines nibbled on the bread, before abandoning her sandwich and lying against her aunt. Andre sat huddled in his blanket, staring at the black night on the other side of the kitchen window, as though he longed to run out there. It was near morning when he fell asleep. He had refused to move from his father's side and sat hunched up on the kitchen chair. When Michelle brought Ines to bed the room was dimly lit and the girl had clung to her and asked when her mother was coming back. Instead of answering, Michelle slipped into bed with her and held her close.

Debris

The two slept together, while in the kitchen Andre had folded into himself and held his tears. He had no right to cry. To his uncle's questions of hunger or tiredness he gave a quick shake of his head. His father was a statue beside him, unreachable. All night, Andre waited for his father to ask what happened. He would have crumpled with the memory of his mother's laughter and the fall of her face, but in those first hours before the truth got lodged too deeply inside him, he might have told his father what he had done and not become so lost.

Eventually Andre fell asleep. Eugene made no motion to bring the boy to his room, nor did he move when Ron decided to lift Andre to bed. He was still sitting at the kitchen table, his tea cold before him when Ron went to sleep on the couch.

****

Andre's best friend was a curly haired boy who lived in a two-story house down the road. His mother was a lawyer. The father's employment was as Usao said, "Something to do with finances," though Dolan Hastings had explained his job to her numerous times.

When he came with his son the day after the accident he was dressed in a dark suit and appeared nervous. His hand was on his son's shoulder, which seemed for his benefit rather than the boy's. "I'm so sorry," he said the moment the door opened. He was a narrow man with tired green eyes and a thin mouth. His hair was curly once but was now going bald. Eugene accepted his hand. He'd answered the door in a daze. There had been the phone calls to Usao's parents in Spain. The moment Sophie heard a terrible moan came from her and she started to cry. It must have been seconds before Alejandro grabbed the phone from his wife, but it felt like years. Alejandro refused to believe it was the truth. "There's been a mistake," he'd repeated over and over. Eugene imagined Alejandro a small solidly built man standing stiff in their sunny hall staring at nothing, while Sophie would have drifted into their back kitchen in a daze. In the months to follow she would begin to wander around the narrow streets of her town looking for her daughter. Alejandro would wake to find her side of the bed empty and he would not be able to keep his wife from falling into a world where her daughter still lived. But that day it had been him who insisted that this was a mistake. He said Eugene didn't know what he was talking about and needed to go back to the hospital and see Usao. Alejandro begged until he was silenced by Eugene's tearful plea to stop.

Michelle found Eugene on the couch afterwards, staring at his hands like an old man falling into dementia. He'd seemed not to know himself anymore. "It's my fault," he'd said when she stood before him.

"You can't think like that," Michelle had told him.

His hands had been facing upwards on his knees, his fingers had moved in and out in a weak fist and Michelle had to fight the urge to still them.

"I hope its okay," Dolan said now, "David wanted to see Andre. I probably should have called. I didn't know what to do."

"It's okay," Eugene said. His neighbor noticed how pale his face was and though Eugene looked at him, he felt as if Eugene barely registered their presence. When Eugene stepped aside, the father told David to go on, "I'll wait in the car."

"You don't have to," Eugene said. The snow had lost any whiteness. A scurry of rain had made it a dirty slush. It was cold, Eugene felt the chill on his face and hands and saw how dark the day was, a dull heavy metallic grey. A distant sound of traffic and David's father was walking back to his car that was parked outside the low wall. Eugene felt a tug in his gut, an idea that he should say something, call the man back and offer him some coffee. They'd spoken before, hadn't they? During the birthday parties with the balloons and clowns and the cake there'd been chats in the back garden while Eugene barbecued and other times while the sons played, but it was like grasping falling leaves in autumn. The instances were so small; they were gone before he could feel anything for it. The man was in the car before Eugene could think of a single thing to say. He closed the front door.

****

Andre's room was in darkness. His figure huddled under the covers. He couldn't get small enough, legs were pressed against his chest and his warmth filled the space around his head. The door opened slowly and Andre thought it was Ines and wished he could disappear. She'd come to him already this morning. He'd woken to her beside him. There had been so little light, a slow dawning grey had peeked in from the gap in the curtains but it had been enough to see the brightness of her eyes. She'd pulled at his covers and he'd woken to her face and felt a terrible pain. She had the same bright eyes as their mother and when Andre looked into them he saw his mother laughing, and he was sure Ines knew what he had done. She of all people had the ability to reach deep inside him and he was so afraid that she might hate him. She'd tried to get into his bed and he'd jumped up and said, "No, you can't." She was holding her teddy, orange fur with sweet brown eyes and a faded tired smile. He saw her grip tighten when he told her to leave him alone. He had never spoken to her like that, but the shame was nothing compared with the fear.

"Por favor," she'd said.

He'd shouted for her to go away. "Leave me alone, go away!"

Michelle had rushed into the room and turned on the light. "What's going on Andre?"

Debris

She'd picked up the tearful girl.

"I want to be left alone," Andre said and for a moment Michelle looked at him. She might have thought of reprimanding him and telling him that he didn't need to treat his sister that way, but she'd softened and her pity angered Andre further, because no one had an idea what he'd done. It would have been better to be screamed at and to feel his father's fists on his body, than to have Michelle's soft gaze and his father's silence.

"Andre?" The voice was not Ines'.

Still Andre didn't move.

He felt the weight on the side of his bed. "Hey." Andre knew David's voice and he closed his eyes against it, squeezing so hard it hurt.

While outside his room, the clocks had stopped. The Grandfather clock in the hall, the clock on the mantelpiece in the living room with the small face in a wooden design, and the large clock over the door in the kitchen all read 6:35.

****

Andre stayed in bed for hours after David left. He saw his mother's profile against the steering wheel, remembered the shake of his hands as he pulled the hair back from her face, the blood, the pale skin. He shivered and cried because he was afraid of his mother then.

He rose because his father came in for him and told him lunch was ready. His father took the blanket off him and said, "Come on Andre," and he followed the man up the hallway to the kitchen where sandwiches had been laid on the table. Michelle was there with Ines. Ron had gone home to their children. Martha and Jamie had spent the night with a neighbor. The wake was in three days.

Andre and Ines were told that their mother would be laid out in the living room, so they could give their final goodbyes. Andre wasn't sure what that meant but the thought brought a piercing pain to his belly. His grandparents were arriving that evening.

A quiet had descended on the house that would never fully leave, no matter how loud the television or the voices. It was as if the house had entered another world. They were now down under the hills with the fairies, hiding in a hollow, dark place. Andre could hardly hear the sea, even with the door opened it seemed distant from them now. Every so often Andre would go to the bathroom and step cautiously to the mirror with his heart thumping, the sound a deep resonating beat in his ears and he would look at his reflection, expecting to see some change. Smaller eyes maybe, or pointed ears, or a different color to his skin. He'd read the stories about Changelings, babies being exchanged by the faeries. He'd often wondered where the human babies were taken or if the faeries hadn't exchanged them at all, but cast some spell to bring a change, to signal out this human as bad luck. And wasn't he bad luck? Yet he found no change

9

or mark, though sometimes he would lean towards the mirror and study his reflection for so long he was sure there was something different under the surface.

6:35. He first noticed they had all stopped because of the silence of the Grandfather clock, and then he'd gone from the hall, to the living room, to the kitchen where he saw his mother's profile in the pale face of the clock and felt her presence in the stillness and deep quiet.

****

The house was full of murmurs. She lay in the living room; Andre and Ines were brought in by their father. Silent, his father had a tight grasp on Andre's hand before he was let go and had to step up to the coffin himself. It wasn't her, that's what he wanted everyone to know. The figure before them with the pale face and straight mouth wasn't his mother and that knowledge sat deep inside him and made him want to bury his face in his father's stomach. Ines was crying. Their grandparents sat on stools by the wall. They'd hugged the children fiercely and let them go just as brutally. They had not spoken. The clock read 6:35. No-one had said anything about it, though Andre had caught his father looking at the still hands of the clock and there was a heat in his eyes that made him imagine his father throwing the clock out the window. "Say goodbye," someone said, but Andre would not.

In the kitchen, he stopped breathless from his need to get away. There were people standing by the sink, dark suits and coats. Michelle was by the door in black pants and a blouse. Her eyes were red from crying. There were sandwiches and cakes on the tables. Chairs pulled out, feet coming from under them.

"You need to open the door to let her out," an elderly neighbor said. She was sitting at the table, wearing a black hat and coat. She held a cup in her hands. Her face was wrinkled and her blue eyes bright. "To let who out?" Andre asked and she smiled and shook her head. To Michelle, she said, "She needs to be freed," and Andre thought of his real mother, not the woman in the coffin, but the woman who was light on her feet and whose skin shone. It was easy to imagine her flying away and he wanted that woman to stay with them. He cried out when Michelle went for the back door, but it was too late. The cold drifted in and a part of him drifted out into the night sky with the stars and his Mammy who must have been happier now when she was not tied in these rooms with the clocks and unfamiliar faces. He knew at that moment while he stared at the darkness into which she had fled that he would not stay in this house without her and suffer the guilt brought from Ines's soft trust.

Chapter Two

"Boy Sets Fire to School"

The Bray People – October 26, 1987

The secondary school fire that forced an evacuation of students and teachers was caused by a thirteen-year-old boy who was playing with a lighter, officials have said.

Monday morning, smoke filled St. Mary's school and prompted the evacuation of one-hundred-fifty students. Fire officials reported that they were called around 10 a.m. and that the fire was extinguished by 10:30 a.m. The students were able to return to the school just after 11 a.m.

Tuesday, Nigel Meehan, principal of the school, confirmed that the fire was caused by a second-year boy playing with a lighter. He said the boy first ignited some material in the assembly hall.

"It didn't cause much damage to the school, the hall floor was scoured and there was a lot of smoke," Meehan said. He said the only real cost will be paying for the fire extinguisher residue to be removed. The student who started the fire admitted to his mistake after their return to class. The boy was sent to the principal's office and his father was called. He apparently took the lighter from home.

"The fact that he admitted to the deed makes me comfortable that he wasn't acting out in anger against teachers or fellow students; he didn't have intentions to burn the school down."

Meehan said the student was suspended for the week and a hearing would take place with the school authorities to determine further action, if any.

****

Principal Meehan was a small man with intense navy eyes and stubby hands. His hair was receding and his forehead was broad, which made his gaze remarkable, like sea pools in a desert. "I didn't mean to," Andre said and for a moment he wondered if it was true. The fire when it started had shocked him and he'd run out of the hall and closed the door with the futile hope that the fire might fizzle out alone.

Meehan nodded to the seat opposite him. The walls in his office were dark compared to his bright classroom and it made Andre feel small. While Meehan phoned his father, Andre stared out the window at the empty playground. The day was bright but there were patches of clouds starting to move towards them. He didn't know how long Meehan had been watching him when he finally turned from the window. Meehan's tie was loose and his eyes looked tired. He asked Andre how the fire started.

"I was playing," Andre said, and uttering the word made him feel raw. Playing sounded wrong coming from him. Meehan nodded. He was known for his silences, which was worse than any berating and beating because it pulled things out of the children by making them squirm in discomfort and talk. Andre had lost the ability to talk, but he had an urge to cry, not from Meehan's steady stare or the notion of his father's imminent arrival, but from the idea of Meehan throwing the word 'play' back at him. "What were you playing?" Meehan might have asked and Andre wouldn't have been able to answer. Meehan might have pointed out that in the last months he'd rarely seen Andre doing anything but wander around the school and cause fights. It wasn't the first time Andre had sat in this office. At least once a week, he'd been sent in with a bloody nose and a ripped uniform and he'd sat rigid and stiff and made no comment when detention was given out over and over. Now Andre was huddled in his chair and nothing like the boy who'd stolen the lighter fluid and hidden it in his school bag. He'd imagined he'd be standing when his father came into the room and he would tell him he caused the fire because he wanted to live in his aunt's house, but when his father walked in the door, Andre cowered. His father was too big for the chair beside Andre, too big for this sparse office, and the school, and the house they lived in.

"Andre?" his father said. Andre mumbled that he was sorry. His father nodded. His jaw was tight, but his soft gaze surprised Andre and made him feel like reaching out to the man. "I was only playing," he said. His father's gaze hardened. He shook his head and Andre wanted to take those words back and say that wasn't true. He wanted to say when he went to the shed for the lighter fluid he'd seen his mother. He'd known where the fluid was because last year he'd followed her to the shed on Bonfire night and she'd put the fluid and lighter back in its place. "This summer we'll light a fire on the beach," she'd said then, but last week she'd said nothing. She'd only smiled at him and afterwards he felt cold and numb, like when he and David stuck pins into each other after being in the snow. He didn't cry and this alone made him wonder if he'd really seen her.

He wanted to say that he'd lied the night of the accident. From the side of the road he'd screamed that they'd been driving too fast and his father had lifted him and held him tight as if he might squeeze the lie out of him. Andre wanted the lie squeezed from him now. He wanted to tell the truth, but he'd forgotten how.

"People could have gotten hurt," his father said. Andre nodded and knew his father was thinking of Ines in her small desk at school and how she wandered around after Andre at home.

His father said little to the idea of Andre's suspension. He thanked the principal for not taking further action. He didn't say that Andre would not be coming back to school after the week was up. Decisions had been made since the fire. His father had called Michelle and asked if Andre could stay there for a while. In the last year, Andre had fought to go to Michelle's. When he'd first met the new live-in-nanny Ursula, he'd told his aunt that he was too old for that crap. Ursula was in her fifties and had wide shoulders, arms and hips. Her short hair was grey. She had kind hazel eyes and the few times she managed to get close enough, he'd suffered through the fiercest hug he'd ever known.

"What about Ines?" Michelle had asked and he'd answered by saying, "Ines can have Ursula. I want to live with you."

What had Michelle said when Eugene finally relented. Had she been silent on the phone from the surprise? Had she said yes, of course, or had she asked Eugene why on earth he would take Andre from Ines?

In the car, with his clothes smelling of smoke and his head sore, he met his father's gaze in the rear-view mirror and his father said, "It's what you want, isn't it?"

Andre had no idea what he wanted anymore.

****

Ines watched Andre fold clothes neatly, so unlike a young boy. His precision was bred from his mother. She knew he was going to Michelle's for a few days and she must have known about the suspension, because she was not alarmed that he was going and she wasn't. So easy to explain it now, "You have school, Andre doesn't."

But she asked why he was bringing so many clothes. He was moving quickly, filled with nervous energy that made him afraid to sit still. He had wanted so much to go, but he hadn't realized how hard it would be to have his father agree to his leaving. All day he'd felt the need to cry and it occurred to him now and again that it was right that he should feel so bad. It was his fault his mother crashed the car; his fault the house in Bray was so quiet and sad. If he left, they might get some part of the happiness back. He shrugged, unable to look Ines in the eye. She was so sweet it hurt him to look at her. Ursula was hovering around the house. She'd argued with Eugene. "You can't send him away," she'd said and she'd followed him into the study. Her voice issued from there like a train going through a tunnel. She was unafraid of Eugene, and in turn Eugene only vaguely listened to her. When she stood at Andre's door and saw him packing, her face was red with temper. "You'll have to go to school there," she told him. "Do you really want that Andre, to have to start somewhere new?"

He told her, "Yes, that was what I want," when in reality he hadn't thought of school until his father told him that he couldn't have his cake and eat it too. "We're meeting the principal tomorrow," he'd told Andre.

"Are you coming back?" Ines asked Andre in his bedroom.

He nodded without looking at her.

****

The principal of Andre's new school was tall and thin with a bush of red hair. From across his desk, he regarded Andre with a look that endeavored to peel layers of the boy. Andre kept his head down. He didn't like Mr. Cullin's bright eyes, or the way his father had shaken his hand and thanked him for seeing them at such short notice. He didn't like the school either with the tiled corridors and the dark grey walls. It was before 8:00 a.m. The grounds of the school were quiet, though teachers had started to arrive and there was a sprinkle of laughter and the shutting of doors.

"I won't tolerate any messing," Mr. Cullin said after the introduction. His voice was soft, almost feminine.

For the first couple of weeks, Mr. Cullin watched Andre like a hawk. He saw him walking around alone a lot. Sometimes he was with two other boys, Ronan and Pete, whom Andre seemed to tolerate more than anything else. In the classroom Andre was quiet. His days of fighting and lighting fires were over. There was nothing to fight for and there was nowhere else to run to. Instead he moved inward, so no one, not even Ronan, whose smart answers would have the class rolling in laughter, reached him.

At home, things were no different. Sometimes Martha could drag Andre out to play or go for a walk, her persistence tough enough to break him down. Other times he would be pulled outside by the sound of a football game in progress on the green in front of the house. Then Andre would wait on the sidelines until he was asked to play. Communication between him and the others consisted mostly of nods and pats on the back. The locals wondered about the new boy, thought him strange and maybe a little slow. The ones who would have liked to form a friendship with Andre would walk to him, nod and shuffle their feet, but be unable to pierce the silence that surrounded him. Even the local bully, Henry Morgan, fifteen and large-boned, who did not tire from shouting abuse at the people he had grown up with was wary of Andre. The first week, he'd gotten no response when he'd shoved Andre. "What's your problem? You don't say a fucking word. Are you dumb or what?"

Ronan had stood up for Andre then. "Leave him alone," he'd said and got a chase around the field for the effort, while Andre had felt nothing but heaviness in his limbs.

Debris

On his fourth week, Andre came home from school to see Eugene's grey Mercedes with the black leather seats parked outside Michelle's house. Usao had liked her Golf that had ended up crashing into a stone wall. The driver's side caved in like paper in a toddler's hand. Before the accident, they had always driven the Golf to Michelle's house. The Mercedes was put away for weekends with the suits and ties, and Eugene would drive Usao's car and she would relax with her shoes off and her feet up. To Andre it felt wrong to have his father's car parked in the housing estate. He had never lived in a housing development like this before. The car looked conspicuous and arrogant, and all Andre wanted to do was disappear. The grey hood sparkled in the sun. Above Andre was a blue sky and in one of the houses a baby's cry issued from the open window. Andre's bag was heavy on his back and his father's car was pointed towards home, so Andre imagined his father driving around the cul-de-sac at the end of the row of houses so the car would be facing the right way. For some reason, this gave him hope.

Martha usually ran out to greet him, but she wasn't there that day. She may have been at a friend's house, or it's possible that Andre left school early and hoped to find the house empty and have a few moments of quiet when he could forget that this was not his home. He hadn't considered how out of place he would feel in his aunt's house. His mother had told him about cuckoos once and it had fascinated him that the other birds could not see the difference from this huge egg to their own small one. "Nature works like that sometimes," his mother had said and at seven Andre had told her that he didn't think it was fair, but in Michelle's, he'd lain awake at night wishing he could be as tough-skinned as those intrusive birds.

Andre's father visited often during the weekend with Ines, but never during the week and expectation made Andre on the verge of tears. It felt like a torrent rising in his belly, but he didn't trust it, because in front of his father the feeling would grow still and morose.

"Do you want to come home with us today?" his father had asked Andre the previous Sunday and Andre had shaken his head. For a moment, he'd felt his father study him. They'd been in the living room watching football and Andre had wanted his father to take the choice from him, to stand and say, "I'm sick of this nonsense." Andre had felt tense with the possibility, but Ron came in asking for the score and the moment was shattered. Andre was starting to hate Sundays and the forced get-togethers where his mother's absence was keenly felt.

Sometimes it felt like Andre was two different people or rather a younger, less certain boy was hiding inside him and he went from hating that boy to wishing he could let him loose. What would it be like to speak easily to people like he used to. He remembered walking with his father on the beach and talking non-stop about Selkies. He'd just read a story about them and he'd dreamed he would find a seal skin on the beach. His father had told him his mother was a selkie, but she didn't want to go back to the sea after Andre was born. "She loves you more," he'd said and for weeks Andre had looked for his mother's selkie skin. It was shocking to recall how disappointed he'd been when he couldn't find it.

He felt something of that disillusionment now. His uniform sweater was baggy on his thin frame. His hair fell over his eyes. He'd refused to get it cut no matter how much Michelle pleaded because he liked to hide behind it. At the wall of the house he paused with nerves. When finally he continued, he went slowly and quietly. Later he would wonder what would have happened if he'd stormed inside, rather than let the door click quietly behind him. His father and Michelle were in the kitchen and immediately he could tell something was wrong from the quiet hushed way they were speaking. Jamie was upstairs, Andre could hear his vroom vroom, and it may have masked his entry. A drumming had started in Andre's ears and he had an urge to leave, but he moved forward instead. The kitchen was at the back of the house, looking into a small square garden. The window was covered with net curtain and a quick glance showed his father sitting on one end of the table, his long legs spread in front of him and his coat hanging on the back of the chair. Michelle was sitting opposite her brother. Bags of shopping lay on the floor beside her. Andre leaned against the hall wall, squashing his school bag and the few books he carried on his back.

"Jesus, why do you keep repeating that?" Michelle asked and Andre closed his eyes. His mouth was dry and he felt a trembling in the pit of his stomach.

"Because it's true, he hasn't been in any trouble at all. There used to be a fight every week, sometimes more, but there hasn't been one since he got here, has there?" Eugene's voice was soft and there was an edge to it Andre didn't like.

"I'd tell you if he had. If anything he's too quiet. He keeps to himself a lot, he goes out most evenings just to hang around the estate but I rarely see him with anyone."

In the quiet, Andre imagined his father looking out the window. He imagined stepping into the kitchen and saying "Hi Dad," but he couldn't move.

"He's like his mother; you know that," his father said, "He may look like me but God he has her way—remember how he used to make up silly stories about everything and anything.

Michelle might have nodded. Andre had to bite his lip.

"And have you ever heard of a child cleaning his room at three?"

"No," Michelle said and there was a light tone to that word that felt wrong to Andre. He knew she should be stopping his father from saying anything more, but he wasn't sure why he knew this.

Debris

"Mind you that was throwing all the toys under the bed, but he has the orderliness that was so much a part of Usao, the determination too, the way she seemed to need no one at all," he paused and when he spoke again, Andre heard the shake in his voice. Was his father crying? The thought made Andre want to disappear. "But she wasn't an island. She needed people and he does too Michelle. He needs you. I can't fight this anymore."

"Eugene, what are you saying?"

"I'm saying he wants to be here with you, not with me."

"But it's not his choice to make, he's a boy, you're the one who has to make the decisions."

His father said nothing.

"What about Ines?"

"She's staying in Wicklow."

"Jesus, Eugene I didn't mean that. She's already lost a mother. She doesn't need to lose a brother too."

"She was losing him when he was with us. We all were. If he wasn't locked in his room, he was fighting with everyone—you remember what it was like. You know he caused that fire to get here and someone could have gotten hurt. Last Sunday I asked him to come home and you should have seen his face. He looked so scared. He wants this place to be his home."

"Do you really want this, have you thought of what it means?"

"Of course I have, I've thought of nothing else and I want the best for him."

"But the best for him is to be with you. God, you only have to think of the schools. There's a difference between the Grammar and St. Joseph's."

"He was moving towards expulsion, what would that do for him? Besides I went to St. Joseph's and I'm doing okay."

"Yeah and you went to college so your children would get a better chance and I helped you do that for Christ's sake."

"What's that supposed to mean?"

"I am just stating the fucking obvious. We live in a council estate, you don't."

The silence moved out from the kitchen like a wave, and Andre was caught up in it, though he didn't understand it.

"What does that matter?" Eugene said.

Michelle's laugh was gruff. "You're on the right side to say that."

There was a shuffle of movement and Andre imagined his father leaning over the table the way he used to whenever Andre got into trouble at school, getting so close he could feel his father's angry breath on his face. "He's happy here."

"He's not happy and besides life is not as simple as just being happy. There's more to it than that."

"Is there Michelle? Like what, like not seeing your mother die in front of you, or trying to survive it afterwards. All I know is there has been no trouble. He has settled here and he's doing well in school. He might not be happy, but it's the closest to it I've seen and I'm afraid to ruin it, but if you don't want him to stay, just tell me because I don't know what to do."

Andre stood in that carpeted hall. He wanted to pound the walls. His teeth hurt with the effort to keep his mouth closed. For once sound was moving through him, needing to be released. It would have come out as a deep wail.

"It's not a matter of what I want. We need to ask him," Michelle said.

A quiet descended that made Andre want to burst in the room. He imagined his father and aunt staring at each other like statues. "Oh my God," Michelle said. "You've already asked Ron, haven't you?"

His father must have nodded because Michelle said she couldn't believe his nerve going behind her back to ask her husband.

"I had to make sure it was okay with him first, it would be rude otherwise."

"Rude," Michelle repeated as if she'd never heard the word. "I can't believe this."

There was the sound of the chair being pushed against the floor and a rattle of shopping bags. "What did Ron say?

"That he had no problem with it if you didn't. He said it was your call."

"No it's not. It's Andre's call."

Eugene said, "Okay, we'll ask him Sunday?"

Andre found himself at the kitchen door. His body had moved of its own accord. He hardly knew what he was doing, though when he saw his father in his suit and tie by the kitchen table and the surprised, almost embarrassed way he was looking at his son, he felt an intense hatred for the man. "You don't have to wait until Sunday," Andre said. "I'm staying."

****

Andre darted out of the kitchen and Eugene went after him, though Michelle didn't see the point when this was what he'd wanted. She heard her brother call for his son and the slam of the bedroom door and it was impossible to understand exactly what was rising inside her. It was more than disbelief or anger. Her life had changed in the space of an afternoon. No it was not a life, she thought, but her perception of it, as if she was looking from the outside in, and she didn't recognize anyone.

Eugene appeared at the kitchen door and she told him he should go. She felt adrift looking at his face and slightly dizzy, a hint of vertigo, of

Debris

looking down from a height with the fear of falling. He said something, but she wasn't listening. Tired, all of a sudden, she managed a nod and told him she would call later when she knew she wouldn't. The shopping was left on the floor and when Jamie came to find her she put on the television, counting the minutes until Martha's arrival so she could escape upstairs. Andre had come home early. The thought came and left without the residues of curiosity or irritation. She did not cook dinner that night. When Ron came home from work she was curled up on her bed and Martha and Jamie were eating cereal. Andre had not emerged from his room and Michelle had not gone near him, though she'd experienced a tightening in her chest when she'd stumbled past his bedroom door.

"Are you okay?" Ron asked and she hated her temptation to glance at his feet. So many times she'd had to badger him to leave his muddy shoes at the front door and she didn't want to care about the dirt today. "Why didn't you tell me Eugene talked to you?"

"He didn't want me to," Ron said.

She wanted to laugh, but was afraid that she would cry instead. When the resentment settled back, she said, "Well I don't want to cook dinner."

"Michelle."

"And I probably won't want to tomorrow either."

Ron stepped closer to her and she sensed his uncertainty in the slow trod of his step. "I'm sorry, Michelle, I should have said something."

She closed her eyes and felt the tears behind them. What would have happened if he'd told her? Would she have felt guilty about Andre? Would she have felt it was her duty to help, or would she have felt the same betrayal as she had when looking at the face of her brother? It was hard to know.

"How about some fish-n-chips and a six pack, or maybe I'll just get you the six pack?" Ron said and Michelle didn't want to. Still she couldn't help but smile.

****

Andre liked to roam. His favorite time was the gloaming when everything was turning grey and obscure, becoming a world of shadows and movement. During those hours he was sure he would see his mother again. The idea thrilled and scared him. He remembered how he'd believed she was a selkie with her long dark hair and the accent that was so different to everyone else. Of course he knew she was from Spain. He'd been to the town with narrow streets surrounded by a yellow desert, but that had always been quickly forgotten once he'd come back home to the sea's greens and greys. But he knew now that she wasn't a selkie and had never been. She didn't belong to the sea. She was in the air, in the trees. In the

evening he could feel her in the breeze that touched his cheek and in the cold on his fingers.

In his father's house, the thought of her had been oppressive, like a hand squeezing his heart. She'd always seemed too far out of reach. He was struck again and again with the idea that she'd abandoned them, taken flight the first chance she got. So many times he'd gone back into the shed, hoping to get a glimpse of her face with the soot on her cheeks, but she was never there and he had begun to think that he'd freed her by opening the door. She'd fled because there was too much to hold her down, too much weight in memory and pain.

But in the estate it was different. In the last months he'd found so much possibility. Michelle's house was a narrow attached house held behind a stone garden. From her front door, identical grey houses spanned left and right and there were two more rows on the opposite side of the green, one facing Michelle's house, the other row faced the main road. To drive into town, it was necessary to go around the green and then past the two rows of houses towards the main road. To walk, it was possible to go through the field at the back of Michelle's house. Not everyone liked to walk there, especially at night when there were few streetlights to guide the way. The path was muddy and went past two large warehouses that had once been used for storing flour and corn. They'd been vacant for many years and had broken windows and large cavernous dark rooms littered with wood and empty cans and cigarette butts. Fires had been lit there in the past and the furthest building from the estate had the corner blackened out. At night, lights from the town spread upwards to the area to give a semblance of clarity. The traffic was audible during the day, but at night the irregular sounds of cars barely dipped into the quiet.

The muddy lane led past the warehouses and into town. Coming back towards home, Andre was greeted by back gardens behind wooden fences, clothes hanging on lines, the curtains closed on lit bedroom windows and he liked moving freely behind everyone. He liked the open field in front of the warehouse with the overgrown grass and the trees that looked like old gnarled giants spreading their arms outward. Older kids hung out in the area most nights. Sometimes they would gather in the warehouse and Andre would see the flickering of lighters and small fires from outside, or they would sit on the grass smoking and drinking beer and Andre would hide in the row of tangled bushes that cut across the field to watch.

Andre tried to go there alone as often as he could, skipping out of the house before Ronan would appear. Ronan lived across the green from Michelle's house with a little sister and mother. He had light hair and bright blue eyes. He could hardly sit still. In class his legs would be going constantly and he was always berated for tapping his pencil on his desk. He talked non-stop. The first time he and Andre wandered to the back of the

estate, it was straight after school. They were still wearing their school uniforms. Ronan's laces were untied and Andre noticed without saying anything, though the carelessness annoyed him. Ronan was talking about the kite that he'd built with his father when he used to come to visit. Ronan said, "I haven't seen him in ages," and then proceeded to describe how he and his father had spent weeks working on the kite, only for it not to get off the ground. They had no idea why and had messed with the bridle and side-slip but nothing worked. "Da ended up getting pissed off," Ronan said. For a moment there was silence. Andre breathed it in, but it didn't last long. Ronan started talking about the kite he intended to build by himself. Andre hardly heard what he was saying, but he felt every word as if it was spit in his face. They were near the warehouses and the building made him think of the shed at home, his mother smiling and telling him they'd have a fire next year. He was sure she was in the warehouse, maybe watching them from the large window, or running around the place, and the discomfort of Ronan's incessant talking was wearing on him. It felt wrong, as if this place, the field and the warehouse and the backs of the houses and the sky above, was one big church that needed silence.

"Shut up," Andre finally said and for a moment Ronan looked at him with an open mouth, then the surprise passed and he shoved Andre. There'd been fights before in his old school with boys he had suddenly found a terrible loathing for. Those boys had hardly said a word before they'd gotten thumped or kicked and a scuffle would start, but Andre had gone passed such high feelings of hate and anger. He merely kept walking. Ronan caught up with him and walked beside him. "What are we doing here anyway?" he said. He'd wanted to play football on the green.

Andre didn't answer and felt Ronan's glance every now and again. The warehouse gaped in the sun-light. Opposite the front door someone had made a makeshift bench with upside down buckets and a plank of wood. Empty cans of beer were tossed on the ground beside it, the silver peeking from the overgrown grass. Inside the building, there was a musty smell. Ronan walked behind Andre and pretended to vomit when he pointed out a used condom. The floors were littered with debris, but Andre kept his gaze upwards. At one point Ronan asked, "What are you looking for?"

Andre didn't answer.

The next time he went to the warehouse he made sure to go alone. He wanted to feel as invisible and lost as the ghosts he'd read about. He sought his mother out in those stories as much as the open air.

He thought of these stories whenever he wandered in the dark, always towards the back of the estates where one night he came across a couple in the corner of the field. The girl was lying on her back and the boy was writhing on top of her, his hips fast and furious. The sounds she made frightened Andre and he thought of the Sea Fairies he'd read about, the female being beautiful, while the men were monstrous and his fear kept him still until the boy moaned into the girl's hair and grew still.

After this he stayed close to the warehouse walls and watched the older kids from inside through the broken windows and he'd imagine that he was on a different plane. He thought of places he might have come from. He could be a visitor from the past when the warehouses were in use and there was nothing but fields all around. He knew there had been mills in the town and a river that had long since dried up, though in the evening, he would never stay in the echoing darkness of the warehouse for long. At night, the place seemed thick with presence and it scared him to think of other ghosts watching him.

A dog started to bark. There was laughter from the green and darting shadows that Andre didn't bother look at. The breeze ruffled Andre's hair. It was dark, but he knew this path by now. The dips and rises were as familiar as his skin. The barking dog reached him from the estate and he waited for that moment when it would finally stop. For a few seconds, there would only be the squelch of his boots on the mud and his breathing and then there might be laughter from the fields, or rising voices. Sometimes there would be nothing from there and he would continue on in the quiet towards the warehouse and the fields dimly lit by stars and he would sit at the wall and smoke cigarettes he'd stolen from Ron until his mouth grew dry and dirty and he grew tired of the stillness. In the last few weeks, he'd started to buy his own cigarettes, thanks to his father's pocket money, which he'd used to buy presents last Christmas, too. He'd hated everything about that holiday, the first year of his mother's death and had started to dread it from the first day of October.

A fire was lit in the middle of the field. Andre stepped off the muddy lane onto the grass. Between the fire and him was a line of small bushes where Andre liked to hide. It was from there he'd watched the couple. Now he looked at figures highlighted by flames. There were four people, two were sitting on the makeshift bench with their backs to him, and two were on the ground on either side. He could make out no faces.

"After fifteen fucking years, they're let out and that's it, is it? They should be fucking happy," The voice was male and angry and Andre was sure it was one of the seated boys. Andre stepped closer to the bushes. His heart had moved between his ears.

"Don't start that now," another boy said.

"Fuck off," the first said, "I'll say whatever I want."

The smoke was drifting toward Andre. He smelt hash and heard the click of a can opening.

"It's not as if it's the first time this happened either, Conlon died in prison."

"We know, alright. Christ." There was a shove between the boys on the bench and the angry boy said, "Don't be disrespectful."

22

Debris

"To you or Conlon," someone said and everyone laughed.

"I have to go."

Andre sought out the owner of the female voice but couldn't find her.

"Skin up first," the angry boy said.

"I don't have any gear."

"Come here and get it."

"Colin?"

"I said come here."

The girl rose then from the grass. She'd been sitting furthest from the warehouse. Her pale face was lit up by the fire. Her hair was short and her eyes were big. She walked to the boy closest to her and he handed her something Andre couldn't make out.

"Erin, you know you're good for something," Colin said and laughed. The girl's face looked like stone with the firelight. "That's not funny," she said. She sat on the ground beside him with her legs crossed and started to make the joint. Andre couldn't keep his eyes off her. There was an impish quality to her that he loved. He couldn't remember seeing her before, but she must have been present on other nights. If she hadn't spoken, he might have taken her for a boy and he'd probably done so several times before. He liked the short hair and the way she sat as if alone. He would have liked to go to her and sit beside her. He imagined she would keep skinning up without a glance and be hardly fazed by his presence. If she was alone, he would have approached. Andre had had a few encounters with the girls in school. He was good at hiding his nervousness with them. His latent sociable personality, the boy he'd been before he killed his mother, rose when he was with the girls so he managed to look them in the eye and smile and ask them questions. Twice he'd gotten notes to meet a girl at the back of the bike sheds after school. Sinead Neary was the first, and though he was nervous, his body seemed to move of its own accord, pressing her between the wall of the shed and him. They were red-lipped and tousled by the time they'd finished. At home lying in the bed he would imagine the girls in his class naked and masturbate with guilt from the idea of his mother watching. He would lie stiff as though a body lay next to him that he didn't want to disturb. Afterwards he'd want to cry with shame and would have to leave the house as though he were escaping the scene of the crime.

"What are you doing?"

Erin was putting the joint in her mouth and Andre's stomach lurched when he saw that there was only one person on the bench. He'd been so busy watching the girl that he'd completely forgotten about everyone else. The boy might have gone off for a piss and spotted him in the bushes.

"I asked you a question?" he said. He was small and could have been taken for a twelve-year-old if not for the size of his head and the seriousness of his eyes, which held a hard steady gaze. He smelled of beer and smoke. Andre shrugged and said he'd just been going for a walk.

"I've seen you before," the boy said. Andre didn't know if he wanted a response, so he stayed silent.

"You're staying with the Moran's, right?"

"Yeah," Andre said.

"What's your name?"

"Andre."

"Do you always sneak around like that Andre?"

Andre said no. The boy laughed and told him his name was Colin and not to be so bloody worried. "I don't bite," he said, "You can join us if you want, unless you're more comfortable spying like a perv. Is that it, are you a perv?"

Andre had a flash of the couple in the grass and felt his cheeks grow hot. He mumbled no, but Colin had already started back to the fire that had been built within a circle of rocks. Some wood lay to one side waiting to be thrown in. Erin was blowing out smoke while watching Andre approach. He wondered how old she was while the other boys asked about him. Colin explained that it was the lad staying in the Moran's house. "The nephew isn't it?" Colin said and had to give Andre a shove to get his attention.

"You're the nephew right?"

Andre nodded. The fire was hot on his face and Colin tapped the bench and told him to sit. The gesture made Andre stiffen because it seemed to be more order than offering. He didn't want to sit with the boys, but there was a tension in the air that made it impossible to plonk beside Erin. Colin remained standing beside her. He had a nose ring and looked old to Andre, maybe twenty. He was wearing a leather jacket and had his brown hair sleeked back. There was a piercing interest in his eyes that Andre didn't like.

"Is your Da the one with the Mercedes?" Colin asked.

"Yeah," Andre said, "He's a fucking wanker."

Everyone laughed and Erin tapped his leg and handed him the joint. Andre took a pull and felt the heat in his throat before coughing it back up. His eyes watered. Colin told him to hold it in for Christ's sake. Andre did what he was told and felt the smoke waft through him before exhaling and spluttering to cause more laughter.

"Alright, hand it over," the guy sitting next to him said. He was sitting on the seat with his legs spread out. He had long red hair and eyes that looked like water. Andre passed him the joint and he asked why Andre wasn't staying with his Da. Andre shrugged. He sat up a bit, and said, "Come on, tell your good-buddy Manny your troubles." He seemed impatient and Andre imagined him springing from his seat. He said that he'd gotten expelled from school. Erin laughed and said, "Cool."

Looking at her in the firelight, he was sure she was close to his age. She was small boned and her eyes had a shining interest that wavered on innocence. When Erin asked why he was expelled, he didn't have to lie a second time.

"Jesus," Manny said, "We have an arsonist in our midst."

"Why did you do it?" Erin asked.

"To get away from the wanker," he said.

"Did anyone get hurt?" Erin asked. Andre shook his head. She nodded and looked at the fire and he wondered if her attention would have lingered if he'd said yes.

A skinhead with a denim jacket sat on the ground beside Manny. He drank from a beer can and gestured towards Andre with a smile when Manny went to pass him the joint. Manny laughed and handed Andre his joint again. Only seconds had passed since his last smoke and he felt a muffled confusion and a heavy weight on his head, like the night was pressing down on him. It made words hard to form. He had no idea what to say anyway. Still he took what was offered, unable to find the will to shake his head and suffer the insults that might follow. He took a drag, this time managing to inhale and exhale without the cough. "Go on, have another," Manny said. Thick heat flowed down Andre's throat and chest and spread throughout his body. After a moment, his legs felt watery and he was glad he was sitting down. He lost the gist of the conversation. Distant sounds of cars reached him from the main road. Every now and again he thought he heard a shout from the estate, and it felt as if the volume was put up high and lowered again. Erin spoke little. She sat with her legs pulled up and her arms around them, watching the fire, her face aglow. He would have liked to know what she was thinking and where she came from. He knew without her there, he would have wanted to leave. Others arrived. A tall man with his arms around a blonde girl came from town and stopped by Colin. Andre noticed the shake of hands and the lingering touch and the girl's glance towards him, which held a touch of mockery. Andre's heart was beating too fast. At one stage the guy with shaved head said something to him, but Andre didn't know what it was. He'd been watching a piece of wood burn in the shape of a face. Colin tipped his shoulder. Andre swayed and was told that Vinnie asked him something.

"What?" Andre managed to say. Vinnie was smiling but his thin mouth looked sharp and cruel. He asked if Andre got pocket money from his Da. Andre asked why.

"You can't smoke everyone else's gear." Colin said.

Erin sighed.

"You have something to say?" Colin asked and Erin stared at the fire and said no. Andre felt a tight ball inside him, not quite fear but resignation, as if he had known from the first that the Mercedes was what interested them. He said he didn't have any money on him. "That's okay, we'll be here tomorrow," Colin said and glanced around him. "We have nowhere to go, eh boys."

"Speak for yourself," Vinnie said and a thick silence ensued. Andre felt as if he'd fallen into a deep hole and had no idea how to get out. This sensation of being trapped was made worse when Erin stood and said she had to go home.

"Stay," Colin said and there was an edge to his voice that made Andre more alert.

She said she couldn't, and Colin told her to fuck off back to her Da then. His tone was gruff and petulant, and Erin's glance was filled with something Andre couldn't read. He was sure there was anger but there was something soft too that made him crumple a little on the seat. She stepped back from the fire and Andre was pulled by her retreat as if it was a newly opened door. "I have to go," he said, or at least wanted to say, but it was more a nod and a mutter when he rose shakily from the bench.

Manny said, "Night, night, little man."

Colin stayed still and was staring at the fire. His small frame was enlarged by his silence so Andre walked away from him, passed Vinnie and onto the path, where outside the reaches of the dying fire he caught up with Erin.

"Hi."

Her glance was furtive but she said nothing about him joining her. She walked with her hands in her pockets and her shoulders forward, which reinforced his idea that she was not much older than him. She had a vulnerable air. "I'm sorry about them," Erin said after they'd walked for a bit. Andre shrugged and said it was okay.

"I don't like them too much. I mean they're not really friends of mine." She paused and sounded hesitant when she said, "They used to know my brother, that's all."

"Used to," Andre said.

Erin nodded and said he died.

"Do you ever see him?" Andre blurted and he wished the ground could open up and swallow him when Erin stopped walking to look at him, which forced him to pause too. Her face was made up of shadow when she said, "He's dead."

The words held more curiosity than criticism. Andre shrugged and nodded and was about to continue walking when she grabbed his arm. The touch surprised him. Although he wore his jacket and sweater he was sure he could feel the heat of her fingers. She was his height. He wondered what color her eyes were.

"But you knew that already so what did you mean?"

Debris

"Nothing," he tried. But she said, "Come on, tell me. How would I see him?" And it might have been her interest, the way she clung to his arm or the fact that he didn't want her to walk away in a huff, because it was easy to imagine being left alone in this lane and after all these months he didn't want to be without her.

"His ghost, alright, I meant his ghost," in an annoyed tone that wasn't exactly honest, because it was more fear he felt at that moment. He expected her to scoff, but she nodded and there was sloppiness to her expression that reminded him that she was just as stoned as he was, which might have been why the idea of ghosts didn't seem so ludicrous. The dark night and open space added to the atmosphere. There was a shuffle in the grass. It might have been a cat or a mouse and it made Erin turn around. He felt her grip tighten and then ease before she released him.

"Maybe I have," she said.

"What?" Andre asked.

"Maybe I have seen him," she said and it was surprising how relieved he felt. He was lighter suddenly. "How about you?" she asked and for a moment he was confused, "Who did you see?"

There was a surge of worry that this was a tease and her interest was only to make fun, but the dread that she would get impatient with his reticence and walk off was greater so he told her that he'd seen his mother.

"She died?"

He nodded. His head was a mess, flying in all directions, while his guilt stayed stagnant in him. He could almost taste it. Erin was still watching him, as if waiting for something more so he blurted, "I killed her." And the confession brought a dense emptiness. Still Erin didn't walk away. She asked how. Her voice was low, as if there might be eavesdroppers laying low in the ground around them. Andre saw his mother's face, the laughter and the fall, and felt incapable of explaining. All he managed was, "It was an accident," and her silence gave him the impression that she didn't believe him, though there was no will to argue. He would have liked to know what she thought, why the nod as if she understood what he had said, but he couldn't say anything. A need he didn't think he possessed anymore, a feeling that had died with him after the accident, caught somewhere in those fifteen minutes, had been resurrected and it brought a sweet scary pain. "Do you have a smoke?" she asked and he took out two cigarettes and lit one for her. They walked and smoked in silence. They were near the estates when he said he hadn't seen her in school before. "That's 'cause I don't go."

"Why?"

"It's complicated," she said.

He would have liked to ask about her brother and how he died, but if she didn't want to talk about school, she'd hardly want to talk about that.

Behind the houses, there was the smell of fried food, bedroom lights burned, and he saw her eyes were a deep dark color. Erin took the last drag from her cigarette; she smoked it right down to the filter. Andre had thrown his on the ground moments ago. She was stamping on the butt when he asked if he could walk her home.

"Walk me home? Jesus what planet did you come from?"

Andre shrugged and wished she would say something instead of watching him. Eventually she started walking, which he hoped meant acquiescence. They were at the end of his row of houses and went towards the green. The grass was soft and muddy in places. A horn blasted from somewhere.

"What do you do all day then?" he said. The green was empty and silent and he kept his gaze on the skinny girl in a jeans and navy hoodie. Her skin was pale and when she looked at him she seemed tired. He would have liked to reach out and touch her hand, but he had the feeling she wouldn't like that.

She said, "My Da's Dan McEvoy," as though it should mean something to Andre.

"My Da's Eugene Nolan," he said and she paused before crossing the road to the row of houses with their identical gardens to Michelle's and the lights on, the flicker of television. "Don't be smart," she said.

"I'm not being smart," he said.

"So no-one's said anything to you about Da."

"No," Andre said, "Why would they?"

"Swear."

He did the sign of the cross over his heart. "Cross my heart and hope to die."

She smiled and told him he was weird. She hadn't heard that in years, though she seemed to have eased slightly.

"Why should I have heard about him?" Andre said when they'd started walking again.

"You can see for yourself."

Chapter Three

Her house was on the row behind Ronan's, facing the main road. It was the same narrow attached house as Michelle's, but the likeness ended there. With the street lights, it was possible to see that the place needed a paint job. The garden was over grown. An old bike was thrown on its side near the path. An old Volvo, looked as if it hadn't been driven in years. Erin saw him looking at it and said she took it out sometimes at night. The windows couldn't roll down and there was a hole in the back floor, but it wasn't too bad when it wasn't raining. She tried to sound light-hearted, but her voice had tightened and he felt a tension in the air with his reluctance to leave her. Yellow, jaundiced light spread behind the front door glass.

"Do you want to you come in?" she asked. She reminded him of Ines at that moment; her fright when she used to crawl into bed beside him and murmur that she had a bad dream, only he couldn't be this way with Ines anymore. He could not expect Ines to forgive him for what he had done, and yet he'd told Erin and she was letting him follow her to the door towards sickly yellow light. He wanted to ask if her father was at home, but she already had the door open and was stepping inside.

The hall smelled musty and dirty, it made Andre think of locker rooms. There was newspaper on the stairs, not in a neat pile, but sheets of paper lying across the steps as if they'd been thrown from a height. A coat was bundled on the floor by the bannister, the wallpaper was yellowed, and the floor, a pale brown carpet, needed a hoovering. The click of the door closing seemed loud and he realized there was no television on or any other sounds coming from the rooms. The silence was uncanny and made him think that he was being watched. To the right of him was the door of the sitting room, draped in darkness. He could make out the couch by the window and the corner of a television. He didn't feel like moving to investigate. Outside he hadn't noticed what lights were on elsewhere in the house because the garish yellow hall had taken his attention and he wished now that he had looked. "He must be asleep," Erin said and she started towards the back of the house. The kitchen door was opened. It was a different lay out to Michelle's house, whose kitchen door was to the right of the main hall. Here the door was straight ahead. Andre could make out a sink and the kitchen window, which was uncovered and let in some light from the houses at back. Erin walked slowly as if this was not her house at all and she froze with the sound of footsteps from upstairs. She kept her gaze on the ceiling, tracking the movement of whoever was coming towards them.

L.M. Brown

Months ago, Andre would have told Erin that he had to leave, but then he wouldn't have been living anywhere but his own home. He would have been making up stories, rather than fixated on ghosts and he would have been uncomfortable with Erin's silence, instead of feeling familiarity with her stillness, so it would seem somehow that he'd been drifting towards this place without even knowing it. She hadn't moved by the time the man appeared at the top of the stairs. From her viewpoint, she would have seen his body cut in half by bannisters. His head was probably lost to her, too high in the gloom of the upstairs hall. The man didn't address her, but asked Andre, "Who the fuck are you?"

"Andre," he said and the man repeated the name in a mocking tone, "Andre, what's wrong with John or Michael or bloody Patrick? Andre," he laughed and told him it sounded like a girl's name. The man was skinny and his eyes were small and sunken in his narrow face. He wore a stained t-shirt and sweatpants and the skin was pulled tight on his arms. His hands were large and red, and his grey hair was wild on his head.

"Erin, are you there?" The shout made him wobble on the top stairs. His eyes widened and it took a while before he got his balance. His laughter was a wheeze in his chest. "Yeah Da," she said and walked towards the end of the stairs. "The paper is complete shite, there's nothing good in it at all. Why do you bother getting it?" he growled.

"You asked me to."

"As if you do everything I ask you to," he said and Andre felt sick with the way he was looking at his daughter with narrow critical eyes.

"So you like boys?" he said. His attention was on Andre now, who had no idea what he was talking about, though the man's piercing stare made him shake his head.

"But isn't she just like a little boy with her short hair and flat chest?"

"Da?"

"Da, Da," he said in that mocking tone again. His head rocked back and forth on his long neck. "Isn't it the bloody truth, no amount of Da will change it."

He gripped the bannister and Andre thought the man was trying to scare him with his near-falls and laughter. Once still, the man asked if Andre had anything to say. There was a glint in his eyes that wasn't there before. "Are you not going to stand up for her honor?" Andre wanted to say something, but had no idea what it should be. It was like trying to communicate in a different language. The man in front of him made him forget how to speak.

"No, I wouldn't either if I were you, they're not worth it. They'll take whatever ya have and then fuck off. You can't trust them, can ya Erin. Come on now, tell the boy."

Tell the boy; Andre glanced at Erin, who had stiffened.

Debris

"Fuck it, I need a drink."

He started down the stairs and Erin moved to Andre. There was a slight shuffle of her feet and they were side by side. Her hand brushed his and he wanted to believe the graze was deliberate. Andre felt nervous and scared, but also bigger than he ever had in his life. He resisted the temptation to look at Erin's face because her father was getting closer and he needed to keep an eye on him. Andre could smell drink and sour sweat. He saw the man's eyes were red and his lips flaked and dry. His legs were unsteady and slightly bent. He was not a tall man but the sharpness of him was frightening. His bones seemed dense and Andre imagined that his large skeletal hands would give an awful stinging slap. His eyes were a misty blue. He paused at the end of the stairs, and smiled to show discolored teeth. His upper body jerked forward and he screeched, "Boo!"

He laughed when Andre flinched. The hair at the back of the man's head was flattened, as if had laid on it all day. He was still laughing when he disappeared into the kitchen.

Erin smiled sadly when her father left them, though they didn't move until the light had been turned on in the kitchen and there was a clatter of glasses. On their journey upstairs Andre couldn't help glancing down every now and again, wary that her father might follow them. The thought brought a tightness to his chest and made his legs feel shaky, similar to how he'd felt after a few joints, only he was aware of every sound now as he had not been by the fire; the dripping tap in the bathroom, the slight tick of the overhead light on the medicine cabinet. Towels were on the floor. The bedroom beside the bathroom had the door open and revealed a tossed bed and an ashtray on the floor. The room smelled like her father.

The house was smaller than Michelle's with three rooms upstairs. Erin's bedroom was at the front. She twisted the handle of her door and stepped into a small room lit by streetlights. There was something about the way she threw her jacket over the chair and walked to the window that made her look less like a child. She seemed distracted when she walked to the window and flicked at the curtains. The television was on downstairs and a barking laugh came from there. Her gaze was still held on the window when she asked if he missed his mother.

It was a physical pain to hear her say 'your mother' with such ease. No-one had spoken of her to Andre in a long time. The first months after the funeral, Michelle had sat with him in his bedroom and whispered that his mother would not want him to blame himself. He'd told her that she had no idea what she was talking about and when she'd tried to reminisce about Usao, he'd pushed Michelle away and told her that he didn't want to remember what it was like. To remember only made it worse.

Erin was watching him quietly, so he nodded.

31

"Me too," she said, and it hit him then, the absence in the house. Erin smiled and told him to close the door. He obeyed and the room's darkness was pierced here and there with the flicker of orange streetlights. The single bed was against the wall and neatly made. A wooden chair was by the window with clothes draped around the back and there were some more clothes folded on the floor. To his left was a chest of drawers, which looked white in the dim light, covered with a few knick-knacks that he couldn't see properly. She asked if he had any more smokes and took an ashtray from under her bed. She sat heavily on the mattress with her back to the wall, facing the door. He sat beside her. The ceiling was damp in places; her breath was on his cheek. She smelled of smoke from the fire. Close to her now, with the light from outside streaming onto the foot of her bed, it was hard to make out the full features of her face, but her eyes stood out. They lit their cigarettes, boots hanging from the end of the bed, and were easing a little when a crash came from downstairs. Within seconds, they heard her father shout her name.

"Erin, come here, do you hear me!" Her father was in the hallway downstairs and his voice made the house seem much smaller. "Should you go down?" Andre asked and she shook her head.

"I don't want to," she said and blew a smoke ring into the dim room.

The father called her again.

She said, "I used to run down all the time, and then one night I was so tired I didn't want to get out of bed. After a while, he stopped screaming at me. I thought he might come up and give out, but he went back to his drink. He probably forgot what he wanted me for. He doesn't remember things, but I do."

Andre felt like his heart had expanded in his chest. It wasn't pity he felt, but a terrible helplessness beside her. She continued to smoke and blow rings into the dim room and her father stopped shouting just like she'd said. He could be heard rummaging around downstairs. There were banging doors. "Please God, let him have another bottle," Erin groaned.

He must have found one because eventually the banging doors stopped. Andre asked where her mother was.

Erin glanced at him and he wished he hadn't asked that question. He put out his cigarette in the dirty ashtray that rested on her outstretched legs. His mouth was too dry to smoke and his stomach too unsettled.

"She used to sing all the time," Erin said. "She liked having people around too."

Erin told him that there was always someone chatting with her mother in the kitchen. The front door was never locked. The house was always clean and it smelled nice too. For a while Erin had tried to keep the place like her mother had, but there was hardly any point when her father kept making a mess wherever he went and no one wanted to visit anyway. Her father scared her friends off.

Erin put out her cigarette.

"You're the first person here in ages," she said. "Are you not worried?"

"No," Andre said, "I'm not."

"Tell me about your Dad?" Andre remembered Eugene at Michelle's kitchen table, large and vacant and was hit with a surge of sadness that had been denied him until then. "He doesn't care about anyone."

"Does he hurt you?" she said.

"No, he just ignores us."

Erin rested her head against the wall and said, "God, I'd love to be ignored."

****

Between streetlights, the sky was black and Andre wondered if all the stars were held over his father's house. He had the stars and they had the silence. There was no rush of waves to cover his breathing. He'd used the bathroom in Erin's house to wash his face and had put some toothpaste on his fingers to rub against teeth and hide the smell of smoke, though Michelle would hardly notice with the amount Ron smoked, it was more a way to keep the truth to himself. Michelle appeared at the kitchen door the moment the front door opened. She was in her bathrobe. Her hair was down and her cheeks were red from anger. "Where the hell were you?"

"Ronan's, I'm sorry, I lost all track of the time. There's no school tomorrow."

"That doesn't mean you can disappear and not tell us where you are."

Andre apologized again. He'd learned the best way to deal with Michelle was not to argue.

"Don't do that again," she said.

He said he wouldn't.

He wondered what Michelle would say if he told her he'd spent the last half hour in Erin McEvoy's house. "Don't tell anyone you were here," she'd said when he was leaving. "They mightn't let you come back."

"Why?" he'd asked.

"Why do you think?" She told him that her father wasn't well liked. They'd been standing at the front door. The television on in the living room, smoke wafting towards them and Andre thought Erin's mother drifted between them, a faceless absence that he forgot the moment he stepped out into the cool air.

Chapter Four

Andre spent hours wandering up and back from the estate to the warehouse, sitting every now and again on the make-shift bench with his walk-man and listening to The Cure. All the while keeping his attention on the path. He'd thought it best to be there first, so he would not have to approach. He was fourteen and the type of person who would think about things like this for a long time. He thought about the best way to stand at the kitchen door when you don't want to enter the room, or how to walk through a house without glancing at the photos hanging from the walls that showed a family that no longer existed, or sit in a once familiar kitchen and eat when all he wanted to do was smash his plate on the ground and scream. He had to count quietly in his head some Sundays in Bray, one, two, three, until he felt calm, though no matter how much he counted he could never stop himself from looking at the clocks. He expected them to say 6:35.

He stood when he saw Colin and Manny approach. They were coming from town. He'd expected them to come from the estate and the difference threw him off. He was nervous as it was. Earlier, he'd remembered the ease in which Colin had snuck up on him the night before and wondered when Colin had become aware of his presence. It made him feel stupid to think all those other times he'd been visible while he remained on the sidelines. He recalled the boy and girl he'd seen writhing on the ground. They must have been aware of his figure in the bushes watching them. Maybe they'd laughed afterwards.

The boys were nearly at the bench and Andre clutched the money in his pocket. Every Sunday his father gave him money, his eyes never meeting his son's, the quick thrust of cash and the awkward pat on the shoulder. Andre had brought forty with him now, but he had no idea how much hash cost.

Colin walked with a swagger. Manny's blonde hair was standing up at the back and he was smiling at Andre. "What do you want, little man?" Manny asked.

Before Andre could answer, Colin asked, "Did you have fun last night?" His voice was tight and strained and Andre could feel the ice in his gaze. Manny glanced at his friend, but said nothing, waiting for an answer. He looked amused with Andre's shrug. A crow cawed overhead and a breeze rustled the grass and Andre pulled his money from his pocket. "I want a quarter," he said. He wished he knew how much it cost. Forty pounds was in his hand and Colin took it all and said it was extra for last night. His amusement made Andre certain that he was being robbed of a fair amount of money.

Debris

"Nothing is free," Colin said and a blast went off in his head, *nothing is free*, as if he didn't know what life was like. "Next time I'll go somewhere else then," he said and flinched when Colin stepped closer.

"What was that?" Colin's face was in his. Andre smelt cigarettes and a musty scent of unwashed clothes. Andre had turned his head sideways. His body was stiff, but he wasn't afraid, though he knew he should be. "I'll go where I won't be fleeced," he said.

The smack rang in the air and his cheek stung. Watering eyes made him blink.

"What was that?" Colin said again. Manny wasn't smiling anymore. His green eyes were narrow and focused. Andre had an urge to look at Manny's hands, to see if they were curled in a fist or relaxed by his side. The place seemed too quiet and Andre's voice was low when he repeated what he had said.

His cheeks burned with the second slap and he had to hold back tears. "What was that?" Colin said again. His voice was sharp and cruel. He raised his hand and Andre flinched.

"Nothing," Andre said.

"That's what I thought."

Colin's hand dropped and he nodded at Manny, who handed Andre his quarter of hash that had been cut into a rectangular shape and wrapped in tinfoil.

****

There were some people waiting by the bus stop on the Main road, a baby wailed from underneath the shelter and the noise made the quietness of the house more sinister. It wasn't that Andre was afraid as much as unsure. Now that he stood in front of Erin's house with the curtains that looked dirty in the sun he wondered if she really meant for him to come back.

Ronan hadn't helped matters. Andre had stopped at his house on the way to Erin's. "Don't tell anyone," Erin had said, but Andre needed a cover. He'd told Michelle he was going to Ronan's house and they were planning to go to the cinema. The mood Michelle was in lately he wouldn't be surprised if she came storming over to the house looking for him. For the most part, Andre stayed out of her way.

From the door, Andre had heard water running from the kitchen, which would have made him guess Ronan's mother was cleaning up after dinner, though the tomato sauce smeared on his face left no doubt. "I just finished dinner," Ronan said and was about to go for his jacket when Andre told him to wait. "I have to ask a favor," he said. "I need a cover."

Ronan's disappointment was easy to read. Although he tried to hide it, Andre saw the dullness in the bright eyes. The same thing happened whenever Ronan talked about his father.

Ronan asked what the cover was for, just as the water stopped running and made Andre aware of the little girl humming in the kitchen. The sound saddened him in a way he didn't want to think about. "I met Erin McEvoy last night," Andre said, as Ronan's mother appeared at the kitchen door. Andre smiled at her and said hello, but he got no smile back. The woman was short with long dark hair and a round face. Her arms in her t-shirt were wide, the flesh wobbled under arms as she dried the plate. She wore a long navy shirt and was barefoot.

"You planning on helping?" she asked Ronan.

"I'll be there in a second," Ronan said. Hs mother lingered for a moment too long before retreating. "Go on," Ronan said.

"I'm going to her house and she doesn't want anyone to know."

"Her Da's crazy," Ronan said and Andre didn't like his frown, which seemed theatrical. He shrugged and said, "Yeah, I know, I met him last night. If Michelle's looking for me, can you tell her I've just gone down to the shops for something?"

"I can't believe you were in the house."

"Will you cover for me or not?" Andre asked.

"I will, if you tell me what it's like in there."

"Don't be a bollix."

"I'm not being a bollix," Ronan said, "No one's been in there in ages, not since the wife disappeared." He leaned forward to whisper, "Rumor has it she's buried in the garden."

Ronan laughed and his mother appeared again. Andre had no doubt she'd been listening to the conversation. Her eyes were a bright blue like her son's and they were glaring at Andre. "He's not going anywhere near that house," she said.

"Ma."

The girl had stopped humming and she called her mother, but was ignored.

"You stay away from the McEvoy's," the mother told Ronan. She looked at Andre and added, "You would too if you knew what was good for ya."

"What will I sing?" the girl said from the kitchen, to no one in particular.

"Bad people," the mother said, and it seemed as if she was not talking to anyone at all. Her voice drifted towards the ground by her feet. Still Ronan said, "We know Ma."

Andre wanted to say he didn't know. Erin was nice to him last night. At one stage she'd laid her head on his shoulder while she talked and he felt better than he had in a long time. But instead he patted Ronan's arm and told him he'd see him later. On the driveway, he heard Ronan's mother say, "You stay well away from them."

Debris

Andre was turning the corner towards the front row of houses when Ronan caught up to him and asked, "How will I let you know if Michelle comes looking for ya?"

Andre smiled and told him to knock on Erin's door.

****

"I think he's crashed out," Erin said when she opened the door. She led Andre into the kitchen. The window was uncovered and showed a square shaped garden with overgrown grass. Erin was telling him about the mess of gin she'd had to clean up this morning. Her father had broken a bottle. It must have slipped from the table, which was the cause of all the commotion last night. She was surprised he hadn't cut his feet with the glass, though the bottle had fallen towards the back door. She spoke in a low, sad voice while Andre stared at the garden and thought of a pale and lifeless body with dough skin like the body in the coffin at his father's house and it seemed too real, as if he could actually see this woman through the ground. He was surprised with his lack of feeling, and that he could nod and ask Erin if she was okay in a calm voice. She said she was fine. It had been horrible cleaning it up, stinky and sticky. Her clothes were ruined and then she'd had to run out and get more drink for her Da. Andre pulled his gaze from the window. Erin's large eyes were so lovely and she looked younger than him now, frail and timid with her narrow wrists and the way she tilted her head slightly to the side, looking quizzical and unsure.

"How did you get drink?"

She shrugged and said she had fake I.D, and anyway they all knew her Da and would prefer her coming in to get the drink than him. "He hasn't left the house much in the last year," she said.

A year, was that when her mother disappeared? Andre wondered, and what about her brother? So many questions he could feel them weighing him down because it was impossible to ask without telling her that he'd talked to Ronan about her.

"Anyway I'm glad you're here. I was waiting for you," she said. It was nearly five now. Andre had spent so long waiting for Colin and Manny that the day had slipped by. He'd gone back to the house after and had eaten some stew before running to Erin's and now his stomach felt queasy with the stale smell of drink and dirty dishes. It was hard not to glance at the garden. Erin said she'd wanted to look for him, but her father was in one of those moods. Andre had no idea what she meant by one of those moods. She'd rolled her eyes as she said it as if her father was nothing more than a cantankerous child. He didn't believe her, because when Erin smiled, it didn't reach her eyes. Her glance down the hall reinforced the idea that this was an act.

"Where were you?" she asked and he fumbled to get the hash from his pocket. He didn't trust the silence of the house and yet he had no urge to leave. It was like the world stopped once he stepped behind her front door. It felt good to be with her. He was a different boy to the one who slipped in and out of Michelle's house or wandered the fields alone. Andre unwrapped the quarter.

"When did you get that?"

The gear was dark brown and crumply. "Today, that's why it took me so long."

"Oh," she said, and she dropped onto the chair by the table. He'd imagined she'd be delighted with the gear and that she'd take it off him straight away. He didn't know what to do with it. There was no way he could bring it to Michelle's house. He took the seat facing the hall.

"You shouldn't go to the field without me. Colin is bad news."

"I won't go near them." Outside it started to rain, the pitter-patter sending shadows over them. The room had grown dull and he realized it was colder here than Michelle's.

"It's not as simple as that," she said. "Promise you won't go."

He said he couldn't promise.

"Please," she said. "You don't know what they're like."

He could still feel the heat of the slap on his cheek and thought he knew well enough, but he shrugged and said okay and was rewarded with her smile. He uncrossed his fingers.

She thanked him and leaned forward to touch his knee. "I'm sorry," she said, "But I need to ask what happened to your mother?"

He heard the worry in her voice and sensed an uncertainty in the retreat of her hand. The rain had gotten heavier and he told her it was a car accident.

"You said you killed her," Erin said and the words were like ice on his chest. He didn't know what she expected, if she hoped for details that were as yet impossible to dredge up. He could see it all, but to put into words and lay it out in front of him was too much.

"It was my fault."

"Is that why you see her ghost?" Erin asked.

"I don't know," he said. "How about your brother? Why do you see him?"

But Erin didn't seem to hear him. She was looking out of the window and she said, "He keeps seeing her whenever he goes out. That's why he hasn't been out in a year. He's guilty, I know it. I always have."

"Who?"

"Da."

Andre could feel the garden breathing down at him. Still he asked, "Guilty of what?"

Debris

Erin said, "One day Ma just up and disappeared, no letter, no nothing. Who does that? Who just leaves without packing anything?"

****

Erin stopped going to school after her mother left. She said it was just so weird, like a hole had been put into the world. It was impossible to concentrate on anything or to pretend interest. "Still," she said, "It's not like I made a decision not to go back, one day turned into a week and all of a sudden it was three months and to put on that stupid uniform was impossible. It's been over a year at this stage and no one gives a shit."

They were in her bedroom. There'd been movement from upstairs and Erin had jumped from the table and told Andre that they needed to get to her room. She locked her bedroom door this time. The silver key was kept on the rim on top of the door. Maybe she hadn't done so the previous night because she didn't want to worry Andre, or it might have been today's talk about her missing mother that frightened her more. It made Andre jumpy.

In the bedroom next door Erin's father had started a racking, phlegm filled cough that lasted minutes. The sound settled deep under Andre skin and made him restless. Once the coughing stopped, Andre smelled cigarette smoke wafting towards him. Andre had a couple of cigarettes, but no rizzla papers. "I didn't think of that," he said once they'd settled on the bed and Erin asked for the works. Erin told him not to worry. She knew ways around that. She was sitting on the bed and had pulled up a small table Andre hadn't noticed last night. In the day light, the bedroom's yellow walls looked like they could use a paint, but she kept the room clean and neat. On her dresser, there were some photos that Andre did not look at. He was sure her mother was in one of them and he felt uneasy with the idea of putting a face onto this missing woman, as if her absence would become more solid then. It was already enough to fill the house. Andre had brought no photos of his mother from his home. It hurt to look at her smiling face.

"Where did you learn that?" Andre asked when Erin started to rub the cigarette between her fingers to empty it of tobacco.

Erin shrugged, "Around." Andre thought of her brother then. Every now and again he would sweep through Andre's mind, but Erin appeared unwilling to talk about him. It was hard to believe she hadn't heard the question in the kitchen and Andre had no idea how to broach the subject of him again.

Andre sat on the bed close to her and watched as the tobacco rained from the tip of the cigarette. Erin kept some of the tobacco, the rest she scattered onto the floor so it blended with her light blue carpet. The hash hardly needed to be lit. It was crumply and soft. She smiled at Andre and said, "This is good stuff."

"Yeah, I know," he lied.

"Might as well make a strong one," she said and her dexterous fingers kept breaking off small crumbs. Once she was satisfied, she mixed it all together and began to put the tobacco back into the empty cigarette paper, pushing it down with a match. Her father's coughing had stopped and the silence was worse because Andre expected a knock on the door or her father to start shouting. Andre cringed with the thought of that face and the smell that must be worse now. He didn't know how Erin coped with living in this place, where the silence was only an overture to trouble and Andre felt himself floundering for something to hold onto. He was used to being alone and wandering, but not this, not the ignorance of waiting for someone to do something.

"And anyway," Erin said, when she had nearly finished putting the hash laced tobacco back into the cigarette, as if there had been no lull in the conversation. "I couldn't leave Da alone. He was knocking on everyone's doors and stopping people in the street asking where his wife was."

She glanced at him before taking the cigarette filter between her teeth and pulling the white bit out that looked like cotton. She was beautiful, Andre thought, with her short hair and pale skin. She spit the filter out and made her own filter with some cardboard from Andre's cigarette box. Then she shuffled up on the bed, to sit with her back against the wall.

"What's he doing?" Andre said. It sounded as if her father was stamping around the room and a strange low keening noise was coming from him. Erin lit the make-shift joint and exhaled before telling him that he was probably crying. "Some days he cries for hours. He never comes near me when he cries."

Andre watched Erin's mouth settle around the joint. She took another long drag. The low keening noise continued and she passed the joint to him. The filter was slightly wet but he didn't mind it coming from her. He took a drag and felt the warming heat on his chest. His eyes watered and he managed not to cough and splutter. It was strong, already his fingers tingled a bit and the heaviness had started in his head. He didn't know if he liked the sensation, but he took another drag because she was watching him with a smile. Her eyes were ablaze with mischief and he didn't want to let her down. He wished he had some water when he passed the joint back to her.

"Do you have any music?" he asked and she shook her head and said no. She had no money for music and besides it would probably bring her father to them if they made noise.

"Better to keep quiet so he can forget about us," she said and Andre nodded, though he couldn't understand how she could go through her days without music. All of his spending had been on tapes, The Cure, the Smiths, Blondie, Green Day, Dead Boys, Therapy, to name a few.

Her father started to call Erin's name, but in a low voice that seemed to suggest more chant than command and made Andre think of the Pookas, the most feared of all the Faeries, who were known to stop in front of certain houses and call the names of those they want to take with them. He had an image of her father dragging Erin away from the room with his cruel bony hands. "What does he want?" Andre said and took the joint that was nearly done. Although he wished he was more clear- headed now, he still smoked.

Erin shook her head and Andre saw a shadow cross over it. Dullness came to her eyes that made the man's voice next door sound grotesque. "Erin, do you hear me?" her father said. Then he stopped calling her and started to shuffle around the room next door, so Andre thought of an old man he'd seen once in his mother's town in Spain walking up and down in front of the supermarket, shaking his head and muttering to himself. The joint had gotten hot, but Erin took it off him and squinted as she took the last drag. Andre wanted to stop hearing the movements of the man next door. It seemed slightly perverse to him, like listening to someone use a toilet, but when he took out his Walkman to share with Erin, she brushed it away and said she didn't want to listen to music. His hand tingled with the feel of her fingers. She'd put out the joint in a dirty ashtray she kept under the bed. Outside it was getting dark and gloomy. Streetlights were starting to come on and her father was outside her door. Andre felt heavy and useless on her bed. He had an urge to lie down and pull her with him when her father started tugging at the door handle.

"Why the hell are you locking your door?" he demanded.

"Open the door Erin, why aren't you opening the door?" The voice was petulant now, a hint of tears held in there and before Andre could think he was standing. Erin grabbed onto his pants. "What are you doing?"

His head was light from standing so quick. The walls of the room had a tendency to move in and out and he hated how aware he was of every part of his body. He wanted to get out of his head. "I'll just answer the door," he wanted to say, "I'll tell him to leave you alone. It'll be okay." But instead he shook his head and pulled away from her and she jumped and grabbed his arm. In a low voice, she told him, "No, don't, please."

Her fear worried him.

"I'll be there in a minute," she shouted to her father.

His knock was hard and steady. She said, "Please, Da."

There was an uneasy silence before he said, "Be quick about it."

They listened to his unsteady steps down the hall and stairs before Erin asked Andre, "What would you do if you were me?"

He was thrown off by the question. "I don't know," he said, "Probably go downstairs."

She sighed, "I don't mean that."

"What do you mean?" he asked.

"Never mind," she said. He hated her father then, for the screaming and the knocks and making Erin do things she didn't want to, but mostly for making him look like a stupid kid.

She was going for the door when he called her. "Erin."

She seemed impatient now and he hoped it wasn't towards him. "Yeah," she said.

"What do you want to do?" he asked and knew it was the right thing to say when she smiled. "I'll tell you later okay."

Chapter Five

The room was sliding into darkness. The end of the bed and segments of the wall were illuminated by street lamps, so there was an infusion of sick yellow light that seemed to reach towards the voices downstairs. When Erin left, Andre had wanted nothing more than to lie in bed and listen to the music. In his Walkman, there was Siouxie and the Banshees. He'd taken his time trying to decide what music Erin might like and had figured Peek-a-boo would be a good choice.

Slinking into dark stalls,
Shapeless and slumped in bath chairs,
Furtive eyes peep out of holes.

The lyrics of the song seemed to fit Erin and he'd imagined that she would want to listen to it over and over again. But she hadn't wanted to hear it once, which surprised him. How could she survive without music? In Michelle's house that was all he did. He had a tape player but he preferred the Walkman so he could feel the music rush into him. It made him feel separate from the world. Sometimes one of the family would come up and ask him to join them for a movie, which he did every now and again, though he never wanted to. He felt too conscious of his rigidity on their couch watching television. This was not his family, his family had broken apart and splintered and no one was good at acting. Everyone was a little stiff. He didn't feel that way in Erin's house. He might be a little on edge, but he didn't feel out of place, or that he was pretending to be someone he was not. For the first time in nearly two years, he had some kind of purpose, and for that reason he could not hide behind his music. He was aware of the clatter of dishes and the voices from downstairs. Although he couldn't hear what they were saying, he had the impression that there was an argument because of the brief bursts of dialogue.

From the top of the stairs, he heard the father say, "What am I supposed to do?"

Andre stepped down the stairs slowly.

"Do you hear me?" the father said.

"Yes, I hear you," Erin said with impatience. Leaning over the bannisters, Andre saw her father's legs reaching out from behind the door. He must have been at the table, where Erin had sat earlier, facing the garden. Andre had forgotten about the garden and the thought of it made his heart quicken. "Why don't you answer me then?" her father said.

Andre saw Erin when she stepped in front of the door. She held a sandwich and was looking towards her father with a tight jaw and she shook her head and said, "I don't know what you should do, okay!"

"Don't you talk to me like that," her father said and his legs disappeared, though Andre didn't know what was going on until he was standing in front of Erin. He grabbed her and she must have felt the spit on her face when he shouted to have some respect. She turned her face towards the door and Andre jumped back from the banister so she couldn't see him.

"Okay, Da. Let me go."

Andre had his back against the wall and listened to her father say in a lower tone, "I'll have respect in this house."

"Eat your sandwich Da."

"Sit with me."

"But Da."

"I said sit."

Andre heard the chair being pulled against the floor and then nothing but quiet. He went back to the bedroom, where he switched on the lamp by her bed and turned towards the dresser. On top of it was a hairbrush and he could see even in the dim light that the bristles were full of hair. He picked it up and brought it to the light. He'd often stood at the door to his parent's room and watched his mother brush her hair. The memory of it now made him feel displaced, as if the time between watching her and now was nothing and he'd suddenly found himself in this room. Under the light of the lamp, he saw the hair was closer to blonde, and hence a lighter shade than Erin's. A mumble came from downstairs and Andre pulled one of those hairs out. It was long and he let it drop behind the bedside cabinet. It was hard to understand why he was irritated with Erin for leaving the brush out with her mother's hair. He would never have kept something so private of his mother's for others to see, and in any case he would never have kept her brush. He'd pushed everything of his mother's away and maybe it was this that got to him, his emptiness compared to Erin's possession. He plucked one more hair out and let it fall. He heard Erin say something. Her father was laughing and it was not unlike the sound of his racking cough. Andre stepped out into the hall and heard the water start to run and a clatter of dishes.

Andre put the brush back and finally looked at the photos he'd been trying to avoid. There were three framed photos on the dresser. The first showed a young woman sitting at a table that Andre assumed was the round kitchen table downstairs. She looked young and had long blonde hair that fell over her shoulders and was parted sideways. Her head was tilted to the right and her chin rested on her hand. She was smiling, but not looking directly at the camera, so she seemed distracted or caught up in a world outside. Her eyes were the same color as Erin's, a deep grey, almost black, but they were smaller, more pensive looking.

The second photo was taken outside. The woman was in jeans and a sweater and had her arms around a younger Erin whose hair was shoulder length. The two of them were standing on a beach, it was a cloudy day and their hair was blown back from their heart-shaped faces by the breeze. They were smiling at the person taking the picture and Andre wondered if that might have been her brother because he could not imagine Erin had ever smiled at her thin, half-mad father.

The third photo showed an empty street on a grey day. The image startled him. It looked as if it was taken just outside Erin's house. He could make out the cracks in the pavement and had a strange idea of the photo being inhabited, that somehow he was missing somebody standing there.

"It was taken from Ma's camera," Erin said. She was standing at the door. He hadn't heard her approach.

"She left a roll of film and I thought maybe she'd left some kind of hint as to where she'd gone, but there was only this. I think she was trying to say that she wanted to leave and when I see the picture, I see her outside her house with the camera, so it's empty but it's not, if you know what I mean." Erin stepped into the room and closed the door and the dim light made the photo come to life, as if it was a moving image.

"But I don't think she walked away," Erin said from her place on the bed. A chill went through Andre. He was afraid to ask what she meant and was quick to put the photograph back. It made him uneasy now, as did the picture of the woman staring into space and the woman beside Erin when Erin was a different girl. These people didn't exist anymore, just like the people in the photos in Bray. The television had been put on downstairs, the volume was loud and the noise was oddly comforting coming through the floor.

"When Da first started acting weird I spent hours looking for clues. I searched everywhere for a blood stain, or a mark on a wall where she might have fallen. It was crazy because after a while I realized I wanted to see something. I wanted to know what had happened even if it meant something real bad," She paused to take cigarettes out from under her sleeve. She must have stolen them off her father moments ago. Andre took one and she lit them both. While she pulled on the cigarette and her cheeks moved in Andre didn't recognize her. Then she brought her cigarette away and it was Erin again and he thought the change was just because of the joint they'd shared.

"I wondered how he did it if there was no blood. I started to imagine his hands around her throat. He must have come from behind her and grabbed her so there was nothing she could do. I'd look at the photo of her in the kitchen and think of Da waiting to pounce. "

The rain had gotten lighter and fell muted on the glass, while obscuring the world outside.

"Do you really believe that?" he asked.

Erin said that her Da was not always like this. He wasn't always crazy.

"It's the guilt that's eating him alive," she said, "Or maybe Ma is getting him back, maybe she's haunting him here. I haven't seen her, but I have heard some weird noises and at the beginning we kept losing things and he kept saying, she's back, she's come back."

Andre believed this. He imagined the woman in the photo hiding in the house and that was the reason for her father's crying earlier and movement around the room. He might have been trying to get away from her. "Not all ghost are good," he said, when really what he meant was he was not afraid of his mother. She didn't hide things or follow him around, she walked beside him. Erin didn't seem to be listening or at least she made no response. The television was still on high and every now and again there was a clatter. Her father seemed incapable of sitting still. "The other night I woke and Da was in my room looking down at me."

Her voice had gotten low. Andre stood before her smoking, not willing to sit down yet. He was a little jumpy with the thought of the photos behind him and the man downstairs. Erin told him that her Da looked so weird, lit up by the street lights, just staring at her with a hateful expression. She'd asked her Da what he was doing and he didn't answer, just stood for what seemed like ages, not caring that she'd started to cry and then he'd turned around and left the room. That was the first time she'd locked her door.

"What are you going to do?" Andre said.

"I need to find some proof, but I haven't been able to go into his room. It's too dangerous with him downstairs."

Her head tilted and Andre noticed the long ash on her cigarette that might fall on her bed and grabbed the ashtray. She flicked carelessly and asked if he would help her.

"Why don't you go to the guards?"

"If you don't want to help that's fine!" she said and her anger surprised him.

He put out his cigarette and a blue stream of smoke rose from the ashtray. "I didn't say that."

"Yeah you did, you wanted to hand it over to the guards as if they give a shit."

"A woman's missing."

"Yeah, my Ma and my Da isn't right in the head and I'm fifteen and haven't been in school for months. What do you think will happen if I go to them? Do you really think they'll have any sympathy and they'll drop everything to escort me home and go through the house to find a clue to as to where she is? I'll probably be taken to social services, no thank you."

"You're fifteen?"

"Yeah and when I'm sixteen I can live by myself."

"Where?" He felt weightless with the thought of her going away.

"I don't know," she said, "I can't just make a choice, my Da doesn't drive a Mercedes."

"I don't have a choice either," he said and she studied him for a while in the dim room with the television booming under their feet and the rain sending shadows over them.

"You can't go home if you wanted to?" she asked and he felt a ripple of anger with her simplification.

"No, I can't," he lied and was sure she didn't believe him when she nodded and said okay. Her voice held a touch of irony that he refused to dwell on.

"I can't go into his room. I have to keep watch," she said, "It's much safer that way."

Was she serious? She wanted him to go into that room. The thought made him feel sick. "Why should I be the one? I don't have a clue what to look for."

"You need to look for anything that might belong to her, or anything that's out of place."

"It's been a year. He'd have gotten rid of it all."

"Yeah cos he's really smart, isn't he?" she said.

It was a relief to laugh.

"Why can't we just wait until he leaves the house?"

"He doesn't leave, he can't." She shuffled up on the bed to sit with her back to it. Andre saw headlights on the main road and had a sudden yearning to leave the house, but he knew he wouldn't enjoy his wandering thinking of her stuck at home.

"He causes problems whenever he goes out, it's one of the reason's I stopped going to school"

She sat forward and grazed his hand, the gesture was shy and uncertain and made him want to sit beside her, but he stayed where he was.

"We can do it tomorrow, after lunch, when it's still bright outside so you don't have to worry about turning on the light. I don't know why but turning on the light in that room freaks me out, I think he would know."

She shrugged, as if was just a small thing. Andre couldn't imagine setting foot in that dark dank room or opening drawers and wardrobes, but it didn't seem he had a choice. If he said no, he was certain Erin wouldn't want him back and it made him feel a sinking sensation similar to when the boys had asked him about his pocket money, though he didn't want to dwell on it too much.

"Da usually crashes out in the afternoon and if I sit with him he'll stay in the living room. I've tried to go into his room whenever he fell asleep down there, but I barely get upstairs before he wakes up and calls for me. I think he's worried about me getting in there, so it would be better if he didn't know you were here. I'll leave the door unlocked and you can go straight upstairs, okay?"

It took a moment for Andre to nod. The lump in his throat made it impossible to say okay.

Later while he lay in bed in Michelle's silent house he would realize he'd seen no photos of Erin's brother.

Chapter Six

Yesterday's rain made the grass glisten and Andre's steps squelch on the green. Michelle had been putting the finishing touches on dinner when he left. He'd stood at the door and told her he had to go out for a while. "You can't go now," she'd said. His father and Ines were due any minute. Ines wanted to spend every minute with Andre and it was exhausting. Usually he'd be lying on his bed and the music would block the sound of arrival or her footsteps up the stairs, but they were like clockwork and Andre didn't need to hear them to know when they'd arrived. Eugene was never late and he'd held that custom, as if punctuality mattered.

Ines would appear at Andre's door and gauge his mood. Sometimes he'd rise and walk to the door and tell her to go find Martha, other times he would remain lying on the bed and she would enter and lie beside him with a book. She was a quiet, thoughtful eight-year-old. Eventually they'd be called for dinner and at the table his father would ask Andre about school and this and that. Andre had become an expert at shrugging and finding one word answers, until eventually the conversation would move away from father and son to involve everyone, though they would remain aware of each other throughout, like two points in a compass, father and son heading in different directions.

"I'll be back soon," Andre said.

"You better be," Michelle called after him.

****

Andre didn't bother going to Ronan's house. A red Ford Fiesta was parked outside, which meant his mother was home. Yesterday's interaction had left him reluctant to see her again. Plus he didn't need any more reason to worry about Erin's father. Still it bothered him that he hadn't been able to phone Ronan from Michelle's house to tell him where he was going since the phone was in the hall and everyone would hear. Andre hoped to be quick in Erin's house, not only because Erin wanted their meetings to be secret, but because he was sure that Michelle would be against him seeing Erin.

The sky was blue over his head. Last night's rain had stopped by the time he'd left Erin's house. They'd had another smoke and had sat in the bed while she'd talked to him about her mother. Her name was Cathy, though everyone called her Cat for short. She didn't like being called Ma, so Erin had called her Cat too. She used to sing all the time. When she was cooking or doing anything in the house there was always music. She used to say life was too short for silence. Andre had felt lazy on the bed and at one stage his hand had drifted towards Erin and she'd let him hold it. It had been wonderful to be cocooned in her dark room and feel her skin. "Da was much older than her," Erin had said. "They met when she worked at Geraldine's drapery and he came in with a huge bunch of roses. No-one had bought her flowers before, she was eighteen. They went out for a year before they were married."

"Any snacks?" Andre asked.

She'd gone down to investigate and came back with a bowl of dry cornflakes and nearly dropped them when Andre's disappointed face made her laugh. The cornflakes stuck between his teeth and he'd sworn to bring some food the next time. "Munchies," she'd said.

"What are munchies?" he'd asked. "Chocolates?"

Which started her on a laughing spree again. "You have *the* munchies," she'd said. He'd forgotten about her father, but he'd appeared at the living room door when Andre was leaving. "Who are you?" he'd said. His eyes were red and half-shut. Andre told him his name was Paul. Erin held in her laughter until they stood outside.

****

There was a soft breeze, hardly strong enough to ruffle his hair. Erin's Volvo was a dark red color, almost purple and its license plate was 79, he would have been 4 when it was made, and Erin 5, living their lives on other sides of the city, maybe she'd been happy too, in her clean house and listening to her mother's singing.

With the sight of the open front door, he felt as if he'd swallowed a block of lead. The heaviness in his stomach was weighing him down and made his steps slow and reluctant. No sound came from the house. The stillness reminded him of an old stone ruin his family used to pass in the Wicklow Mountains that never had any birds around it. When he'd asked his mother why it was so quiet there, she'd told him it was haunted by a woman who'd been starved to death. Her figure was often seeing wandering from room to room. Every time he'd passed, he'd hoped to see a ghost, though that thought frightened him too. He felt the same sensation now, an element of excitement and dread. The door was on the latch and he had to take a deep breath before pushing it inward. He was expecting to see Erin's Da at the living room door with his red eyes, down-turned mouth, and the hard boney hands that were difficult to forget because they were bigger than they should be. There was nothing, but the musty smell of drink and cigarettes. Maybe a clock ticked somewhere. He'd forgotten to ask Erin about the clocks and if they'd stopped, and as he stepped inside this detail seemed suddenly important so his throat constricted with the need to talk to her. He stalled for a moment hoping to see her.

"Go on," the soft whisper startled him and then he saw her sitting forward on the couch. Sun light draped her head. She looked tired, maybe she'd been crying or she'd fallen asleep when her father had. He must have been there with her, but Andre couldn't see him and it made him aware of every move. He looked towards the kitchen with the sticky floor and the dishes still in the sink, no matter the sound of the tap running yesterday. Maybe they'd been washed and re-used moments later, so Erin's life was a repetition of the same acts; cleaning and re-cleaning and still all anyone saw was the dirt that kept re-appearing.

Andre stepped as quietly as he could. The stairs creaked on the third step and made him stop for what felt like several minutes and he imagined Erin on the couch, staring at the wall opposite, scared to move in case she might alert her father. Andre took the next step and half-hoped that her father would wake and save him from going into his room, but he didn't wake and Andre found himself at the door. It was closed and he had to turn the handle. It was hard to breathe; his throat seemed to have gotten smaller when he imagined the father on the other side of the door. It opened to nothing but the tossed bed. Andre stepped inside while the silence issued from downstairs. The sheets were dirty. There was a cigarette hole on the bedspread, ash on the floor, a bottle tossed on its side, clothes in a ball in the corner. Did Erin have to wash these clothes? Did she knock on the door like Michelle did with Andre and ask if there was anything that needed washing, or did he shout at her to come in and pick everything up? Had she gotten used to the smells? He stepped over the clothes to the bedside cabinet. He didn't want to touch anything. He'd never had to finger dirt before and his hand stopped inches from the bedside cabinet. There was a book on top and he picked it up to see it was the bible, the cover was light blue leather. The name Dan McEvoy was written in an untidy hand. Andre's hand was sticky from holding it and he felt nauseous. He opened the top drawer of the bedside cabinet and found it full of papers. He picked up the pile to see some bills and an open envelope with no name or address, and a letter inside that held indiscernible writing. He let them drop when he noticed the old tissue at the bottom of the pile and gagged with the thought of Dan McEvoy's bodily fluids on him. It took some vigorous rubbing of hands on his pants before he felt steady enough to close the drawer. The cabinet underneath held nothing but scraps of paper, a few coins, and an old black comb with teeth missing. Andre went to the chest of drawers that was in front of the door. The first row was made up of two half drawers and the second and third had one drawer. He opened the small ones first and found underwear and socks in one, vests and white t-shirts in another as well as a crumpled empty packet of Major cigarettes.

The second drawer was harder to open, and his heart was thumping with the noise made from the stiff hinges. Some sweaters and pants had been tossed inside. There was a musty smell from them, Andre lifted them up and searched between garments. He was about to close the drawer but decided to dig a bit deeper. His flat hand was sliding under the clothes when he felt the paper in the far corner. He opened the drawer further and looked at the very back where he saw a white envelope. He pulled it out. There was no address for Dan or anyone else written on it. At first he thought it was empty, but while trying to put it back exactly where he'd found it, he felt a hard object in the corner and stilled for a moment because he knew exactly what it was. The silence ticked and his breathing filled his ears as he pulled the envelope out again. It wasn't sealed and inside he found a silver ring with a small diamond. He put the empty envelope back and closed the drawer. The noise grated his senses. His steps were not as cautious in his hurry to Erin's bedroom, which seemed foreign in the day light and sad too, like a place abandoned, and he went straight for the picture of the woman staring out of the kitchen table with her chin in her hand. He lifted it up and brought it closer to the window, though he didn't have to. He'd known from the moment he saw the ring that it was the same one that Erin's mother had worn.

****

The ring burned a hole in Andre's pocket. He would have liked to talk to Erin before he left the house, but they'd already made plans to meet after his dinner. When he got downstairs she gestured towards the door. "Go," she said and so he did.

Once outside the house, he started to run and he didn't stop when Ronan darted out of his house to call for him. "I have to get back," Andre shouted at him, not out of politeness, but because he didn't want Ronan to follow him. He couldn't imagine having to keep a normal conversation or feign interest in football when the ring was in his hand searing his skin. His father's car was parked outside Michelle's house and it looked obnoxious. 'Da', Andre called him when he was with Erin. He wanted to suffocate the Dad, the politeness in the word, though Da felt wrong on his tongue. He had never called Eugene, Da, to his face, and he realized whatever way he referred to him didn't matter. He would not go into that house today and slot into his role, whatever that was, the wayward son who was not wayward anymore, the Lost Boy? How did his father view him? What did he think when he thought of his son? He didn't cause trouble anymore, was that it? Was that enough?

Forward on, that was the only way for Eugene, but Andre was not looking forward today. He was looking back. In his mind's-eye he saw a young blond woman sitting by a kitchen table staring off into space. What had she been thinking of at that moment? Had a question been posed to her? Maybe she was looking outside at her daughter, maybe Erin was out there beyond the window playing, oblivious to the moment, only to be brought back to it again and again because of a click of a camera. Every time Erin looked at the photo she was back there, and she was trying to understand something that was already done. Already gone.

Debris

Andre would not be able to stop thinking of her mother. She was light where his mother was dark. She sang songs instead of stories. She was young and vibrant, like his mother had been. Her presence must have been felt in every room. Whenever Andre had gone into the rooms at home, he'd known if his mother had just left from the scent in the air. What would he have done if she'd just disappeared, one day he'd come home and called to her and there was nothing. How would he have felt if that evening they'd waited while it grew dark and every time he saw his reflection on the black window his heart jumped thinking it was her, but she never came, that night or the next? Eugene would have gone mad looking for her. They all would have. It would have killed them not to know, but what if she'd gone and she'd left her ring behind? Didn't that mean something else entirely? If it had been out in the open, if Erin had showed him and said Ma left this, he would have known it was goodbye. But it had been hidden in an envelope and in the back of a drawer because Dan McEvoy didn't want his daughter to see it. Andre remembered Dan's keening noise and the walk around the room and thought it must have something to do with the ring. Maybe at certain times Dan felt it more than others, maybe in his drunkenness he was prone to take it out and study it, or maybe, there was something of the woman kept in the ring, like the hair had been kept on the brush. Andre wondered if that was why he'd kept nothing of his mother's in his room. To be aware of her in the house or to feel her presence when he walked was one thing, but he didn't know if he had the strength to bring her into his room and close the door and is that not what Dan McEvoy had done. A cold dread started inside Andre and he stopped before the fields at the last row of back walls. Waist high walls separated the square gardens from the open space and Andre thought it pointless to have a meager wall to keep that tiny space away from the wider sky and fields as if to say this is what I'll take for myself, this is what is mine when in reality anyone could jump those walls and cause havoc. He stayed on the other side of the wall and slid down to hide. There was no evidence that Erin's mother had died, nothing but her disappearance and the ring, yet the ring seemed enough for him, holding it in his hand he was sure he could feel her, like he'd felt his mother in the clocks that had stopped, or in the breeze that had come through the door the night of the wake and it scared him. He held the ring in his palm. His fingers curled tight as if it was her hand he held and without him she might fall away.

Chapter Seven

The table was pulled out into the middle of the floor, set and ready with a roast chicken, potatoes, gravy and carrots. Michelle wiped down the sink and finished the few used saucepans. She was still in her Sunday clothes, black skirt, blouse, and an apron had been tied over them to protect the good clothes while cooking.

Ron had gone for a pint after mass on Main Street. Most Sundays, he walked down the hill from the church to The Snug bar, which might have stood by itself years ago and looked out on the field but was now sandwiched between The Cottage, a fast food restaurant, and the drapery store that had closed down two years ago. Less than twenty years ago, women weren't allowed in the pub alone. When Michelle, in the navy school uniform that did nothing to flatter her legs, heard she had walked past the pub with dark tinted windows and felt a helpless kind of anger that made her turn around and burst through the front door. She was hit with the smell of stale smoke and drink. An old man wearing a peaked cap and grey suit that had seen better days sat at the narrow bar and turned to look at her. They watched each other for a while, the man with watery blue eyes and lines etched into skin and the school girl who wanted to say so much but whose voice failed her. The bar man was wiping the counter, though Michelle hardly noticed anything of him. The old man was the one who'd remained in her head because of the lack of curiosity, the pure blankness of him. It was the same kind of indifference hat she now saw in Andre.

The television was on in the living room. Eugene was on the couch pretending to watch whatever was on. He didn't care for pubs and neither did she. They'd never talked about their parent's car accident. There was no need to voice the fact that their parents were drunk. For weeks and months afterwards the knowledge hovered like static around them. The lightness of her parents when drunk was what Michelle remembered most about them. Her mother changed from having solid feet on the ground to a floating apparition of light touches and a sing song voice. Their father grew quiet and his mood dipped in his silence. Michelle used to wish for any other emotion. Screams and slamming doors would have been easier than the way they faded.

Blankness. Indifference.

And now she had Andre's silence to deal with. He wandered around the house and gave no trouble, at least nothing that she could put her finger on. But there was the quietness that got to her, the way he looked at her with a vacancy that suggested not a boy who was lost and troubled but a boy who'd given up trying. He lived with them without participating, though when she said this to Ron, he told her to give the boy a chance.

54

Debris

"He's lost his mother, for heaven's sake." And she'd wanted to ask why that was suddenly her responsibility and when was the choice given to her, not when Eugene phoned her and said, Andre wants to stay with you, or later when he sat at the kitchen table and said, Andre needs you.

She dried her hands on her apron and took it off, slowly, unwillingly because it meant putting some part of her away, the woman who could hide behind her chores, the cooking and cleaning while her brother sat in the living room, probably glancing at his watch every few seconds. Andre was fifteen minutes late. Ron should have been home by now.

"Where did Andre go?" Eugene asked from the kitchen door and Michelle's grasp on her apron tightened. It was like having a nail screwed tighter in her gut. Outside sheets fluttered in the breeze, the day looked close to rain but she knew it would hold back for another hour or two. She had gotten so good at reading the weather, a lick of her finger to measure dampness, no, she wasn't quite that bad, but she felt she was near it sometimes, staring, waiting, prophesying. Was it when she was twenty-two and Eugene nineteen that she started thinking about rain? Maybe it was between the secretary job and taking care of the house, and her younger brother who was lost, or maybe not lost, or helpless like she'd assumed, but bloody spoiled.

"Do you remember when I told you to iron your own uniform?" she asked without looking away from the window. "You must have been 14, maybe 13, I don't know, I'm pretty sure I was in my last year at school."

His silence forced her to turn to him. She saw his form take up the doorway, tall and wide. His dark hair was cut short and there was hardness around his eyes that had only come in the last few months. No, not hardness she thought when she studied him, but reservedness, similar but lesser than their Da when his moods dipped and he sat in his chair by the fire listening to no-one.

"You were in here."

She glanced at the far corner, opposite the door and saw a younger Eugene, thin and loose of shoulder, serious-faced, as he tried to get his sweater to lie flat on the ironing board.

Eugene was frowning now. He said he had no idea what she was talking about and his anger caused a ripple in the room. They could have gone for a swim on the tension. He asked again where his son was and she had to bite her tongue before she stepped away from the sink. The rim might have left an imprint on her back. She felt as if there were imprints all over her. The apron was in her hands. And she had to fight the urge to throw it at him and scream.

"You'd nearly finished your sweater when Da came in. Don't tell me you don't remember?"

She saw a loosening around his eyes, a relenting that came in the shape of a shrug. "That was years ago."

"It was and it wasn't," she said. "Not much has changed."

After a minute she said, "Da gave me a slap and said he never wanted to see his son ironing again."

A Sunday evening, a lifetime ago, yet not long ago either, she can still feel the sting and remember the smell of the pub.

"You laughed," she said.

"I did not."

"Yes, you did, you laughed and you left the room with your sweater half done and by God, I wanted to burn the thing but I didn't. I did my duty, and I did it again when they died."

The front door opened. They heard it through the cracks of their silences, the places where they had fallen away from each other and Ron's humming was there too.

"Is everything alright?" Ron said.

"No, everything is not alright," Michelle said.

"We don't know where Andre is," Eugene said.

"No, you don't know where Andre is." She didn't mean to shout but she felt better for it. The men were looking at her, Ron surprised and worried. He would have liked to tell her to calm down. She could see it in the wide probing eyes, but he was smart enough not to. Eugene's blank expression infuriated her further. She would have liked to poke his shoulder with a sharp finger or hit him on the face and chest, which made her afraid to move. "He is your son. Why do you think you can just give the job to me?"

"Michelle?"

Michelle glared at Ron and said, "Don't Michelle me," before turning her attention to her brother.

"'I should have burnt that uniform. I should have left the iron on it until the whole house went up in smoke, but I didn't, and God help me but I'm not going to make the same mistake twice."

****

Andre jumped up when he'd seen Ron in the distance. His figure was easy to make out because of the loose walk and the way his head hung low. He had a tendency to watch his feet while he strolled. Andre ran to the far side of the fields to get away from Ron's happiness. The ease of him was an affront and made Andre trip over his feet. He'd promised Erin to meet her beside the houses. She'd asked him not to go to the fields alone, but he couldn't think of that now. He waited for Ron to disappear around the front of the houses before running up by the side of the field. The rain had left the grass muddy in places and it wasn't an easy run, sinking a little in the worst places. It seemed a long time since he'd stood in the bushes watching Erin, hard to believe only two days had passed.

The benches were empty, cans had been left in the grass. The air was still, the trees unmoving, but there was a chill in the air that settled under Andre's clothes. In the warehouse, he stopped inside the door. The gloom was thick and dense. Outside the day was full of clouds. They seemed to have drifted into the building to linger against the walls and he realized he was scared. The ring seemed like something from another world, brought back by Erin's mother. There was an idea that she wanted him to find it. He'd been about to close the drawer when he'd shoved his hand inside. The thought made him shiver and feel slightly claustrophobic. He went to the far corner where the darkness seemed thicker and sat on the dirty ground, and wondered what he was running away from. A strange feeling had risen in his belly and he was on the verge of crying.

"I'd love to be ignored," Erin had said the other night and Andre's stomach had tightened with the knowledge that it was not as simple as that. His father didn't ignore him. There was not blankness when he looked at his son, but a terrible deep anger and resentment that made it impossible to speak during those Sunday dinners in Michelle's house and all other times. His one-word answers were not from rebellion, but to get his father's attention away from him.

Andre wanted to forget that moment when he'd sat in the back of the car and met his father's gaze in the rear-view mirror. He'd caught his father staring at him as if he was something foreign that he didn't understand and had no care to. His father had said, "It's what you want, isn't it?" And Andre thought *no, it's what you want*, but to say this would have brought him deeper into the truth and he wasn't strong enough for that. He still wasn't; taking the ring out of its hiding place, that's when he'd felt the sorrow unfold within him.

His father had not hidden away his wife's rings. He'd hidden Andre away. To think of this made him feel ugly and helpless and there was no way he could face his father today. Was it the ring that had finally made him acknowledge the truth or the way Erin hid from her father and looked at him when she'd stood by the kitchen door, her body tense with anger and impatience? In the last two years, his father had showed little else towards Andre and he'd sought escape. His stomach grumbled. Soon it would be dark. He crouched down in the warehouse while outside the March day dimmed and fingers of light barely reached his feet. He looked like a wooden statue or a bundle of clothes, guarding his treasure like the leprechauns his mother had told him about.

He knew his father blamed him for the accident and that was why they never spoke about what happened. There was no way around it. Andre hadn't been sent to live with his aunt because of the fights or the fire. He was sent here because his father couldn't stand looking at his face. The night his mother died, Andre had waited for the questions and the following days, too. They never came because his father had seen his son huddled on the side of the road with the man's jacket over him and he'd seen what Andre held in his hand. The parishioner John Marrow was crying beside him while the sound of sirens filled the air and the spectacles Andre had stolen from the hall table were lit up by headlights. Andre should have dropped them while he'd reached for his mother and minutes later as John pulled him out of the passenger seat, but instead shock had tightened his grip. When his father arrived on the scene, he'd run straight for his wife, but was held back by the medics. They were the first phone call John had made. He'd taken Andre out of the car and wrapped him in his coat before he went to the driver's side to look at Usao. He was crying when he came back to the boy and sat beside him and only when the sirens were approaching did he ask Andre for his father's number.

Usao had to be cut out. The sound was sharp and cruel and his father's screams rose with it and made the boy shake and cry. And only when Eugene had stood before him did he realize that he still held the spectacles.

Andre wrapped his arms around his belly when he remembered how his father had stared at them. For a moment Andre was sure he'd vomit and was hardly aware of the tears on his cheeks. Eugene had stood frozen before his son processing what the spectacles could mean. Then John was beside him telling him he was so sorry and Andre managed to stand and drop the glasses at the same time. "Dad?" he said, "We were going too fast," and his father took him in his arms and squeezed him so tight Andre cried out. He heard the glasses shatter under his father's feet and he did again now. The sound traveled through the years, glasses that had splintered into tiny fragments and were left on the side of the road with some essential part of the boy and man.

****

"You should keep a better eye on him," Mrs. Neary said. Her eyes were a stunning bright blue and might have been beautiful if not for the stern way she was looking at Michelle and the fact that her thin mean mouth was below them. She held onto her front door as if she needed to bar Michelle's entry. The day had not been a good one and Michelle had to take several breaths in order to calm down and not tell the woman where she should bloody well go.

"I take it he isn't here,' Michelle said.

"No he isn't," Mrs.Neary said. "He's probably at the McEvoy's."

Michelle saw a burst of satisfaction on Mrs. Neary's face and refused to feed into it by showing a reaction. Michelle thanked the woman and walked away. It took several seconds before she heard the door close. Michelle knew about the McEvoy's and their troubles and she'd heard

Debris

some things about Erin that did not bear repeating. It was hard to know how she felt going to their house, indifferent maybe, certainly not as shocked and offended as Mrs.Neary and her ilk would presume. *Jesus*, she thought, *the nerve of some people.*

It was dark and cold so the green was unusually silent which fed into Michelle's ill-humor. Even in the meagre light the McEvoy's home was worn and shabby looking. Standing in front of it, Michelle couldn't help wonder what had brought Andre to the house in the first place, but more importantly why a girl like Erin would take an interest in Andre, and then she considered the term 'girl like Erin' and felt that she was just as bad as Mrs.Neary. 'A girl like'….what the hell, Michelle thought. She was limp-limbed from the horrible run in with her brother which rather than bringing relief had brought a shocking guilt and no satisfactory solution. Eugene had refused to say anything about her tirade and had eaten his dinner without looking at her, a dinner that would have grown cold if not for Ron saving the day and rallying everyone and convincing Ines that there was no need to wait for her brother and he'd be happy with a plate kept for him when he got home. There was the hour of waiting afterwards where Eugene sat in the living room with Ron and watched the Sunday game and avoided his sister, as if his refusal to see her point would make it disappear and his determination alone could make this situation go on, which he seemed capable of doing for now because Michelle was so bloody exhausted she couldn't bring herself to tackle her brother again. She would have stayed in the house without regard to Andre's absence if Ron hadn't come to her and insisted they should look. Insisted that she should go to the Neary's since the wife was the only one there. Michelle knew this was Eugene's instruction as her husband would have thought little of a teenage boy out after dark. He thought little of anything that wasn't in front of his face, but still she rose and left the house and if it was not for all this, she might have knocked on Erin's door with a little bit of antagonism towards the girl who was known to be a trouble-maker, but instead when Erin opened the door, Michelle had an urge to cry and for a moment she didn't say anything. Erin didn't either, because the woman was looking at her softly and in a way she hadn't been looked at in a long time. Michelle said, "Is Andre here?"

And Erin remembered not to trust, it was not hard to remember since the memory was in her skin. At least that is how she felt. She bristled and her gaze hardened. Michelle noticed and drew back. "I don't know any Andre," Erin said.

"Who is that?" Her father was behind her now. His hair was tossed and his eyes were red. He had a downturned mouth and Michelle was angry at the girl for lying. "I'm looking for Andre, is he here?" she said and Erin didn't flinch with the impatient hard tone.

"Andre," the father said absently and shook his head. "Paul was here," he said. Erin remained stone-faced.

"Andre, what kind of name is that anyway?" the father said, absently. The front door closing was answer enough.

Chapter Eight

He woke, startled and stiff. For a moment, he thought he was in the car because of the hardness under his legs and the darkness, too. His head had been black when they'd first crashed, and he cried out years later in a way he hadn't then, because then he'd had no idea what it meant. Erin called to him again and he remembered where he was when the smell of the dank warehouse reached him. He jumped up to look for the ring that was not in his hand. He flicked his lighter, but there was so much debris, wood and stone and so little light.

"What are you doing?" Erin said. "They were looking for you an hour ago." She sounded panicked and Andre's heart had quickened and his mouth was dry with the thought of the ring being lost. There was laughter from far off. It was so dark. He could barely make out the outline of his hands and he was on his knees, searching. Erin was getting impatient and the voices were getting nearer.

"Shit," Erin said, "Andre, we need to go."

He couldn't see the ring. His fingers were sore. He'd rubbed something sharp, not glass, maybe the side of a can and it had torn the skin of his thumb. He felt the warmth of the blood, and saw the black red whenever he flicked the lighter, though his focus was on the ground. Silver, why was it so hard to see it among the dull things. If he didn't find it he would question its existence just like he'd questioned his mother's presence, or the way his father looked at him. It was hard to keep anything together. Erin was coming towards him. She had a flashlight. He hadn't noticed because she kept it shining on the ground, lighting her way, and she was moving slowly and carefully, as if afraid to make noise. "We have to wait in here for a minute," she said. "Be quiet." But he was already moving towards her, tripping over a lump of wood, nearly falling forward. The blood was running down his arm, warm and slippery like a living thing. "Give me the flashlight," he said.

She told him to be quiet.

"No, don't," she said, but he'd grabbed the flashlight off her and brought the light upwards.

"Who's in there?" the voice was from outside and Erin moaned, stalling Andre for a second. He looked back to see her pale face. She stood frozen and he might have said sorry, though he had no idea what he was sorry for. He was concerned about the ring since Colin was in the vicinity. Andre was sure Colin would take it for himself. He would put a piece of Erin in his pocket and walk off. He scrambled for the corner, and Colin was at the door. His figure appeared wide in the dim light. His flashlight gave shape to Erin.

"Hello, Erin."

The light was weaving in circles on the floor and finally shone on silver and Andre picked it up. The blood had run down to his sleeve.

"Who is that with you?" Colin asked.

"I didn't know he was here," Erin said.

"You didn't know he was here," Colin repeated. He'd stepped inside and Manny was visible now, tall and faceless in the dark night.

"That's really interesting isn't it Manny, that she didn't know he was here. Do you think I should believe her?"

"I don't know Col, but if that's the case I would ask why she's here. Was she investigating a strange noise? Did she, for example, think that the wee man was a rodent, and if she did, does that not mean that he is a fucking rodent?"

Andre stiffened, the ring that had seemed so important felt tiny in his hand. Manny's voice had been brutal. Erin had her back to Andre now, and Colin's flash-light shone on the floor so it was impossible to see her face. She seemed far away, even though she had not moved. There was a change in her stance that made him feel alone and trapped.

Colin laughed. "I think therefore you are."

Erin said, "I found him asleep in the corner like a little baby." She tried to sound carefree, but there was a quiver to her voice and Andre knew she was scared. Only now he became aware of her telling him to hurry up while he'd searched for the ring and he would have liked the ground to open up and swallow him whole. His cut stung and he was still bleeding. He wondered if that was what made him light-headed or if it was his strong desire to go to Erin and hold her hand, though somehow he knew that would only make matters worse. Colin stepped back from the doorway and said okay and Andre felt such relief he thought he'd vomit, until Colin said, "Go on home little man."

Erin a small figure given shape by the flashlight in Andre's hands standing in the middle of the floor was so still, he had the impression that she'd stopped breathing. He started walking, and was trembling so badly he nearly fell when he tripped over the same piece of wood from earlier. The flashlight was shaking in his hand and he thought this heart might burst from his chest and half-wished it would so he could find a way out of this. He paused beside Erin to ask if she was coming. She didn't look at him, and Colin said, "No, she's staying. Manny will walk you home if you need, won't you Manny? Make sure the baby gets back safe into his cot."

"No." Andre wanted to say that he wasn't a baby and he wasn't going to leave without Erin, but he was choking on the words. They were clawing animals in his throat and Erin said, "Go home Andre." The way she said it with such final submission made him grab her hand. "You're bleeding," she said.

Andre would never forget the concern in her voice.

Debris

Colin shouted, "Jesus Christ, I'm losing patience here." And he came for Andre, a bull with his wide shoulders and large head and Manny was laughing, a grotesque clown, thin legged and long haired and mouth opened, so his teeth flashed in the dim light. Andre's head went back from the force of Colin's slap and Andre cried out with the sensation that his skin had been torn from his cheek. His cheek bone throbbed and he felt more than saw the movement of Colin's hand going back again. "You shouldn't do that," Erin said. She sounded breathless, "His Da's here, I saw the car."

"So fucking what?" Colin said.

Erin said, "He won't let you away with that."

"He won't know," Colin said and grabbed Andre by his jacket. His breath stank of tobacco. "Will he, little man?"

Andre hated that he was crying. The tears blinded him and made him sniffle when Erin was quiet beside him. Colin tapped his cheek and Andre flinched, the pain was under his skin and the touch brought it rushing upward. Andre was pushed towards the door. He stumbled and fell forward and was sure he would land on his belly but he managed to right himself and the ring burned his hand, but for a different reason than earlier. Now it reminded him of his stupidity and carelessness, how naïve he'd been fifteen minutes ago. He turned to Colin and tried to sound firm when he said he wouldn't go. Colin charged and somehow he knew the exact spot that he'd slapped before. Andre's pain was blinding. Erin said. "Go home, Andre."

"I can keep going," Colin said, "I don't have to stop. You want another slap."

Andre said nothing. The heat traveled from his cheek and down his throat.

His head hung on his neck and it felt huge, an iron weight. Another smack and Erin screamed for Colin to stop. Andre's head was light. He felt his eyes flutter to the back of his head.

Manny had him now. He was pulling him out of the building and Andre was trying hard to focus on what was going on. The pain ebbed and flowed, it seemed to have the ability to breathe under his skin. It was so hard to think, but he pulled away from Manny. From inside Andre heard Colin's murmur and he didn't need to hear the words to know it wasn't good. The very air had turned bad, the world had changed. Andre was sick and scared, "Do you need directions little man?" Manny said and Andre's head cleared a little. Manny shoved him and might have hit him again. The silence was tight enough to hold intention but Andre didn't give him a chance. He started running. Manny laughed when he fell. Andre was up again quickly, sinking into the mud, running and stumbling, more scared than he'd ever been before. He wasn't aware of the rain that fell on him..

His father's car was still there. If Andre had thought to look, he would have seen that it was just after seven. An hour ago, Michelle had stood at the door of Erin's house and once she'd returned home, Ron and Eugene had walked into town through the estate. They were not long back and were trying to decide what to do. Ron and Eugene were at the kitchen table. Michelle was standing by the kitchen sink. She had refused to offer the men tea. She would not make another damn thing for her brother, so they sat empty-handed, a dry Irish house, tipping the scales of argument. Andre's absence and Ron's chatter about the possibility of Andre going into the city and getting delayed, or maybe having a girlfriend on the sly were the only reasons Michelle had not thrown something at Eugene.

They heard the crash of the door opening and Andre stumbling through the hall. The adults were so pale and still, compared to his purple and red panting body. He was in the room seconds before Michelle could push herself from the counter and the men were able to stand.

"What happened to you?" Eugene said. Andre's left cheek was a deep red. He pulled away when Eugene touched his chin. The thought of any heat on that cheek made a cry start in his throat and he couldn't cry. He couldn't think of how sore his cheekbone was, running it had felt loose, though he knew it couldn't have been. Eugene was trying to get a proper look at his son's face but Andre kept pulling away. Ron was asking who did that. His voice was low and had a level of rage that seemed unsuited to Ron.

"It doesn't matter," Andre said. He was aware of passing time with every beat of his heart. Minutes ticking on the clock that he would never get back. He needed to act quickly and help Erin, but it was hard to think straight with them crowding around him. Michelle had gone for his hand and exclaimed when she saw the deep gash. The dried blood was dark red.

"Jesus Christ, talk to us," Eugene said. Andre stepped back. He wanted to scream at them to shut up, but they must have seen the fear and frustration on his face because there was a brief stillness. "You have to come now," he said. His voice was slurred from the exertion of his run. Ines and Martha had run out from the living room. "What's that smell?" Martha said. Michelle told her to be quiet and go back to the movie.

"Andre?" Ines was beside him and he couldn't look at her.

"She's in trouble," Andre said. "Please. You have to help."

****

The men left the front door open in their hurry, which brought Michelle to the hall. From the doorway she looked across the fields and her gaze went in the direction of Erin's house and she wrapped her arms around her belly and would have remained at that spot until the boys came back if Martha had not come out to say that she was cold.

Debris

Michelle closed the door and waited in the kitchen, unable to sit still, caught between the fury that had been lingering all day and a deep resonating sadness that seemed to be bigger than her.

Chapter Nine

Andre made it as far as the field before his legs gave way. It was so hard to run. His legs were like jelly and a pain had started in his head, burning behind his eyes. He stumbled and Ron tried to hold his arm. Andre told him to go.

"She's in the warehouse."

He was sure Eugene stared at him for a moment too long and Andre couldn't care. Stumbling in the mud, he watched Eugene and Ron disappear into the darkness ahead. It was like being in a nightmare, the lights from the estate could not reach him and he kept stumbling. He wanted so much to run, but his pants were heavy from falling in the mud earlier and his body felt hollow and his steps seemed to be in slow motion, to lift his feet and step forward was so cumbersome and hard, one after the other, it was like being stuck in quick sand. His tears were from frustration. The men had disappeared and it was so tempting to stop and wait for them, though in the next instant he imagined Colin with a knife, or Manny hiding behind the door of the warehouse, jumping his dad and uncle. Eugene and Ron didn't know what to expect. Colin was small, but vicious and if he got one of them on the ground he wouldn't stop hitting. In their hurry, Andre had said nothing about the presence of two young men. His father and uncle were running towards them now. Andre shouted for his father and uncle to be careful, only it was not a shout but a small pitiful sound.

****

Time was measured by his deep uneven breaths, everywhere else was silent, nothing came from the warehouse and then he saw the two figures coming towards him as if they'd stepped out of a deeper darkness. One was tall with broad shoulders, the other walked with a loose limbed rapidness. Andre's chest tightened and his body froze from his crippling urge to flee. His fear tasted like the sweetness of rain because fear was not bitter; the aftermath was; the shame when it passed and he recognized the two coming for him as his father and uncle and he saw Erin was not with them. He started to run.

****

When the front door opened Michelle darted to the hallway. Ron was the first to enter and took the time to hang his wet jacket on the hooks by the door which he never did. Usually he'd throw it behind the back of the chair where he'd grabbed it just over a half an hour ago. Eugene kept his attention on Andre as the boy shuffled through the door behind him and Andre kept his gaze planted firmly at his feet, a bent figure with clothes weighed down by mud. They were all muddy. Boots were thrown off by

Debris

the door while the silence was almost visible. Michelle held herself straighter. Her arms wrapped around her waist for the umpteenth time as if she was afraid there might be some hole where everything she'd been feeling throughout the day might leak out. She didn't grow scared until Eugene closed the front door. "Where is she?" she blurted and Andre stood straight. Through the dirt she saw the bruising on his face was not so livid, though his eye was still red and one side of his lip was swollen.

"It was a mistake," his voice sounded raw.

"Your hand," Michelle said. She had forgotten about the blood and went to check it now, but he stepped back and said he was fine.

"Let me see," Michelle said, and felt Ron and Eugene's stillness and might have been annoyed with their inaction if she didn't feel their worry and confusion and the drift between the three of them.

"It was a mistake," Andre said again and he sounded on the verge of tears, but he straightened and his eyes flashed when she tried to get at his hand again and he made her think of a spooked horse she'd seen once rearing up in Wicklow.

In the living room, the sea witch Ursula was singing about the poor little souls for the second time. "Watch it again," Michelle had said when Martha wandered in to tell her the movie was over.

"But Mammy," she whined.

"Watch it again," Michelle snapped. Martha slunk back to the living room while Michelle waited for the men to come back.

Andre lurched towards the stairs and said he needed to shower.

"There was no-one there and he won't talk," Eugene said when the bathroom door slammed. "He won't tell us a thing. Who it was or what happened?"

Erin's name was on Michelle's tongue and she wasn't sure why she kept it there. She'd said nothing about Erin's house earlier, such had been her mood, and something of it had lingered. "Where did he take you?"

"I need to change," Ron said, "Can you put on the kettle?"

"The back of the fields," Eugene said.

"You could do with a change of clothes," Ron told him.

Eugene started upstairs and Michelle held his arm to stop him, "Was it the warehouse?"

She saw the fall of his face and wondered what he was thinking in the seconds before he nodded yes.

"He's just a kid," Eugene said and Michelle was thrown by the words. She wanted to say "Of course he is," but she couldn't voice it. The shower was running. Eugene said, "We ran up ahead. Andre was so tired and kept stumbling. He wanted us to go."

Michelle had a feeling Eugene was taking detours, that there was something that he didn't want to reach. "So we ran ahead. By the time we came out Andre had almost reached us. He wouldn't accept that there was no-one there, we told him it was empty and that we needed to take him home, but he wouldn't listen."

****

The water hurt his face. When Andre closed his eyes he saw the darkness of the warehouse and the flash of his lighter. He'd hoped to see Erin waiting for him unharmed and smiling and he'd thought of his mother then, how he'd come into this building searching for her along the ceiling as if it's height meant a level before heaven instead of a ceiling in Hades.

His father had been behind him.

"Come on," he'd said and he'd touched Andre's shoulder and Andre brushed him off. He'd flicked the lighter again. His father said, "Andre."

Andre took a step away. His attention had been on the ground. He had no idea what he was looking for, but he'd wanted to see something of Erin, have her appear before him with her tattered jeans and rain jacket and say, "Andre, we need to go," so he could listen to her this time. It reminded him of the hours he'd spent waiting in his shed at home while his father and sister slept and he'd begged his mother to come back and give him a second chance.

He'd wanted a second chance with Erin, but his father and uncle had been there, reminding him that the moment was lost.

Where was she? At home, was she siting on her bed, waiting for him?

"Can you tell us what's going on?" his father had asked.

"I made a mistake," Andre had said.

He'd been going for the door and his father had asked, "Who hit you?"

"No-one," Andre had said and had a sudden need to get as far from this place and his father as possible. He shouldn't have gone to them. He couldn't remember why he did, his helplessness, his inability to listen to her? Although she was probably laughing at him now; the boy who had run home because he'd gotten a few slaps, and to his father of all people. Ron had been waiting outside. "What about the girl?" he'd asked, "We need to see if she is okay?"

Andre imagined him going to Erin's door. She would not open it. She would watch from her unlit bedroom and he wondered if that was why she never turned the light on, so no-one could see her looking out.

"I made a mistake," he'd said.

He'd refused to say anything else.

****

In the mirror, he saw that his cheek was turning yellow and his lip was swollen.

Debris

"We need to stay here," Erin had said and he'd pulled the flashlight from her.

He wanted to shake the memory from him. He knew he wouldn't be able to stop thinking of this all night and he thought of sneaking out to Erin's house to see if she was okay and beg forgiveness, only it was too risky after everything that had happened. Michelle would be alert throughout the night, just as she'd been the first weeks of his arrival, always appearing whenever he went to the bathroom or downstairs for a drink to make sure he was okay. She would be at the stairs before he reached the front door and the last thing he could do was bring anyone to Erin. At least he could keep his promise of silence; he could do little else. There was no denying that he was too ashamed to face her.

"Go home," she'd said, but had she really meant that? Now, hours after the slaps, he'd forgotten how dizzy they'd made him, but he recalled how he'd run from Manny. "Go on then," Manny had said and Andre had felt winded when he'd heard the shuffle behind him, Manny was at his heels, like a wild dog.

"Walk him home," Colin had said, though Andre was chased.

Michelle knocked on the door and asked him to come down to eat while he was sitting on the rim of the bath with the towel wrapped around him, heedless of the goosebumps on his skin.

On the stairs, he heard the mumble of the adult's voices. They were sitting around the table. Ron nursed a beer, while Eugene and Michelle were drinking tea. Andre took the seat at the head of the table and folded over his food. He'd forgotten about his non-appearance for dinner and the hours that he'd spent in the warehouse before Erin's arrival, until Eugene asked where he'd been all day.

"Went into town," he mumbled an apology.

"That's not good enough," Michelle said. "I've asked you to let us know where you are at all times. We went looking for you."

Andre recalled Erin saying something like that. Had they gone to her? Maybe she'd seen them walking around looking for him. He hoped so.

He said that he'd fallen asleep on the way back from town. He'd gone into the warehouse for just a minute and he didn't mean to take so long. He saw the exchange of glances and knew they wanted to ask what else happened there, but for some reason they didn't. Michelle asked how he could have fallen asleep in the warehouse. "Not the most comfortable place," she said.

"I don't know," Andre said. "It was okay."

Her smile surprised him. There was a hint of conspiracy in it. He thought of Ronan and his mother and had no doubt Michelle had gone to their house when she went out looking for him. Ronan's mother could have said something about Erin and this made him uneasy.

"The warehouse is not the best place to go," Ron said.

"I think he knows that now," Eugene said. Andre put down his fork. He'd eaten a few mouthfuls, but wanted nothing more than to leave the room. The television grew quiet next door. His father sat forward and seemed on the verge of speaking when there was a burst of laughter and Ines and Martha came running into the room with Jamie on their heels. He was nearly five years old and had in the last six months moved away from the sanctuary of mother's skirts. She missed him now, though he was only a few feet from her. With a wide grin, he told everyone that Martha was the sea witch. "I am not," Martha said. She was ten and held herself as if there was a bad smell in the air whenever her brother was around. "Ursula, Ursula," Jamie teased and dodged his sister's thumps while Ines stood close to Andre, "What happened to you?" she said.

"Nothing," he said.

Michelle said, "He fell, now go on and brush your teeth. It's nearly bedtime."

"I don't have a toothbrush, how did you fall?"

"That's enough, Ines," Eugene said. Andre glanced at him and saw that he'd sat back again, whatever he was going to say had been forgotten with the children's arrival.

"Jamie hit me," Martha said. Ron told them to stop messing around and go upstairs.

"We'll need to take him to the doctor tomorrow. He has to get that cheek checked out," Michelle said.

"No I don't," Andre said, but he got the impression Michelle didn't hear him.

"Will you be around?" she asked her brother.

"I don't want to go upstairs with Martha, she's mean," Jamie said.

"Do I have to do everything myself," Michelle asked and Ron was up like a shot, telling the kids to get upstairs before they drove their mother crazy.

"You too," Michelle told Ines, who was standing by her father's side. At eight, she was still petite, but there was seriousness in her gaze that made her look older. She repeated that she didn't have a toothbrush. Michelle said she was sure her hands could do with a wash and waited for Ines to drift away, before saying. "Well, will you?"

"I have meetings all day tomorrow, but I'll try to get away," Eugene said.

Michelle nodded but not in agreement. Eugene bristled and stood. "Jesus, alright, you've made yourself clear."

He turned to Andre and told him to get his things. "You're going home."

Three days ago, Andre would have obeyed with relief. He would have wanted nothing more than to believe everything would be okay, but he didn't think so now. After today, he understood that life would only

Debris

revert back to how it was before. His father would continue to look at him with that tight-jaw and Andre would want to escape again. He would be trapped, just like Erin. He shook his head and said no, he wouldn't go. He looked on the verge of tears.

"He's just a kid," Eugene had said earlier and Michelle had realized she'd forgotten that during the last few weeks. And she'd gone and forgotten it again, because of her antagonism with her brother and her temper. Her need to force a point made her overlook the boy beside them who might have paled, only it was difficult to see under the yellow bruise.

"I said get up," Eugene said and went to pull his son up and was blocked by Andre's hand. Michelle saw the bandage on the thumb covering the cut that she'd forgotten about. Andre must have taken care of it alone in the bathroom. She stood too and said, "This isn't about him."

"What is it about, a jumper you ironed years ago?" Eugene said. "I don't remember that day, but I'm sorry I laughed."

He reached for Andre again and something snapped within the boy. It was as if he was brought back to that first night when his mother had just died and he'd sat beside his father all night waiting to let his secret loose, his hurt was just as great. He said, "You never asked what happened."

"What are you talking about?" Eugene said.

"The accident," Andre told him. "You never asked."

Eugene stalled and it was obvious he was taken aback, but in the next minute his face retained its blankness and he told his son it didn't matter how it happened. Usao was gone and talking about it wouldn't bring her back.

"You never asked because you know it was my fault," Andre said.

"Don't be ridiculous," Eugene said, but his force was missing. He seemed uncomfortable and reluctant to meet his son's gaze. Martha squealed upstairs. There was the clatter of feet above their heads and Ron shouting at them to calm down.

"You saw the glasses," Andre said. "You know what I did."

Michelle felt a stone in her throat. Her brother's face had softened and it was easy to see the pain, but it was the silence that was worse, the ticking of the clock, the boy's anxious breathing.

Michelle said, "What is he talking about?"

"I don't know," Eugene said.

"Don't lie!" Andre was trying hard not to cry. His hands were clenched into fists.

The moment stretched and Michelle wanted to scream at her brother to say something, but Andre was the one who spoke. "I'm not going home. You can't make me."

Eugene didn't say anything. When the boy stood to leave, Eugene made a motion to go after him but Andre screamed at him to go away.

Michelle was too shocked to speak. Andre looked like a coiled wire and she couldn't imagine him reacting well to anything.

"What's he talking about?" Michelle asked after the Andre had run out of the room. Eugene started to shake his head and Michelle said, "What was he doing with your glasses? Why does he think it's his fault?"

She'd seen Andre's self-blame from the beginning and had always thought her brother was blind to it, now she wondered if that was true at all.

"Jamie's asking for you," Ron said. She hadn't heard him come down the stairs and was surprised to see him at the door.

To Eugene, Ron said, "Ines is asking to stay the night."

"It's a school night," Michelle said.

"I know that Michelle, don't you think I know that?" Eugene said.

Ron was taken aback. Michelle thought he'd been ignorant to what was going on today, or if not ignorant, hopeful that the tension would right itself. Now he was watching Eugene with uncertainty.

"You can't stop yourself, can you?" Eugene said to Michelle, "And then you blame me for lack of choice."

"What is that supposed to mean?"

"You always have something to say," Eugene said.

"It's late. I think you should take Ines home," Ron said.

"Where's Mammy?" Jamie shouted from upstairs.

Eugene said, "If I thought it would offend you Michelle, I wouldn't have asked."

"You didn't ask," she said, "But it's too late to do anything about it now.'"

"Is it?" Eugene said.

****

Later that night with the children in bed and Andre's bedroom light off, Michelle replayed her conversation with her brother over and over again. Was it a question, or was it him telling her that it wasn't too late? All evening her brother had said stuff she couldn't grasp. It made her feel stupid. But he'd said nothing more about Andre going home. Luckily Ines had hit a wall of exhaustion and didn't complain about going home and not being allowed to say goodnight to her brother.

Ron was undressing when he asked Michelle what the hell was going on all day. "You were like a bull," he said.

She sat up in bed. "What about Eugene? He hardly said a word and then got pissed whenever I said anything."

"I don't blame him," Ron told her. "There was steam coming off you."

"That's not funny."

He crawled in beside her.

Debris

"Your feet are freezing," she said.

He laughed and said he was hoping she'd warm them up. She lay beside him in the dark with the hall light shining into their room and asked, "Why would Andre take Eugene's glasses?"

Ron said, "Don't you remember?"

Michelle stiffened. 'Don't tell me,' she wanted to say because she was suddenly afraid to learn what Andre had done.

"He used to do great impersonations of Eugene talking on the phone. He had us in stitches laughing."

Michelle closed her eyes. Ron's hand slid under her t-shirt and she turned to him and hoped he could erase the image of Andre putting his father's glasses on in the car. He might have pulled at her arm, intent on showing her his joke.

"Look, Mammy, look," he probably said.

Chapter Ten

Andre was up and dressed when the house was still quiet. It was drizzling and the morning was dreary and grey. He might have left the house otherwise. He wished he had when Michelle insisted on taking him to the doctor to make sure he was okay. His bruise was a paler yellow, but there was no swelling on his cheek and his lip had gone down. Still none of this mattered to Michelle. She talked about concussion and not taking any chances and Andre insisted that he hadn't been hit on the head.

"Ronan will be waiting for me," Andre told her, so she phoned Ronan's house to tell him Andre would not be walking to school with him this morning. Usually he crossed the green and together they left the estate and turned right towards town and left up the steep hill towards the secondary school, a twenty-minute walk when they hurried.

The doctor visit was quick. Count down from ten Dr. Jones ordered and then shined a light in Andre's eyes and advised him to be aware of any dizziness or nausea. It was all nonsense that Michelle made him go through so she could tell Eugene that she'd taken him to the doctor. Andre knew this because Michelle phoned Eugene on the way to the school. "The doctor said he was fine." His father's phone must have gone straight to message because she hung up straight away. Andre stared out the window, unwilling to look at his aunt while they drove down the empty avenue to school.

Inside, he found Ronan in the hallway amid the dark red tiles. Boys and girls drifted between classes in navy uniforms. The rain persisted and added to the gloom of the old school. Andre had stolen some cigarettes from Ron's pack that lay on the mantle in the living room while everyone else slept and he let Ronan glimpse them under his sleeve before asking if he wanted to skip first class.

The bike shed was at the back of the school beside the basketball courts. It was a small concrete building made of three walls and held bike stands along the back wall. The place was half full of bikes. The boys stood at the back of the building, hidden from the view. They'd run out and had waited for several minutes before lighting their cigarettes in case they were spotted by a teacher.

"Ma got to the door before me. There was nothing I could do," Ronan said when Andre asked if Michelle had gone looking for him. Ronan was leaning against the wall. Andre stood beside him. He could glimpse the road that led down towards the town. Cars passed every now and again, their roofs visible.

"Did she mention Erin?"

Debris

"Why do you think she ran to the door?" Ronan laughed. "She doesn't run often." He looked comical when he smoked, his cheeks caved and his eyes squinted.

"Michelle never said anything to me."

Ronan said. "That's weird. She went straight to Erin's house. Maybe she wasn't there or didn't bother to answer the door."

Ronan threw his cigarette on the ground. There were butts everywhere. The bike shed was not the best kept secret.

"Seriously what happened to your cheek? Did Erin beat you up?" Ronan asked.

Andre told him to get lost. Earlier he'd told him he'd fallen down the stairs and Ronan's eyebrows had lifted in a 'yeah right' gesture.

"Did you know Erin's brother?" Andre asked after he'd thrown his cigarette on the ground and stamped on it. He was trying to appear casual when in reality he felt as if he was doing something wrong, broaching a subject that should be left alone. Since last night, he couldn't help wonder if Colin had something to do with her brother's death. Ronan was frowning. "What brother?"

"Her older brother, I think he died or something."

"Who told you that?"

Andre shrugged. He was starting to feel a weird sensation in his stomach, not unlike how he felt waking in the dark yesterday. He wished he had another cigarette just to have something to do.

Ronan said, "She never had a brother. It was just her Ma and Da."

Andre knew he shouldn't have been surprised. Erin had never mentioned the brother again and there were no photos, but still he felt adrift. Ronan checked his watch and said class would be over in ten minutes, "We should get back. We have Henderson next and he knows I'm in."

"You go ahead," he said. "I'm not up for it."

Ronan stalled for a moment and Andre prayed he wouldn't stick around. He had no intention of staying at school. Ronan said okay. Andre watched him leave and waited until the next class had started before heading towards the main road.

"I mean they're not really friends of mine. They used to know my brother, that's all."

More than anything he wanted to know why Erin had lied.

****

There was a chance he would see Michelle driving before he got to the estate and he decided he'd tell her he felt light-headed and needed to go home. He kept an eye out as he went down the hill onto the intersection with Daley's corner shop and turned right for the estates. His bag was heavy on his back and Erin's voice rang in his ears. Maybe I have seen him. Wasn't that what she said? She must have been laughing at him, this idiot talking about ghosts and seeing his mother, while he'd thought that he'd finally found someone who would understand. He'd told no one else about seeing his mother in the shed, or the clock stopping, or all those other strange things. After the funeral, David had tried to act as if Andre was just the same. The first day he'd gone back to school, David had run up to him and said it was about time he came back. He'd been bored without him. Andre felt like telling him to fuck off but bit his tongue. Getting ready for school without his mother had been terrible, there was a huge hole in everything. David had acted like Andre had been away on holiday. He was trying to be funny, to bring Andre out of his shell. Andre knew this even as he hit him. David was the first fight, though no one could have called it a fight, more like a beating that David took. He stayed away after that so Andre could not talk to him about the shed or anything else. Andre's father was out of the question too and it was too easy to imagine Ines's fright. So he'd blurted it to Erin because of her dead brother who didn't exist and she'd played along, when she had no idea how he felt.

The curtains were closed in Erin's house and it looked quiet and too still and all at once he remembered the previous night; Erin in the warehouse shouting at him to go and his stomach turned, because he didn't know if any of that was true. She'd lied already, so why not lie again. She could have pretended that she was scared of Colin, so they could have a good laugh. Maybe she found Andre asleep and had gone off to get Colin in order to have some fun. She must have known that Colin made him nervous already. He thought this and then he thought of the way she'd stood so tense and rigid, her exclamation when she saw he was bleeding, and his anger fizzled to leave him confused. He might have stood there for a long time gazing at the house if Erin hadn't appeared at her bedroom window and then seconds later opened the door.

"What are you doing here?" She was in sweatpants and a long shirt. Her short hair was not combed and her eyes were tired. He didn't answer and she didn't seem to expect him to, because she had already stepped back to let him enter. The door closed and he was beside her in the dim hall with the television on. "Who is that?" the father shouted.

Erin told him Paul. She'd laughed when Andre first said that name. She'd said it was a brilliant idea. But there was no laughter now. "Michelle was here yesterday," she told him. "How does she know?"

Andre shrugged. "She doesn't live far, maybe she saw me."

"Did she say anything?" Erin asked.

"Not yet."

She touched his cheek, her fingers were cold. The house was cold, worse than outside he thought. "Does it hurt?" she asked.

He shrugged again "Not anymore," but dropped his gaze when he recalled crying in front of her. "Come on," she said and led him upstairs.

Debris

She walked slower than usual. In the room he stood behind the closed door watching her climb back into bed. "It's cold," she said and he wanted to hold onto his anger and frustrations, but it was hard while looking at her pale face. "Why did you go there?" she asked. "I asked you not to."

He told her he couldn't go home, not after finding her mother's wedding ring and he saw some of her lethargy fade. On his way to her house Andre had imagined asking her about her brother straight away, but her drawn face made him hold back. Instead of accusing her, he sat on the edge of the bed and took out the ring. She was propped up by a few pillows and she sat forward when she saw the silver band in his hand.

"Oh my God," she said and her voice sounded wispy and light.

She seemed afraid to touch the ring. Her fingers hovered above his hand. "Where was it?"

He told her about second drawer with the musty clothes and that he nearly hadn't found the envelope and wouldn't have if he hadn't skimmed the surface with his hand. He said he'd thought it was empty at first, but discovered it wasn't.

The ring was in her hand.

"Ma would never leave this," she said. Her full attention was on the ring as if there might be a secret written on it somewhere. Finally she looked at him and there was a sparkle that wasn't there before, but a sorrow too, which made him think of his sister, though Erin was not eight years old. She didn't see the world like Ines, and Andre didn't know if he could trust her grief.

"She used to say it was the only beautiful thing she owned in the world," Erin said. "She wouldn't have hidden it away. If she wanted to leave it she would have given it to me, not to him so he could hide it with his underwear." The anger was a relief to Andre. "Was there anything else?" she asked.

"Like what?"

She shrugged and said she didn't know, "Letters maybe, an address, something."

He thought of the page with indiscernible writing. It never occurred to him that her mother might have written those words, but at that moment he refused to care about her mother. He needed to know what happened last night. He asked Erin and she said it didn't matter. They needed to think of her Ma, yet Erin was pale and different. She seemed to drift away and bring herself back. He wasn't able to explain, but he knew something was wrong and she was lying. "What did Colin want?" Andre said and Erin stiffened and stared at him. Her eyes were blazing. "Can we stop talking about Colin?" she said. "It's not him I am worried about!"

"Something's wrong."

"Who said it was Colin's fault?"

Andre felt winded. Erin pulled her legs up to her chest.

"I went back!" He would have liked to stand and walk around so he could get rid of the restlessness, but he was fixated with her face, the large tired eyes, the limp mouth, it was like looking at a different girl and he was waiting for the other Erin to emerge. "I was worried, I didn't like that you were alone with Colin."

Her smile was limp. "I'm alone with Da every day."

He stood now and she watched him with a feline interest. Outside was getting blustery. Clouds glided by. There'd been a blue patch in the sky when he'd waited outside her door, but he couldn't see it now.

"What about your brother?" he asked and for a moment he didn't think she heard, though he'd said it loud enough and her lack of response made him nervous.

Finally she said, "What about him?"

"He's not real."

"Who told you?"

"That doesn't matter."

"Yes it does, it means you were talking about me."

"You lied," he said and was surprised with her smile. The way it narrowed her eyes made him feel he was the one who'd done wrong.

"Do you know what would happen to me if I lit a fire in the school?" He shook his head. "I'd probably be sent to juvenile detention. I certainly wouldn't be brought to my aunt's house and given pocket money every week to do whatever I want."

She paused and glanced at the ring in her hand. "I don't light fires to get away, I make things up instead. I used to pretend I had a big brother. His name was Jim," She shrugged, "It's not like I was planning on telling you, and I didn't mean to say he died either, that just came out."

She seemed embarrassed now. A color had come to her cheeks. "I used to talk to him when my parents argued. Did I tell you that?" She was bristling now. "Did I tell you how they used to scream at each other?"

Andre shook his head.

"There's a lot you don't know," she said.

For once her father was quiet and Andre didn't like his silence, the lack of noise made it possible for him to be in every room of the house. He wondered how old Erin was when she first imagined her brother. Was she five or six when she pretended to snuggle with him at night while her parents shouted? The thought saddened him. "I told a lie," Erin said. "What's the worst you've done?"

Her gaze ruffled him. She seemed expectant, as if she knew the answer already and he felt a stirring inside him, not unlike those first days after the accident when he couldn't bear to remember.

"I told you," he said.

"No, that was an accident," Erin said. "You didn't mean that. What was the worst thing you've done?"

"I don't know."

"Yeah, you do," she told him.

She was still watching him when the doorbell rang. "What did I do?" he asked.

She said, "You know already."

He didn't want to believe her and think there was nothing to her words. He wanted to think she was trying to take attention away from her lie, but he couldn't. Darkness spread through his chest. The doorbell went off again, a prolonged buzz that made Erin curse. Erin's father was downstairs, but he didn't go to the door.

Andre asked what was wrong and she said she was afraid it was social worker or someone from the schools investigating her absenteeism. Every day she expected someone to come and it worried her. On the fourth ring, Andre crept to the window.

"Shit," he said.

"What?" she was off the bed now. Outside was blustery and the wind made Michelle's hair fall over her face. She was in jeans and a long jacket and had stepped back from the door to glance at the sitting room window. "What is she doing here?" Erin asked. She was standing behind Andre.

"I don't know," he said, though he remembered the way Michelle had asked, "Where is she?" Andre had not grasped that she knew the girl was Erin. The doorbell went off again.

"She won't go," he said, "Not if she hears the television. She'll probably start knocking on the living room window next."

"Why?" Erin asked.

He shrugged, "Because she's stubborn."

"No, why is she here?"

He said he didn't know. He couldn't begin to tell her about running into the house and dragging his father and uncle out. The doorbell went off again.

"Tell her to go away," Andre said. When Erin didn't move, he looked at her and she was gazing at him with narrow eyes and a tight mouth. "What did you tell her?"

"Nothing."

"She never came here before and now its two days in a row."

"I didn't say anything."

They were whispering and he could feel the pressure in his chest. Times like this, he felt he could hate Michelle with her set ways and authority and her belief that she had to know everything that was going on, only he knew she had her heart in the right place. She probably spent the morning worrying about Erin and debating whether or not to come, as if she would ever be able to stay away.

"I'll see what she wants," Erin said and stood. The doorbell rang again. Erin's father shouted, "Piss off."

Andre heard him from the upstairs landing. The front door opened and there was a second of quiet before Michelle said hi.

"What do you want?" Erin said.

"I wanted to see if you're okay."

Andre could hear the distant whirr of traffic and the house was getting colder.

"There was a bit of commotion last night," Michelle said. "Andre was a bit shaken up."

Andre could imagine Erin's blank face. She would give Michelle nothing, which would only make the woman more determined. He should have told Erin to be nice, tell her you're okay and thank her for coming.

"He'd been beaten," Michelle said and Andre recognized that stern, righteous voice.

Say something, Andre thought.

"I don't know Andre," Erin said and Andre cursed under his breath.

"I know he's here. Mrs. Neary was happy to phone and let me know she saw him."

"Mrs. Neary can go to hell," Erin said.

"Maybe," Michelle said. "She seems a likely candidate."

Erin might have smiled. Andre didn't find the will to.

"Close that door! We don't want any Jehovah's witnesses on our doorstep."

"It's not Jehovah's witness, Da," she called into the house. Erin returned her attention to Michelle. "Is that it?"

"Who is it then?" her father yelled.

"You know where I live, if you need anything," Michelle said,

"I've survived fine until now," Erin said.

"Are ya deaf?" her father screeched.

"We want to do more than survive," Michelle said, "Don't we?"

"Whatever," Erin said.

"Jesus, do I have to go myself?" The chair creaked loudly.

"What age are you anyway?" Michelle asked.

Andre heard the door close.

****

"Fuck sake," Erin said. She was in the room. The television reverberated under Andre's feet. He was standing by the window. It had taken some time for Michelle to walk away and she retreated reluctantly, looking back every now and again. "I trusted you," Erin said.

"I didn't tell her anything. It was probably Mrs. Neary."

Debris

He hoped Erin would not think of his friendship with Ronan. It's possible she saw the two walking to school together, but she said nothing about that. She said Mrs. Neary had it in for her alright and it wouldn't surprise her if the woman had gone to Michelle about Andre. When Andre asked why, Erin shrugged and said she was just a pure bitch. "People like her don't need a reason."

Her father was shouting for Erin from the bottom of the stairs and Andre realized that he'd been calling Erin's name since the door closed, a repetitive voice rising up with the television, only now he was getting angry.

"I'm coming," she yelled to her father. To Andre, she said, "Maybe I shouldn't trust you at all. Maybe you should leave right now. I can do it all by myself."

"Do what?"

Her father was coming up the stairs and mumbling. Andre couldn't make out what he was saying. His focus was on Erin. "I'm not letting him get away with hurting Ma."

"I'm coming," she yelled to her father and started for the door. Andre was up after her, "Do what?" he repeated.

Chapter Eleven

The house was quieter, either Erin or her father had turned down the television, and a rumble of voices reached Andre. When Andre first noticed the sweet powdery scent of violets, his immediate reaction was fear. His pulse raced and an urge to run, like he'd run from the shed, took hold of him. Back in the shed his mother had smiled at him and he'd felt a crippling dread. Later, he'd regretted his fear and had gone back for a second chance, but there was nothing.

He could not have explained the feel of her to anyone. It reminded him of when he was younger, around five or six and he'd wake in the middle of the night and feel someone in the room with him. The presence had made the air thicker and Andre conscious of his breathing. He'd mumbled prayers, *Our father who art in heaven, Hail Mary, mother of God*, until he found the courage to slide out of bed and run to his mother.

"Who said it was bad?" his mother had said, "It could be your guardian angel watching you."

But he'd known it was bad because it was stifling, like a hand resting gently on his throat. His mother was lightness. She made goosebumps rise on his skin. A noise rose from downstairs and he realized he didn't want her here, not in this house, locked in small musty rooms. He ran to the window to let his mother out. Rain fell on his face and his mother was still there beside him.

"Do you ever hear your name being called," he would have liked to ask Erin, "But there's no one there. It's like that."

The moment Erin reappeared, he knew he could not broach the subject of his mother. There was something about Erin's face that threw him off. Sternness had come to her eyes when her father had come up the stairs looking for her. Erin had been waiting at the top. She had loomed in Andre's eyes then because there was a difference to her face; all girlhood gone, it had scared and intrigued him and kept him rooted to the spot. "Paul's here," she'd said and her father had looked towards the boy in the doorway, a touch of confusion on his face. His eyes were blurry and he'd stumbled on the top stair from his glance backwards.

"Did you see?" Erin said when she'd returned after doing whatever her father wanted her to do. "The way he stumbled, it would be so easy."

Andre didn't want to understand what she meant,

"Why is the window open?" Erin had asked. "It's cold."

She was going for the window and Andre wanted to grab her arm and say, "Don't, she's not gone yet," but his mouth had turned dry and he could imagine Erin's hurt from his need to get his mother away.

Debris

"You think it's your mother?" she might say. "Who said it was your mother? Who said she should leave?"

Erin closed the window. Raindrops had landed on her face and she dried herself with her sleeve. She was watching him in a way that made him nervous.

Finally she said, "I knew who you were before I met you."

He didn't know what to say or if he was expected to say anything, though he felt a sinking sensation and wished she hadn't told him this. She crawled under the blankets again. She said she was sorry she hadn't been honest but she'd known about the accident before she'd met him. She'd heard Andre had been in the car when his mother died, and she'd known the fire was the reason he'd moved to his aunt's. People talk, she said. And anyway he was pretty conspicuous walking around alone all the time. She used to think it was cute the way he hid from everyone. She'd be sitting in the field with the others and would see him among the trees or gazing out of the warehouse window.

When she stopped speaking the silence wrapped around them with a tension that made it impossible for Andre to speak.

I used to see you among the trees, she'd said, and he saw himself in the bushes above the writhing bodies and the paleness of the girl's legs against the night grass and he felt the same unease that he'd experienced that night—a notion that something was wrong without understanding why. He'd run away from the couple because he'd wanted to get as far away from the boy and girl as possible and he couldn't speak for the regret of it now, for not waiting to see if she was okay, and for running yesterday.

****

There was a story his mother told him once about the devil and his three sons. "Important things come in threes," she'd said, "remember that."

He thought of it and he wanted to share it with Erin, but his head was still a mess with the idea of her being the girl on the grass.

There was the devil, he wanted to say. He came for the soul of an old man and his first two sons tried to stop him, one was a priest and the other was a doctor, one prayed and the other tended his sickness, but it was the third son who beat the devil. The third son looked at the candle burning beside his father's bed and asked the devil to wait until it disappeared completely before taking their father. The devil agreed and the third son blew the candle out and put it in his pocket.

Andre thought of that because he'd already failed her twice, but he couldn't admit it. "What's the worst thing?" she asked again. He said that he didn't know. It was so hard to look her in the eye.

****

Andre shared his school lunch with Erin, while the skies opened up and rain lashed against the window. The scent of violets lingered and when he asked her if she smelled anything she studied him a moment. Maybe she thought of the window being opened when she came back or maybe she was just concentrating, but it took a moment before she said no and there was disappointment in the word.

She decided to have a smoke and he watched her squeeze the tobacco from the cigarette and break up the hash with the sounds of her father rummaging downstairs. His movements were mysterious and oddly perverted, like a rat scurrying about. She said they needed to remember to get rizzla papers tomorrow, though it was also a good thing because it meant she smoked less. She was sitting against the pillow with her legs pulled up and the ashtray beside her. She seemed more at ease, as if all the tension had oozed out since her confession of knowing him, while it was hard for him to stop thinking of her on the ground and the body on top of her.

After he had a smoke he couldn't sit still for the agitation. She laughed at his restlessness, the hand brushing back his hair, the shaking head, while he felt his head would explode. She didn't seem to notice his discomfort. She talked about how boring her days at home had been without him. Sometimes time went by so slowly she thought she'd go mad and she would have liked to go to school. Or she'd like to go back in time to those first months and not have missed so much. "Because after a point, there's no going back," she said, "You make a choice without realizing it. Here…"

"But if you could go back in time why start there, wouldn't you go back to before she disappeared."

"I don't want to think of that," she said.

He took a drag form the joint, the tip was wet and he burned his lip. "You have ants in your pants," she said.

"I need some water," he said, when the joint was smoldering in the ashtray.

"Go on then. I'm not going downstairs again."

On the top of the stairs he paused. The landing seemed higher now in his stoned state. Thirteen steps led to the ground floor inches from the distorted glass that was beside the front door. Andre had counted them earlier. He gripped the banister and thought of Erin's father, the stumble and laugh. The first night Andre was here, he must have looked so small all the way down there, *"A girl's name, what's wrong with Paul."*

Halfway down he heard a shuffle in the kitchen, the chair going back against the kitchen floor and he kept going with his heart thudding in his chest. Slow steps. Was this how Erin felt all the time in her house? The kitchen door was slightly ajar; the light coming from it was ashen. Her father was probably sitting at the table. Andre would walk in quickly and go straight to the sink without even looking at the man. The first night he visited, her father was on the couch with his chin on his chest and spittle

Debris

coming from his sleeping mouth and he imagined the same kind of thing now, but when he opened the door the man was directly in front of him. He had a bald patch the size of a penny on the back of his head. His hair was flattened and when he turned around, his eyes were red-rimmed and angry looking. It was hard to look away from them. "What did you say?" the father asked.

Andre shook his head and remembered the dryness of his throat.

In one hand the father held a glass that must have contained gin. The other hand was pointed towards the window and the afternoon darkened by the lashing rain. Outside was the sodden garden. A stone wall separated them from the back of other houses.

"I'm smothered by them."

His gaze took in the boy, maybe trying to place him and deciding it didn't matter. The father was wearing black pants and a white shirt that had turned brown around the cuffs and collar. His face was lined deeply, his mouth hung. Without warning, he covered the distance between them and grabbed Andre's sweater to bring him to the window. "Do you see them?" he said, with Andre pressed up against the rim of the sink. "Do you think it's normal to live like this?"

The father's breath was foul from cigarettes and drink. There was a hint of sweat combined with the mustiness coming from his clothes. He was looking at Andre intently and sighed when the boy shook his head. He let go of the sweater, but was standing so close, Andre was afraid to move in case it would set the father off again.

He was coiled tight. "They see everything," the father said.

Andre knew the house at the end of the row in front of him was Ronan's. His mother could be watching from the top window now, maybe she saw Andre and she thought he was nodding in agreement. He didn't like the thought. There was a feeling of complicity. By arriving he'd set the father off in a rampage and he'd be leaving Erin to it later, wandering off home to Michelle's house while she stayed locked in her room. The rain lashed against the glass.

"Fucking liars the whole lot of them and she's the worst of them, bet she didn't expect this, oh no, waiting every day for her to arrive. I said she's not coming back. I know for a fact, but she won't believe me. She's still bloody waiting."

Andre was watching him now, trying to make sense of the words. He was talking so fast. "Who's not coming back?"

"I'm surrounded by them," the father said. He drank some gin, silver drops spilled on his chin and he wiped it off before walking to the table to grab a cigarette. "Selfish bitch," he said.

Dirty dishes were piled in the sink. Andre was afraid to rummage through doors for a glass. If he was thinking straight, he might have walked out of the room and ran upstairs, but he'd come into the kitchen for a reason and he needed to go through with what he'd planned. He grabbed a mug from the pile in the sink. The father lit his cigarette.

"They say they don't know where she is, but I don't believe them," he said and Andre looked out at the garden.

****

"What was he talking about?" Andre asked Erin after he'd washed his face and hands in the bathroom to get rid of the smell and the cloying feeling he'd gotten. Then washed the mug as best he could, though the brown rings were impossible to get off, and filled his mug with water.

"I don't know," Erin said.

"He said they know where she is," Andre said.

She gazed at him with soft mocking eyes. "He's drunk."

"But who was he talking about?"

"I don't know," Erin said. She'd sunk lower in her bed and said that her father talks nonsense when he's drunk. Her reaction surprised Andre. He'd thought she would want to know more, or she'd get excited thinking someone else might know about her mother. But instead she'd tensed. She seemed reluctant to look at him, and her discomfort made him bite back his argument that her father knew more than he was letting on.

Chapter Twelve

Michelle could feel the threat of the drops on her skin, any second now and the heavens would open up, but she couldn't bring herself to walk fast. There was a temptation to go back to the McEvoy's house. The girl was so exhausted and wary. She was a child turning into a woman before Michelle's eyes, and then there was that man screaming and the stale smell and Andre there somewhere, a kid hiding in upstairs rooms. What did Erin want with him? Michelle couldn't say she liked it much, but she'd be damned if she was going to be like Josie Neary or anyone else, all these people saying the girl-child was bad news. But Jesus it was hard not to feed into it, hard not to storm back and say that she wanted Andre to come home. She knew something happened to the girl last night, someone beat Andre up and sent him into a frenzy of worry for the girl. What age was she, fourteen, fifteen? Still Michelle wanted to pull him away from Erin, as if she was the one at fault.

Michelle was crossing the road for the green when she heard her name being called. Mrs. Neary was coming out her front door with her navy housecoat and her wide arms crossed to shield herself from the cold. Michelle wished she could feel sorry for her, but there was toughness to Mrs. Neary that didn't sit right and it was hard to know if she'd always been that way, or if events in the last year had caused the bitterness, though Michelle suspected the former.

"Was he not there?" Mrs. Neary said, though she knew full well he was. She'd walked behind Andre when she was on the way home from some errand. She'd watched him go straight to the McEvoy's house. "He was," Michelle said and bit back her 'thank you very much.'

"And you're letting him stay with that man and girl. There's no knowing what's going on in there."

Michelle had a mental image of the girl with her tired eyes and dressed in her large sweater and sweat-pants and was sickened that Mrs. Neary should insinuate such a terrible thing. "She has a terrible name for herself already."

"No thanks to the likes of you." Michelle said and Mrs. Neary drew back. She wasn't impressed when Michelle said Erin was only young girl and they should be helping her rather than bad-mouthing her.

"How can we help someone who doesn't want it?" Mrs. Neary said, "The girl lounges around all day and hasn't been in school for a year."

"She can't just stay at home for a year. Her absence would be reported. Dan would be fined or charged."

Mrs. Neary's shrug made Michelle want to hit her. It was true, she said, Andre hadn't wanted to go to school after the accident. For two weeks after Christmas he refused to get out of bed and a letter was sent from the school. There were tears and screams but Eugene put his foot down when he became aware of the legalities. Michelle didn't want to think of Eugene and Andre's fights in the mornings, how Andre had shouted, and Eugene had watched with a face that she now sees as contempt, but then thought was helplessness.

"Dan McEvoy probably burned the letter."

"Then someone from the Educational Department would have come."

Lucky for Mrs. Neary she didn't shrug, because Michelle *would* have thumped her.

"It's not the girl's fault, you know," Michelle said.

"What's that supposed to mean?" Mrs. Neary said.

"Exactly what I said," Michelle said, "You have no reason to dislike her so much."

"The McEvoy's are a bad lot and you know it. I don't know what you're trying to prove letting him stay there."

"Jesus, they're just children," Michelle said and even as she said it she knew it wasn't true. The girl who'd stood at the door today was not just a child.

****

She couldn't go back, that was the thing, not with Mrs. Neary with her waddling broad body. She'd smiled a wan dry smile, before retreating and Michelle had felt sick to the stomach. If it was her child, her boy in there, would it be different? She didn't want to ponder this, yet the thought came and with it the query of what Eugene would do if Andre was with him. Would he even know? Since Usao's death, the nanny Ursula had been in charge. Ursula baked bread and said "yes, no, maybe so." Would she even know if Andre was not at school? And if he was not at school, who would he be with, David and his financial consultant father, his lecturer mother? It was possible they drank behind doors or beat each other up, but their street would be quiet about it.

Michelle could feel Mrs. Neary watching her and thought she might have been laughing at the sight of Michelle Moran stuck on her sidewalk. And she thought of Erin not being in school for a year and wondered how that could be right. Did the child slip through the cracks or was Mrs. Neary exaggerating? Michelle finally turned towards home and her steps quickened once she realized that she could find out.

****

The school doors had always been imposing to Michelle. They were thick wooden barriers that fronted the convent. When exactly the convent opened its doors to the students Michelle didn't know. She'd never liked history or trusted it. That someone could research past events

Debris

accurately was improbable to her. There was as much fiction in it as anything else. Lately, she could hardly trust her recollections. Had she really hated school? Or was it something else, a need to get away from her parents, to earn money? Maybe she would have left early like Erin if Michelle's mother hadn't insisted she stay on until her leaving certificate at least. But wasn't it her mother who went on about money all the time in such a way that Michelle felt guilty? Guilt was a large part of her adolescence, but most of the time she chose to forget this.

The halls were empty since it was after lunch. Michelle had gone home. She'd had to change from her wet clothes and sit at the table with a cup of tea to calm down before walking to the school with the aid of an umbrella. She didn't want to drive. She felt conspicuous in her car. She remembered a time when parents' coming to pick their children up was a rare thing and she'd considered those kids spoiled. This memory might have made her smile on a different day, and this was exactly how history couldn't be trusted because at the time she'd felt jealous of those girls and boys who slid easily into the passenger seat of cars. Michelle had never done anything easily, except for taking care of people, which seemed like a reflex. The halls were darker than she remembered. Her footsteps echoed amid the large windows and high ceiling. Wide stairs led up to the classrooms. The building might have been beautiful once. Ahead lay the glass corridor and the tiny box rooms where strains of music might be heard at any given time. The secretary's office was at the bottom of the hall. Ann O'Keefe worked there. Michelle had bumped into her at Christmas, "I've been back in that school over a year," she'd said. "Miss Robbins is still around, can you believe it?"

"She'll never retire," Michelle had said.

Ann had agreed. "She's still as moody as ever, and my God she's tiny. She must have shrunk. She's smaller than me."

Michelle couldn't picture Ann sitting behind a desk. In town she'd talked while continually looking around until Michelle asked who she was looking for and Ann giggled and said no one. Bobbed hair and wire rimmed glasses, she was thin and bubbly. Michelle hoped she would be there. She'd considered phoning, but the house was too quiet. Jamie had started pre-school and every Monday he and his best friend took turns going to each other's house. Michelle had never gotten used to the stillness. Alone she imagined sounds that were not there, the trod of her father's slow steps on the ceiling above, a creak of the sitting room door, and besides, to ask about Erin over the phone would have been difficult. She was sure Ann would not be as forthcoming.

The secretary's door was closed. Two doors down was the principle office and this made Michelle nervous. She knocked and was told to come in.

"Michelle, what are you doing here?" Ann asked.

L.M. Brown

Michelle paused at the door.

"Come in, come in." Ann was standing, a petite figure in black. Silver rings glittered on every finger when Ann pointed at the chair on the other side of her desk. "Don't tell me you walked in this weather," she said and Michelle remembered the umbrella in her hands. She would have left a trail of drops from the front door. She apologized and Ann told her not to be silly, "Just leave it at the door."

Michelle obeyed and sat on the hard seat. She told Ann about Andre. She said he'd gone home early because he felt sick. She was going to phone the school, but was getting stir crazy in the house so she decided to walk instead. She said her youngest had started pre-school and it was hard getting used to the change.

Ann said, "Are you kidding?" She'd rejoiced each time one of her boys started. They were maniacs in the house and the rain was killing her now. Two days inside and they had the place destroyed. "Isn't Andre Eugene's boy?" she said after a moment.

"Yes, he's staying with me for a while. There was some trouble after his Ma died. He couldn't settle."

Ann nodded, sympathy in her smile, and Michelle sat forward on the chair and saw the change in Ann's face, the slight lean, "What?" she said.

"He's friendly with Erin McEvoy. Is she in today? He wanted me to tell her he wasn't well. I think they'd made plans."

"Erin McEvoy," Ann mumbled. "I know that name."

Michelle tried not to react, though it felt as if the blood had stopped flowing under her skin. Ann was looking in the drawers of her desk. "I'm sure I wouldn't be able to give information if she was a student here," she said, "But I think she's enrolled somewhere else."

Michelle hoped Ann didn't notice her stiffness. She was tempted to get up and walk out, tell Ann that she had made a mistake, but Ann had already taken out a large brown envelop from the drawer. A white piece of paper was attached to it with a paperclip. "I knew I recognized the name," she said. "Her Mom is Marie McEvoy."

Michelle nodded.

"Did you say Erin still lives around here?" Ann asked.

Michelle didn't want to answer that. She hadn't thought that coming to ask about Erin was tantamount to reporting her. Ann was studying her and Michelle said she wasn't sure. Ann frowned and said she hoped not since Erin hadn't been in the school since last year.

"Her mother came in to tell me the family was moving. I remember her because she was very nervous and she was young, I'd thought that if you put a uniform on her she could blend in with the students. I kind of felt sorry for her, though I couldn't pinpoint why."

"I didn't know her well," Michelle said.

90

Debris

"I don't think she even sat down. She stood the whole time, England I think she said she was going, and Erin wouldn't be back in school. She never gave a contact number, which I've regretted since." Ann stopped and her bright eyes were soft but determined. "Is Erin not going to school?"

"She could be home on holiday," Michelle said and felt foolish afterwards, because it was obvious Ann didn't believe her. Her smile was uncertain, but she shrugged off the lie quick enough. She might have sensed Michelle's discomfort.

"Marie said the new school would send for the records as soon as they were settled." She lifted up the envelope, blank where the address should be, "But no one sent for it, it's been sitting here for that long. I forget about if for months and when I'm reminded I just think," she shrugged, "I don't know what I think, that Erin has settled already and the new school secretary never got around to sending for it. Maybe I should have checked."

"I'm sure that's not your job," Michelle said. Ann shrugged and said maybe, but this was how kids fell through the cracks.

"I'm sure there's a good reason," Michelle said. "I wouldn't worry."

"Maybe," Ann said again and replaced the envelope in the drawer.

After a minute she asked about Ron and the rest of the gang. Michelle said they were all good and Ann started talking about her husband who'd been laid off lately and was driving her mad with schemes around the house. Michelle was only half-listening. She wondered what had happened with Erin's mother. She'd obviously come in nervous and jumpy because she'd decided to leave her husband. It must have been scary to put her plans in action. This was a small enough town, people talked, and to come to the school must have been nerve-wrecking. She'd planned to go to England with Erin, and yet after all the preparation she'd left without her daughter. How could a mother do that? It seemed impossible. The few hours away from her children drove Michelle mad.

When Ann finally paused, Michelle said she hope he'd find work soon. Ann smiled and said, "We'll see."

"It was great to see you," Michelle said.

Ann nodded and said, "You too, we have to get that drink sometime soon."

Michelle stood and felt a slight tremor in her legs. Now she wished she'd brought her car. She was at the door when Ann said, "Since Erin's home, could you get her mother to call me, I'd like to get the records sent out."

****

"You need to stop worrying about everyone else," Ron had said to Michelle many times and she'd wanted to tell him it was not something that she could just switch on and off. She'd start worrying about someone and couldn't walk away; her brother in college with no parents, three years younger than her and still so much the baby, of course he needed her help, and her nephew who'd caused a fire and had been in so many fights to count, he needed her too, but she'd tried to stay back from that. She'd tried to let her brother take care of it himself, though when he'd phoned one afternoon and was hardly able to speak, the words dropping out of him like teeth, she couldn't say no. She wished she had now.

She walked through the school and imagined Marie McEvoy making the same journey. Her steps must have echoed in her head and her heart must have quickened from the thought of getting her daughter out of there. What had she done then? Had she packed? Had Erin packed? Over a year ago had she waited for her mother with her possessions put away in suitcases, only for her never to appear? Had the girl been waiting every day since? The thought made Michelle feel tired all of a sudden. She felt terrible for Erin, but she had to concentrate on Andre. He shouldn't be in that house. Her unease from the meeting with Ann made her look at everything through a darker lens. Rain was falling into her eyes before she remembered to put up the umbrella. She was impatient now to get home and for once glad that Jamie was away until after four today so she could make her phone call in peace.

****

They sat side by side on the bed, listening to music on his Walkman. "One more time please," she said.

Three times Erin had listened to Depeche Mode with her eyes closed and her head against the wall. *I heard it from my friends about the things you said.* She mumbled with the song, rather than sang with it, her lips barely moving, so he would only hear a word every now and again. He would have played it for her all day.

After the fourth time she stopped the tape. Her father was coming upstairs, a plod of footsteps and she listened intently and looked at Andre when her father started down the hall. The rain had eased up a little, though the day was still a heavy grey. "What if he notices the ring's missing?" she whispered.

"He won't," Andre said and tried to smile but it was impossible. The father's steps seemed to get inside his skin, every movement was felt. Her father stopped inside his bedroom door. Then he walked into the room and stalled and there was no movement from the kids in the room next door. They were hardly breathing until they heard the father move towards the bed.

"See," Andre said.

Debris

Erin was about to press the play button again and Andre told her to wait. He was whispering when he told her about the letter. He said it was in the bedside cabinet and it looked old enough. The writing was hard to read and he didn't check the name but it could have been something from her mother. Erin's eyes were wide. She'd pulled the earphone out of her ear and Andre couldn't help wish he'd said nothing. "Why didn't you tell me before?"

"I forgot."

"You forgot? How could you forget? We need to see what it says."

"It might not be from her."

"Then why would he keep it upstairs?"

Andre was saying that he didn't know when the phone rang. "Who is that?" Andre asked when the house was silent.

"How do I know?" she said. Her father shouted 'shut up' from the bedroom when it started again. The third time, he shouted at Erin to answer the fucking phone before he went crazy. She ran downstairs. From the landing, Andre heard her timid, "Hello."

That was all she said before she hung up.

She was looking at him with a frown when she said, "You have to go home."

For some reason, he didn't equate his going home to the phone, up until then he felt untouched by the world in Erin's house.

"Who was that?"

"Who do you think?" she said.

And he imagined Michelle in her hallway pounding the numbers again and again.

Chapter Thirteen

"There was a fight in school today," Martha said. She had a habit of pouncing on Andre whenever he arrived home. She was standing in the living room before he'd closed the front door. Dempsey's Den was on in the living room. Andre heard Zig and Zag's high pitched voice and grimaced. A few days ago this wouldn't have bothered him. He might have gone inside for a minute to say hi to Jamie and see what was on the show.

"Butch had to pull them apart," Martha added.

"Don't call your teacher that," Michelle said from the kitchen door. She was drying her hands on her apron.

"Everyone calls him that."

"I don't care about everyone."

"His nose was bleeding, really bad, his sweater was black from it," Martha said. Andre felt Michelle's gaze on him, "Go on into Jamie."

"Is that what happened to you last night?" Martha said, "did you get into a fight?'

Andre could have killed her then, for reminding Michelle about last night and making him feel as if he'd brought bad luck into the house. There was a sudden chill to him and rather than making him repentant to Michelle and her family, it annoyed him. "Didn't I tell you I fell?" he said and Martha flinched with his tone.

"That's enough," Michelle said. "Go in to your brother."

"And where do you think you're going?" she said to Andre when he'd started for the stairs.

****

She made him tea and sat opposite him with her apron hanging loosely around her neck. Pots were boiling on the stove. The room was steamy and warm. A smell of bacon reminded him how hungry he was and he expected Michelle to say something about the way he spoke to Martha. Now that she wasn't present, he felt guilty. That was the thing about Martha; he liked her better whenever she wasn't around.

"Your father's on his way."

This was not what Andre expected. He'd anticipated questions about Erin, rebukes and threats for missing school, more than likely an order to stay away from the McEvoy house, and he'd rehearsed answers in his head. Erin was his only friend and he liked to talk to her. He left school because he was light-headed and Erin's house was closer than his, and lastly Michelle always hated when people bad-mouthed each other and wasn't that what she was doing now with the McEvoy's and wasn't it unfair since they never did anything to her (which he wasn't exactly sure of since Dan was capable of anything). He'd felt confident when he first sat at

94

the table. Michelle was meddlesome, but sweet too if he got her in the right mood. Mention of his father was akin to pulling the chair from under him.

"Why?" he asked.

"What do you mean why? He's your father and he wants to see you."

"Is that what he said?"

A pause ever so small before Michelle nodded, she hoped Andre didn't notice. The conversation had not exactly gone like that. Eugene had asked the same question as his son.

"Why?"

"He missed school today and spent it in Erin McEvoy's house."

"I know that name."

"Of course you know that name, they're in number five."

Eugene said there was something else about that family. He remembered hearing their name before. Michelle said, "Yes, there was some commotion last year, but that's not the point."

"Then what is?" Eugene asked.

"Your son, I better see you here at 4:30," she said and hung up.

A glance at the clock showed it was 4:15 and she thought maybe she shouldn't have said anything to Andre, in case his father didn't show up. No doubt he'd be late. She still had an hour before Ron came home. Martha and Jamie were laughing next door.

"So how long have you known her?" Michelle asked.

Andre told her a couple of days and was reluctant to drink his tea in case it might show acquiescence to her questions. "Do you know she hasn't been in school for a year?" she asked and regretted it when she saw Andre's face fall. "Did you phone the school?" he asked.

"No one else seems to care."

"She doesn't want your help."

"Maybe so," Michelle said and the lack of argument worried Andre. Why wasn't she laying down the law, telling him not to go back? He wanted nothing more than to get out of the kitchen and away from her soft stare. There was no anger, just concern. He glanced at her hands that held her mug, the fingers of each one touching. She hadn't taken a drink of her tea. The clock ticked and Michelle's quiet was getting to him, it was unlike her.

"Doesn't Da have to work?" he said and saw Michelle's frown and wanted to kick himself.

"Since when have you called him Da?"

"I don't".

"You just did."

"Well doesn't he have to work?" he said and before she had time to answer, they heard the front door open. Michelle smiled but it was a weak smile and only enhanced Andre's discomfort. She rose from the table, but her brother was at the kitchen door before she could make it any further. For once, she wished that he didn't have a spare key. He was in a dark suit and a long tweed coat, his hair brushed back and spotted with rain. He looked tired and aggrieved. There was a sense of being rushed coming off him, like he'd stopped in on the way to an important meeting. "Well," he said.

"Well," Michelle said. "Would you like some tea?"

"No," he said.

His son had not turned around in his seat. He had not looked at the man, never mind said hello and Eugene's gaze fell on him now. Andre's shoulders were bent and all of a sudden he looked so much younger. His confidence seemed to have seeped out of him with his father's presence and Michelle wanted to grab Eugene's arm and lead him out the door, throw him out in the rain. She wanted to say that he was just as bad as Dan McEvoy with his drinking and screaming, no worse she decided. At least Dan gave something solid for his daughter to fight against. How could Andre fight against this silence and how the hell had Michelle not noticed before. Eugene finally came into the room and went to the sink to pour some water

"Rotten day," he said while looking out the window. He rinsed the glass and Michelle realized he didn't know how to behave with his son anymore.

"How were you feeling today?" Eugene was addressing Andre, who sat up and said fine.

Eugene lifted his son's face to look at the bruise. They looked so alike, dark haired and dark eyed.

"I hear you're hanging around with the wrong people." Eugene said. He was still holding his son's face, such a gentle touch, yet Michelle knew it was enough to keep Andre still. After a moment Eugene's hand dropped and Andre glanced at Michelle. She hadn't moved. Her arms were folded over her chest and she had a cold feeling in her body and a sorrow that was not unlike the sadness after Usao's death. Andre's face was like stone. His eyes were so full of hurt, they'd grown still. "Well?" Eugene said.

"What do you care?" Andre said.

"You think I shouldn't?"

The question surprised Andre. It took his rebellion and chewed it up, He looked afraid before he was able to check himself. Eugene pulled out the chair beside Andre. He sat with his knees towards his son and gave Andre no choice but to look at him.

"Eugene," Michelle said.

"I'm talking to my son," he said, and when he looked at Michelle, his face was set and there was a hard determination in his eyes that made

Debris

Michelle wish for once that Martha would interrupt them, come in screaming some complaint about Jamie.

"Should you be able to make your own mistakes, make friends with the wrong people?" Eugene said.

Michelle said. "Stop talking nonsense Eugene."

"It's not nonsense," Eugene said, without taking his gaze from his son. "What do you think Andre? Do you think you should be allowed to do what you want?"

"Of course he shouldn't," Michelle said. She wanted to save the boy from what his father was doing, wrap him up in her arms and say "never mind him," but there was a perverse interest in this too. She was in awe with the coolness in her brother's speech and the cunningness in him because it was obvious the question was double edged.

Eugene said, "I'm not asking you. I'm asking Andre."

The boy must have been thinking of the glasses he'd taken to the car and his biggest mistake, so it was impossible for him to say he should be let alone to do what he wanted. The cruelty and cunning was shocking. "Andre?" his father said and Andre shook his head.

"What was that?" Eugene said. "I didn't hear you."

"No," Andre said. The tears finally came to his eyes.

"Good, then you listen to your aunt, do you hear me?" Eugene said.

"What are you doing?" Michelle's words came out low and heavy. Eugene's frowned; she couldn't believe he looked confused after what he had done. Was that all he would say about his son? You make bad choices?

"Do you think you can just tell him to listen to me and that's it?"

"Stop shouting," Eugene said.

"I'll shout if I bloody well want to, Martha go into the sitting-room, you're too bloody late." Martha looked as if she might cry. Michelle couldn't have handled that, nor could she manage to apologize. "Jamie, you too, go on."

Martha nudged Jamie, who was standing too close to her.

"Both of you," Michelle said. "Go on."

Martha was the first to drift away. Jamie followed. Andre was still at the table. He'd controlled his tears, though his face was tight with the effort and he kept his gaze down and away from the other two present. "Andre, go up to your room."

He looked at her and in the instant before he said no Michelle realized what he was going to do. She felt soft with relief, but helpless too.

"He needs to be home with you," she'd wanted to say and stupidly she'd thought she could say this with Andre present. Maybe she was guilty of cunning too, wanting to put her brother on the spot, but she was afraid to do that now because she had no idea what he'd say. Eugene stood and walked away, running his hand through his hair in an agitated manner.

Drops of rain fell mute on the window. The gun metal grey had a shine to it, the look of the sun trying to get through.

"I didn't mean to do it," Andre said. He had paled. He seemed to be fading before Michelle's eyes.

"I know it wasn't your fault. I know you didn't mean it…" Eugene said. After a minute he said, "I knew you lied. Usao was a slow driver. She used to drive me mad sometimes. She couldn't have been going too fast…" Eugene stopped. This might have been the most honest he'd been since the accident, but Michelle could have hated him for saying all this. A low pained moan had started in the pit of her stomach. Later she'd think she should have said that Usao was a nervous driver, the type to get scared and brake without thinking, but in the kitchen she was incapable of speech or argument. Eugene turned from the window with tears in his eyes. He had loved Usao intensely, Michelle knew that, all his life since he was fourteen years old Usao had been the one, and only now looking at her brother Michelle realized that a large part of him had disappeared with her.

"Michelle is worried about Erin," Eugene said and Michelle couldn't get over the distancing. Why didn't he say, 'we are worried,'? Michelle wondered, though she realized it could be a way to undermine the gravity. Your aunt is worried, I'm not.

Andre shrugged. Michelle thought him incapable of speech, but after a moment he said, "She's my friend."

"She hasn't been in school for a year," Michelle said, though the dread she'd felt earlier with the thought of Erin's mother had left her. Now in front of the broken man and boy, this fact seemed a small distant thing.

"Why?" Eugene asked.

Andre shrugged.

Michelle said her mother left a year ago. "Ann said that Marie had taken Erin out of the school. She'd told the secretary that they were going to England together and she'd sent for the records, but she never did and Erin hadn't been back in school since." Michelle spoke to Eugene. "It's not a good environment. Her mother's gone and her father is a drunk."

Eugene seemed unconvinced. "So was ours," he said.

Michelle hadn't noticed Andre's face, the wide eyes and the surprise when she spoke about Erin's' mother, but she was already regretting her decision to bring Eugene to them. She'd gambled and lost. It might have been different if Andre had left the room when Michelle told him to and before the damage was done. She'd think of this often, the way it could have gone, if she'd spoken to Eugene alone and said, "I can't do this." He couldn't have disagreed or forced her to keep Andre, but instead she said she was worried about Erin and Eugene said they couldn't choose Andre's friends for him.

Debris

Three people in the room and the boy was the only honest one, Michelle would think, though she would realize soon enough she was wrong.

****

The kitchen was empty apart from Michelle. Outside was black and she saw her reflection on the window by the sink. She looked older since this morning. She felt it, a heaviness in her limbs, a slower way of moving. Eugene had stayed for dinner. He'd taken off his coat at some stage, after they'd discussed Erin? When he'd believed he had tucked away the elephant in the room with his apologies.

She served the cabbage and bacon while Eugene spoke with Ron heatedly about one game or another.

She'd thought she would cry for Andre who'd eaten his dinner and had looked uncomfortable with Ron's questions of today. "How was school?" he'd asked.

"He came home early," Michelle had said and it might have been her unsmiling face that told Ron not to probe. So there were lies already, all these adults tangling themselves up. And for what, for the boy to excuse himself after dinner and disappear into his room without any decisions made?

****

Andre was on his bed listening to music when his father came in to say goodbye. He might have knocked but Andre didn't hear. He was listening to Therapy.

"He wants to play Jesus without the suffering."

Drums and guitar up high, eyes closed and singing, not loud. The thought of singing loud scared him because it meant loosening that ball in his stomach. He imagined the words would come out as a roar. His father's touch on his shoulder made him jump. He opened his eyes and looked at his father, before he'd pressed stop on the Walkman and took the earphones off. His father held his coat. He looked tired but relaxed. Andre couldn't remember the last time they'd been alone together.

"Are you doing okay?" Eugene asked. Andre nodded. He wanted his father to leave, because he had started to feel a stirring hatred for the man, who had gone from tears and blame to this forbearance, as if they could fill the gap from one to the other with one dinner and a stupid conversation about the McEvoy's. "I have to go," his father said and waited. For what? Andre thought. Andre found nothing to give him except a mumble of okay.

The next day while he and Erin walked into town, he would agree with her that fathers suck.

Chapter Fourteen

On the way home from school, Andre shared his plan to go to Four Lantern's and offered to buy Ronan a burger. Ronan said he couldn't and Andre knew it was because he'd mentioned Erin. "Why do you not like her?" he asked.

Ronan shrugged and walked with his gaze on the ground. Andre shoved him playfully, not too hard and Ronan said, "She's got a name."

"What's that supposed to mean?"

"It means she gets around."

Andre had to stop himself from shoving Ronan again. His fists had been clenched and he'd felt a rush of anger. "Who says?"

Ronan shrugged.

"You know I lit a fire in my old school."

He was sure everyone knew that by now. People talked. Ronan said, "Yeah, I know."

"And your Ma still lets me hang around with you."

Ronan glanced at him, but said nothing; though it was obvious it was true. After a few minutes Ronan said, "Yeah, well."

He still refused to go.

The day was clear. A few clouds dotted the blue sky and there was a slight breeze. He called into Michelle's house briefly to drop off his bag and tell her he was walking into town. She looked exhausted, as if she had slept little the night before. She nodded and said, "Okay, be back by 6:00 for dinner."

Andre lingered a moment with a desire to say something to make her feel better. She smiled at him and he said, "Okay," because he couldn't think of anything else.

When Erin answered the door she looked less pale and her eyes were clear. Her baggy sweatpants and shirts had been discarded and instead she wore jeans and a black shirt.

"Let's go for take-out," Andre said, and he saw the delight in her face and then the dimming, "I don't have any money."

"I do," he said.

Before his father left the bedroom, he'd taken twenty out of his wallet and handed it to him. Andre didn't want to take it. He'd wanted to stare at the money in his father's hand until his arm grew tired and he was forced to retreat. Maybe he would have left the note on the bed, but Andre couldn't deal with the discomfort, so he'd taken the money, said thanks, and hated himself for the politeness. At least now he could get Erin something to eat. She told him to hang on while she got her things and was back within minutes.

Debris

He wasn't sure what she ate with her Da. She'd shrugged when he'd asked her and said, "It depends." He'd seen her making sandwiches. There was never the smell of cooking, yet the kitchen had a greasy scent to it. She told him her father got unemployment benefit every Wednesday. He'd give her some money that day and she'd learned to shop cheap, a lot of cans, beans, tuna, some bread, pasta. She said it was hard when they needed soap or anything extra, but she managed and she seemed proud of herself for this accomplishment.

"You've been doing that since you were fourteen?" Andre asked. She said of course. There was no one else. She said she'd never met her mother's parents. "I think they hated Da."

Andre would have liked to hold her hand while they walked towards town, but was afraid of her reaction and he didn't need Michelle to spot them hand in hand. Yesterday, her unease had been clear and Andre had no idea why his father stuck up for him, insisting that they give the girl a chance when he'd already insinuated that Andre couldn't be trusted. Maybe his father had felt guilty for that cruelty, maybe he just didn't care. Andre leaned towards the latter.

He didn't think of Manny or Colin and he'd wonder on that afterwards, how he could have been so stupid to believe they only spent time in the back of the estates—in reality the field was an evening occurrence when no one was looking and fires could be lit and beers drank in the dark. The town center was not large with the school and the church, a few pubs, the supermarket; a couple of fast food places and recently an Italian restaurant. The center was like a concrete valley dipping downwards towards the shops. Daly's convenience store was the first place they passed. Students gathered there in the evening waiting for the bus, a sea of navy that had been thinned out by the time Andre and Erin arrived. Erin wanted to walk on the other side of the street. She was afraid of meeting anyone she knew. When Andre asked why, she said it had been so long since she spoke to anyone. She'd kept to herself a lot and whenever she met old classmates she never knew what to say. She seemed a little tense as she walked, less prone to talk or answer straight away and more inclined to glance around her.

She knew that Colin and Manny frequented McCann's bar. She told Andre they sold hash to the kids from school in the evenings and that was where she'd met them first; outside Daly's shop and for some reason they'd taken an interest in her. It was months before her mother disappeared and she liked to stay out late then, away from her parent's fights. Dinner was as haphazard as it was now, so sometimes she'd accept Manny and Colin's offer of a burger or chips. They went there once the town was empty of students and sometimes they'd have a pint in McCann's. When they were close to Four Lantern's, Erin said. "Maybe we could go somewhere else?"

L.M. Brown

She said The Cottage was good for sandwiches or they could walk the extra bit for the Happy Eater. Beside them traffic crawled, it was slow going around town with the narrow roads. Andre asked what was wrong with Four Lantern's. I told you, Colin goes there."

He doesn't want us to be friends. He said that you have a mouth on you and can't be trusted, or you're not loyal, something like that."

"Loyal to what...." Andre didn't know what it meant, but it sat wrong on him, like something his father would have said. They could smell the chips.

She said she didn't know; only he was really angry when he caught them together in the warehouse. She said, Colin got paranoid for no reason and it didn't matter why, but it made her uncomfortable and she wanted to go somewhere else. Andre was quick to agree.

****

They opted for the Happy Eater. It was further, at the other end of town, pass the bus station and near the entrance to the fields and warehouse. They sat at a table in the back where Erin scoffed a chicken burger, fries, and a coke. She told him how she'd met the boys at the corner shop. She'd spent evenings with them while her mother was home, but when she left Erin didn't feel the same. She didn't want to be around the boys as much. She wasn't sure why, but it was like her mother's leaving had made her see them differently.

Colin always had a temper on him and Manny, she paused when she said his name and shrugged and said, "Manny has his issues too, but I didn't care until Ma left."

She finished her burger and wiped the mayonnaise from her mouth.

Andre felt unsettled for the last half hour and was jumpy every time he heard the door open. He thought he knew why Erin spent most of her time in her house and it had nothing to do with her father. "Do you want those chips?"

He pushed his food towards her.

Today at school, he'd thought of Erin's mother walking up to the school and down the corridors. She was a ghost following him around and he'd been impatient to ask Erin about it until she'd opened the door and something stopped him, possibly the man in the house, or the open way she'd smiled and the ease of her that he hadn't wanted to take away, so he'd offered to buy her a burger and waited until she was done before telling her about her mother's visit to the school. He knew with the way Erin froze, chip close to her mouth that she had not known about her mother going to the school.

"How do you know?" she asked.

Debris

He told her Michelle went to school. She cursed and pushed the chips away from her, sat up in the chair and asked what the hell her problem was. Andre shrugged and said he didn't know.

Erin asked, "And what happened?"

It was like rubbing the surface and seeing a sadder, more lost version of Erin appear. She looked like she might cry when he told her that her mother had gone to the school to say they were moving to England. She said Erin would not be back and she would send for the records soon. "I kept expecting someone from the school to come looking for me, but all this time they thought I was in England."

Erin wanted him to go over what Michelle had said in detail. She wanted to know everything about that day with her mother, who she talked to and what she'd said. Andre gave her the details. He'd forgotten how nice it was to make up stories. He said her mother had gone to the school weeks before the end of the school year on a bright day and she had been excited and a little nervous. He asked Erin if her mother bit her nails because he could imagine her sitting in the small office with her hand in her mouth. Erin said no, her mother hated the dirty look of ragged nails. She said her mother would have had her nails painted a subtle color, light pink or white and she would have had her make-up done. She would have been shy in the school.

Erin asked, "Did she say where she was going?"

Andre wished he could make something up here too, but he couldn't and his shaking head brought silence to the table.

Eventually Erin said, "Something happened to her, you know that right?"

Andre nodded.

****

The remains of the chips had grown cold between them and a dot of ketchup had dried on Erin's chin by the time they stood to leave. The evening was cool. Street lamps lit their way, and traffic coming to and from the city weaved through the narrow road.

"Did you see any names on the letter?" Erin asked after they'd walked for a while. He told her no, he hadn't looked. He wished he'd taken it, but it seemed unimportant then. Erin said her father might have intercepted the letter on its way to somewhere else. Maybe her mother had written to someone in England who was helping to sort her out. Maybe that person was still waiting for their arrival, a relative Erin didn't know she had? Someone who might be willing to help her? Andre said nothing then. His hands were stuck deep in his pockets. His gaze was on the ground and he hoped she would not go away. He couldn't imagine life without her.

"Nights or evenings are no good," Erin said. They were passing McCann's now. There were a few people in the fast food restaurant, a

couple outside the pub talking. Erin glanced at them and gathered speed.
The pub's darkened window showed no-one inside and Andre hated that he
should be worried here too. It was enough not to go to the fields. He
missed the place and felt guilty with his lack of communion with his Mom
and he was beginning to feel caged in with the threat of Colin everywhere.
Erin seemed hardly aware of his preoccupation. She was getting excited
with the thought of the letter and was talking about the best time for Andre
to come to the house to get it when Andre asked where Colin lived.

Her frown was given shape by the passing headlight. "Why?" she
asked.

He shrugged and said he was just wondering. Since he couldn't go
to the fields or Four Lantern, he should probably avoid Colin's house.

She gazed at him for a while before she said she didn't know.

He didn't believe her. It was a small enough place for everyone to
know. He'd ask Ronan.

"Seriously Andre, stay away from him."

"Seriously Erin, I will," he said.

She laughed and said okay. Her hand grazed his and he didn't
know if it was on purpose but it helped him forget Colin.

"When can you come tomorrow?" she asked.

"I can come tonight," he offered.

She said there was no point in Andre going to the house after
dinner. Her father woke up at night. He became more energetic and crazy,
tended to get restless before he collapsed with drink. Afternoons he was
quiet and subdued, and tended to stay in the rooms downstairs. He usually
wanted her to make something to eat then, so she could distract him like
the last time. The street was sloping upwards towards the school and the
estate. His feet dragged. He didn't feel like going home. He'd have to eat
dinner, because he wouldn't say that he'd gone for take-out. He wanted to
keep things to himself.

"What do you think?" Erin said.

He hated the idea of going back into that room, but he told her
he'd be there around lunch.

"It's going to be so hard to wait until then," she said. There was
the sound of children playing on the green and from the road they noticed
Erin's front door was wide open. The gap showed the garish yellow light
and the unsightly dark carpet. The hallway was brightly lit, though
somehow Andre knew the place was empty, even before Erin cursed and he
saw her father stumbling down the sidewalk towards the entrance of the
estate. Erin started to run with Andre after her. Dan was a drifting figure in
his black pants and the same shirt he was wearing the day before. His hair
was tossed and he wore slippers on his feet. He was mumbling to himself
and he might have been crying too. There was shiftiness to him, an
avoidance of looking into their faces when they reached him. His head was

down and he was trembling. Andre thought of the keening he'd heard coming from his room and the strange movements.

"It's gone," her father said when Erin tried to stop him. His skin looked yellow in the street lights and he seemed like a confused child.

She said, "Da, come on home." But he sidestepped her by getting off the pavement.

"No," he said.

She grabbed his arm., "Da, please you can't go out like this."

"It's not there," he said and Andre felt cold inside.

"Come back home, Da."

"They took it," he spoke with more force and pulled away from his daughter.

Andre was afraid he was going to hit her when she blocked his way the second time. He was beside the father and gave him less room to maneuver. Andre said, "Mr. McEvoy."

The father whirled around at him. "Don't Mr. McEvoy me, I know your game. I know what you're up to, trying to confuse me."

Close-up Andre saw his cheeks were stubble free. There were several nicks on his skin from when he must have tried to shave.

"Get out of my way," he said to Erin, and he might have moved only the door opened in the house they were standing in front of and distracted him. An elderly woman with legs like needles was standing in the light. "Is everything okay?" she asked.

"Yes, thanks, it's okay Mrs. Giles. I'm just taking Da home."

"He's facing the wrong way," Mrs. Giles said, and Erin said she knew that.

"It's okay," Andre told her. He hated having a witness to this and the way the woman scowled while Erin seemed to grow small. "Thanks very much," he said. He was blocking the father and daughter and the woman had little choice but to nod and retreat.

Erin was still holding onto her father. She asked him where he was going. He said that she could mind her own damn business. He didn't have to answer to her or to anyone else. "It's them that have to do the answering," he said. "I'm sick of their lies."

"Nobody's lying Da," Erin said.

"I have to keep it for her. It has to be there when she gets back. She told me," he said.

"What did she tell you?" Erin asked. Her voice was shaking and her father had caved in with his last words. Erin persisted. "Please, Da."

He said, "I have to get it," though his voice was low and he seemed devoid of energy.

"What did she say? What happened?"

Her father said, "You stupid bitch, you know well what happened."

Erin said no she didn't. Her father's laugh was gruff. He said, "You take me for an idiot, everyone planning behind my back. She came to me and told me what was up. She said it was my fault. She's the only one who knew, so she must have taken it when I was asleep."

"I don't understand what you're saying Da, who told you?"

"Josie Neary," her father said. "She told me everything."

Chapter Fifteen

Andre was trembling by the time he stood at the Neary house and his worry made him stumble when he knocked. Buttery light shone behind the glass as if trying to push its way out, something like the Pandora's Box his mother had told him about. He didn't know why he was thinking about that story, but he knew it was better than thinking about Erin left alone in that house. He'd had no choice but to go, yet he hated himself for it.

"Mrs. Neary's not at home," Erin had said to her father while they were on the street. Her voice had trembled and she'd seemed on the verge of tears with the thought of Mrs. Neary telling her father about her mother's plans, yet she'd still had the presence of mind to add, "She's at mass."

This had brought enough hesitation to be able to maneuver Dan towards home, though it had been an effort to get him there. One minute he'd be fine and the next he'd baulk and start talking about Josie Neary. She gave him no peace and he was sure she'd been in the house. She knew more than she let on, he said, and this had given Andre the chills.

Erin's house had been cold when they'd gotten back and walking into the empty lit rooms had given Andre a sense of foreboding. The quiet had made him remember that house in Wicklow where there were never any birds and the stillness that it possessed, and the thought still lingered. He still didn't feel right.

The curtains in the Neary house were closed. The lights were on in the front room but he could see nothing through the thick drapes. The doors leading into the lit hall were closed. He was sure he heard the television and knocked again on the door. Although he wasn't sure what he would say if Mrs. Neary answered, he knew he wasn't able to go to Michelle's without doing something.

Dan had tired himself out by the time he set foot in the house. He was easy to bring into the living room where an ashtray had spilled onto the couch. There was an empty glass on the ground beside it. Erin had started to clean it up after she'd guided her father into the armchair behind the door and her father had started to get angry then, asking where Erin had been all day, "And that boy, where is he now. Did he go into my room?"

Andre felt there were layers to the man. The tired drunk had been discarded the moment the father had entered the house, In his stead was the angry dominating figure; the man who'd banged on Erin's bedroom door and stood at the top of the stairs laughing at her boy figure and Andre didn't know which part of her father he hated more. He knew which one scared him the most. He hadn't wanted to go, but Erin told him to. She'd said, "Go on, he'll get thick." She'd told him to come back tomorrow while her father had started to rant. She had to push Andre out the door and close it behind him. He'd stood there for a long time, hearing Dan move around inside and waiting for a sight of Erin again. He watched for her to go to the kitchen or upstairs, and when she didn't appear he'd had an urge to bang on the door and scream for her, sure that something was wrong. He'd been about to knock when she slipped from the living room and the relief brought a sick kind of feeling that made him walk slowly away.

The door of the kitchen opened and Mrs. Neary stepped out in her dark shirt and cardigan. She looked like she'd shrunk since he'd last saw her. Her long hair was pulled back from her face and the smell of garlic wafted out behind her.

"It's dinner time," she said and Andre nodded. She was about to close the door, when he stopped her with a hand on the glass. She looked at him with a frown.

"What did you tell Dan McEvoy?" he said.

Her lips parted and she seemed softer all of a sudden.

"I don't know what you're talking about," she said. He was sure she was lying because she showed no surprise or anger. He'd expected her to say, "What would I say to Dan McEvoy?"

There was a moment of pause, where she gathered herself and it was like watching a door close and he realized it was stupid to have said anything to her, as if she'd open up, this woman who was like a brick of resolve. She had a way of hearing everything that went on in her house while keeping herself completely still. She'd made an Art out for reserve. She was stepping back and would have closed the door, but Andre asked if he could speak to Ronan quickly. She frowned. Her eyes went from warm to cold and Andre knew she wanted to say no, but Ronan appeared in the hall with his milk moustache that would have annoyed Andre at any other time. Mrs. Neary was reluctant to leave and she mightn't have if she had a choice, but to close the door on Andre may have garnered questions and Andre was sure she didn't want that. He thought her slightly nervous or uneasy. When she told Ronan not to take long she didn't look him in the eye and she slipped away, her shoulders not so firm. The kitchen door was left open. Andre wanted to ask Ronan if his mother had known Marie McEvoy and if his mother had told Ronan the macabre tale of her being buried in the garden. Dan had said something about the garden that day in the kitchen. He'd said 'they know where she is.' Andre was sure 'they' involved Mrs. Neary, yet there was innocence to Ronan that detached him from the goings-on and made Andre reluctant to ask him much. Ronan asked how town was and Andre said okay.

"Do you know Colin and Manny?" Andre asked.

"Who doesn't?"

"Where does Colin live?"

"Why do you want to know that?"

Debris

Andre said he was just curious. Ronan's frown was different to his mother's; the blue eyes showed more confusion than judgment. He said it was best to stay away from the likes of Colin and Manny. Andre asked how he was supposed to do that if he didn't know where Colin lived.

"All I can tell you is his surname is Mulligan and he lives by the bus station, I think."

"Great," Andre said.

"Ronan," Mrs. Neary called. "Your dinner's getting cold."

"Just get a phone book and look up all the Mulligans in town."

"I can't phone him."

Ronan shrugged, "You don't have to give a name, just ask for him and hang up."

He glanced at the kitchen to make sure his mother wasn't there, before telling Andre that he used to do that to his Dad sometimes when he first left. He said his dad would answer and ask who it was and Ronan wouldn't tell him and his dad would start yelling down the line.

"Why?" Andre said.

Ronan shrugged and said, "I didn't have anything to say."

****

Michelle's phone started to ring just as Ursula and Ines arrived at her house. It was close to six and Michelle answered the door and told them to come in. "Just a second," she said and answered the phone to a high pitched voice saying it was Mrs. Giles from number seven.

"I just wanted to tell you there was a bit of a hullabaloo here…" Mrs. Giles started and Michelle asked if she was okay, "Do you need some help?"

"No, it's not about me," the woman said. Michelle asked if she could call her back shortly—visitors had just arrived.

"Okay, but do," Mrs. Giles said. "It's important."

Michelle apologized to Ursula. Ines was holding her hand and there was something about the two of them, Ines with her timid smile and head down and Ursula with her shy nod and, "I hope you don't mind, I know it's late" that told Michelle that this was Ines' doing. Not that Michelle was surprised. From the beginning, she'd expected Ines to come looking for answers as to why her brother was no longer with them. Most likely, she'd tried her father first. It was easy to imagine Ines at the study door or sitting at the kitchen table watching for a moment when she could ask. "Dad, when is Andre coming back?"

What would he have said? Not now, or Eat your dinner.

"It's fine," Michelle said, and stepped back from the door, but she did mind the intrusion. It was nearly dinner time and she was tired and would have liked to sit with her family without theatrics. There was so much to think about already, Andre and Erin, Erin's mother.

"Andre is at a friend's. He should be home soon."

Ursula nodded. Her grey hair had been cut shorter and Michelle didn't like the pitying look in Ursula's eyes. Although there was a slight urge to take the woman's hand and tell her that she didn't know what to do, Michelle was incapable of asking for her help. She'd tried with Ron when she wanted him to understand how powerless she felt with Andre in the house and always ended up angry and silent. Martha was upstairs in her room. Jamie had run down the stairs when the doorbell rang. He asked Ines if she wanted to play. She said no and he was trying to talk her into playing by giving her his favorite car. Ines hadn't let go of Ursula's hand and the woman told her to go on and play.

"I want to see Andre," Ines said.

Ursula said, "You will, when he gets back, now go on."

The two women watched the children go up the stairs. Ursula smiled and Michelle wanted to say, "What do you want?"

She found Ursula's stare too probing, insulting almost. The women didn't know each other well. There were the Sunday dinners that Ursula cooked, but she'd never joined them. She'd made excuses so the family could be left alone. Her and Michelle's acquaintance was made up of compliments for the cooking or questions about the well-being of the children that never elicited much of a response. It was hard to think Ursula had been with the family nearly three years because it seemed as if Usao had just gone. Michelle still missed her best friend, but she rarely spoke of that to anyone.

She went into the kitchen without a word. The water was starting to boil for spaghetti and she turned it off. The dinner could be delayed. She'd been planning to feed the kids and wait to eat with Ron. She wished he was here now to act as a buffer to Ursula and Ines. Michelle offered Ursula a cup of tea or coffee. She said no thanks. She and Ines had had an early dinner and she'd had some coffee before she left, a detail Michelle considered frivolous. "We wanted to go before Eugene got back," Ursula said and seemed to be waiting for Michelle to rise to it. What did Ursula expect, defense, curiosity? Michelle merely nodded and said that she was going to have a cup of tea.

She'd turned her back to Ursula to get the mug and teabag and needed to take a deep breath. Lately it was so easy to get irritated.

"You haven't asked me why I'm here," Ursula said and Michelle nodded, and went to the kettle.

She poured the hot water before saying, "Do you think I'm stupid?"

Ursula had taken the seat by the table, the same seat Andre had been in the night he'd gotten beaten up. She didn't flinch with Michelle's tone. "No, Michelle, I don't think you're stupid."

110

Debris

Michelle was stirring her tea. The clock ticked beside her and outside it was dark. She was aware that her reflection was caught on the kitchen window and thought it must be made up of sharp edges. "But go on, tell me," she said and Ursula sat straighter. There was a moment of hesitation, the sound of running feet above their heads, Ines shouting for Martha, Jamie screaming for her to come back with his car, and it might have been the reminder of the children that made Ursula blow through the antagonism.

"She doesn't know what's going on," Ursula said.

Michelle sipped her tea and tried not to feel too deeply. It was impossible, stretching her too far. She couldn't take everyone's hurt on.

"Her mother's not there and suddenly her brother's gone, too."

He was gone from Ines before he left the house, Michelle wanted to say. It had broken her heart to see the girl trailing after the boy—ignored by him, but Ursula didn't give her a chance to talk. Michelle probably wouldn't have anyway. She had no reason to dislike Ursula, but she felt aversion welling in her. The woman was sitting in her kitchen as if she was used to the place and she spoke as if Michelle had been waiting for her advice. Now she was talking about the photographs on her brother's wall. The long corridor that faced the kitchen and living room was hard to walk down she said. She said she couldn't imagine how hard it was for Ines. She talked about those photos while Michelle drank her tea.

"I was there when Usao put up those photo's," Michelle wanted to say, "I remember the woman in them, imagine how I feel," but Ursula was talking about the man in those images.

"The old Eugene smiled," Ursula said and the intimacy sickened Michelle, made her turn and empty her tea in the sink. Ursula paused while Michelle rinsed the mug and caught a glimpse of her tight-lipped reflection.

"He doesn't smile anymore, I've never seen it," Ursula said when Michelle turned around. She stood with her arms crossed over her chest. Jamie was banging on the door upstairs. There was pause every few seconds and the girl's laughter. Ursula was telling Michelle that Eugene spent little time with his daughter, which was understandable she supposed, given that he was a CEO. She said this with a mocking emphasis that made Michelle think she was trying to soften her words or be conspiratorial, and when nothing came for her, Ursula sighed and sat back on the seat. She'd deflated and her gaze dropped onto her hands. They were slender hands, no rings Michelle noticed. "Don't they look like strangers to you," Ursula said.

"Excuse me," Michelle said.

"In the pictures, I can hardly recognize the people, it in them, this smiling happy family."

"Their mother's dead."

"Yes, but that's just it, isn't it," Ursula said, "Their mother's gone."

"I don't know what you're talking about," Michelle said. "Old pictures, what it used to be like. I was there, I know what that family was like and they don't have a choice on how to carry on. It just happens, doesn't it? You get up in the morning, you make breakfast. You send your kids to school and you try and forget the hole that's in the world."

"Why are you so angry?"

"What do you expect to happen, everything will fall into place like it was? Except Usao's not there, so that doesn't make sense."

"But why pull the family apart even more, that girl upstairs." And here she gestured above her head, as though Michelle needed to know who she was talking about. The children had gotten quieter and Michelle thought she should be worried, but she didn't feel anything. "She needs her brother," Ursula continued. "She thinks it's her fault, that she did something wrong."

"Well she should join the club. Have you talked to Eugene about this?"

"He says this is what Andre wants," she paused as if waiting for Michelle to say something and when nothing came she said, "Even if that's true, it's not right to let the children decide."

Hadn't Michelle said the same thing to Eugene right here in the kitchen, something about Andre being too young? Maybe Eugene had said it to Ursula and he'd told her, "Michelle was sprouting that nonsense too, but a child knows when they are happy or not." Maybe this was what brought Ursula to the door.

Michelle said, "Andre's doing okay here, he wants to stay and what am I supposed to do— throw him out."

"Yes, exactly." Michelle didn't expect Ursula to say that, and the surprise left her with a sinking feeling in her belly. She went to the cooker and lit the stove under the pot of water because she needed something to do. She would have liked to leave the room, open the door and just keep walking. It seemed everywhere she turned there was someone telling her what to do.

"Can't you see …" Ursula started and Michelle whirled around at her, such anger, that should have been directed at her brother, she'd think of this later of course, but by then it was too late. "No, I can't see," she started, "because everywhere I look someone's needing something and telling me what to do. I can't sit back and look at all photos and lament the change because I'm bloody living it." She paused. The front door was opening, a blast of cold.

"Usao was my best friend, I miss her and I would love for it to be the way it was but it's not and it won't ever be."

The door closed.

Debris

"Hi," Ines said from the top of the stairs. Andre said hello back. Ursula said to Michelle, "We're on the same side."

Michelle didn't answer. To Andre she said, "You're late."

"Sorry," he mumbled.

Ines was beside him, but looking at Ursula. Her face open with questions. Ursula rose form her seat. She still had her coat on and Michelle thought she was getting ready to go. Michelle's inside were quivering and she was scared of the woman before her and the possibility that she might see right through Michelle. She didn't realize that it was early to go since Ines had expressed interest in seeing her brother, or that Ursula's gaze was fixed on Andre in such a way that he'd frozen, waiting.

"Ines wants to ask you something," Ursula said.

Michelle said, "No, wait. What are you doing? Who do you think you are?"

Ines' face fell and revealed layers to her. Andre had taken a step back. He probably knew what was coming; his sister needed him home and Michelle had sabotaged Ines before she'd even been given a chance. Why? Because Ursula was a stranger, coming into her house, because Michelle was angry at Ursula for being so certain of right and wrong and for her ease in pushing through everything. Ursula went to Ines and told her it was okay. Ines wasn't crying, she was more surprised and Andre asked what was wrong. Ursula said everything. She glanced at Michelle, but it wasn't the glance, it was the way she held Ines to her, the softness of the girl that kept Michelle quiet. In the middle of the floor, her insides turned to liquid and she wished she could go back to the moment Ines stood beside Andre, or further to when Ursula spoke about children not being able to make the decisions and Michelle could say, "I know", because it would be nice to have someone in her corner. She hadn't realized it until she'd pushed Ursula away.

Ursula wasn't looking at her. She was focused on Andre and there was a distinct line to her shoulders that wasn't there before. "Your sister wants to talk to you."

There was no missing the glance Ines threw Michelle. "It's okay," was stuck in her throat because she didn't think it was okay. She knew Andre would not listen to Ines' pleas. He was as deaf to them as Eugene was to his sister.

Michelle would ask Ron later why Ursula thought she knew best.

"Can I listen to music with you?" Ines finally said.

Andre said, "Dinner's ready."

"You have time," Michelle said. Andre didn't look at her. Maybe he recognized the apprehension on her face. He wouldn't have known what it was about. He probably read it as the desire for the visitors to go, but he nodded and said okay. He didn't reach for Ines' hand as he used to. He walked up the stairs with her behind him.

Ursula said, "I'll go for a walk."

"No, you don't have to."

Ursula was buttoning her coat. Michelle wanted to say, please don't go, I'm sorry. But she said nothing about Ursula's sad smile, her query of what Michelle was afraid of. "Why couldn't you let the girl speak?"

Michelle couldn't answer her, but Ursula nodded and said, "I'm sorry for stepping on your toes."

Michelle sighed. The water was boiling and she went to the opened packet of spaghetti on the counter. Martha arrived asking when dinner was in the midst of Ursula's buttoning which seemed to go on forever, though Michelle didn't mind. The aggravation was all gone and it made her wonder if it had existed at all.

"Soon," Michelle said to Martha.

Ursula had not moved and was waiting for some response, "It's okay," or "You didn't step on my toes," but Michelle put the spaghetti into the boiling water without a word, not because it wasn't true, but because she didn't want to need Ursula's help. Ursula nodded and walked to the door. Michelle followed her. "You don't have to go, its cold outside."

Later, with the house quiet, she would think of this and cringe, "Its cold outside," as if the woman would say, "Of course, never mind," and take off her jacket.

Michelle would realize with her husband snoring beside her that she should have offered Ursula more than that.

"I'll be back in half an hour," Ursula said and Michelle didn't stray from the hall for several seconds after the door closed behind her. "Stop doing that," she told Jamie, who was running his car down the bannister on his way down the stairs. He ignored her. She'd hardly spoken above a whisper.

"I'm starving," he said.

"You are not starving," she told him, "There are children in Africa who are starving, but you're just hungry."

"I'm starving hungry," he said, and she managed a smile and a ruffle of his hair before going into the kitchen and getting dinner ready. She did not call Andre down, though she thought he must be hungry and it was possible that he was sitting stiff on the bed, sharing his ear-phones with his sister and waiting for their call. Ron was working late, a job needed to be finished and Michelle stood by the sink while her children ate their dinner. When Martha asked about Ines and Andre, she said Ines already ate. "And Andre?" Martha asked. "Mam?"

"What?"

"What about Andre?"

"He'll come down if he wants."

Debris

Michelle was thinking of Ursula outside. Was she sitting in her car or wandering through the estate? What did she think of the place after coming from the large house and the sea? She imagined Ursula was crying for some reason, which didn't make sense because she seemed as tough a woman as herself. The kids scoffed their food. Jamie's face was smeared with sauce. Martha told him he was disgusting. She wanted to go to Andre's room after dinner. Ursula was due back in five minutes and Michelle was tense waiting for the bell to ring. She said no to disturbing Ines and Andre. She said Martha could watch television.

"There's nothing on," Martha said. Jamie jumped from the table and ran into the living room.

"Do the dishes then."

Martha said, "That's okay," and ran after her brother.

The front door opened. For a second, Michelle thought Ursula had a key all this time and she was going to stamp right in and give Michelle a piece of her mind. She was staring at the kitchen door when Ron appeared. "Hey, love."

Michelle smiled.

"Everything okay?"

"Can you please take off your shoes?"

He cringed and disappeared. It was Ron who answered the door to Ursula, Ron and his cheerfulness, his, "Well hello, what are you doing here?"

Michelle waited in the kitchen for Ursula and heard the mumbles from the door. The cold still drifted inside when Ron re-appeared. "Ursula's here for Ines," he said. He was wearing his 'what happened' frown and Michelle understood that Ursula must have declined his invitation to come into the house."

"Can you get Ines? She's in Andre's room," Michelle said and Ron's gaze hardened somewhat. He would have been wondering why Michelle was not greeting their visitor or getting Ines herself and his pause was long enough for Michelle to say, "Oh never mind," and mutter under her breath, "for God's sake."

Ron stepped back, loose with relief from seeing Michelle doing something. Ursula had closed the door. She stood before it with her hands joined in front of her. "Just a second," Michelle said as if she was a neighbor collecting a child. "Would you like some tea?" Ron asked. Ursula said no thanks. She said she was one of the few Irish women who didn't like tea.

Ron laughed and said something that Michelle didn't catch. She was at Andre's door and listening for some sound. The silence made her stall for a moment before knocking. There was no answer. She knocked again and stepped inside. The children were sitting on the bed, not lying back as she'd seen before, but facing each other, legs crossed and an earphone in one ear each. Ines' shoulders were leaning towards Andre and she took the ear-phone out of her ear when she saw Michelle at the door.

Michelle said she had to go.

Ines said, "Can I stay here too?"

"You have school tomorrow," Michelle said.

"But Andre goes to school here."

Andre was watching his sister. Michelle couldn't see his expression but she had an idea that Ines didn't want to look at him, that maybe she'd asked him already and he'd said no, and he was annoyed at her now. "Ursula's waiting for you," Michelle said.

Ines didn't move and her gaze fell on the bed. She shook her head and Michelle felt as if she was a sack of empty organs—she couldn't think or feel.

"Ines, you have to go home?" Andre said.

She shook her head again. Her long dark hair fell like a curtain around her face. She might have been squeezing her eyes shut tight, counting in her head like she used to when she and Andre played hide and seek. "Count out loud," Andre used to tell her, "so we know how long we have." Ines could never do that.

Downstairs, Ron was saying hello to the kids. Ursula probably hadn't moved.

"Ines?" Andre said.

"I'm scared," she said and Andre told her she had nothing to be scared of.

"That's okay for you to say," Ines said. She was glaring at her brother now, "You don't see her."

Michelle saw the effect of those words on Andre's face. It was as if Ines had slapped him. His shoulders came back so the distance between his sister and him had doubled. Michelle stepped closer. "What are you talking about?" she asked Ines, but Ines didn't hear her or if she did she was too concerned with her brother who was getting off the bed.

"Are you scared too, is that why you don't want to come back?"

"I'm not scared," Andre said and Michelle felt invisible, everything else reduced to the two children before her. She didn't know what they were talking about, she didn't want to know, but she thought of the footsteps she heard in this house when she was alone.

"Ines?" Ron was at the door. "Ursula's waiting for you, honey."

"Did you see her?" Ines said. She was starting to cry.

"See who," Ron said.

"No one," Andre said. "I'm hungry." He looked at Michelle who felt drained. "Is there dinner?"

Michelle nodded and Andre ignored Ines calling his name on his way out of the room. Michelle noticed his sneakers thrown on the floor by the bed, his jacket beside them on her way to Ines.

Debris

"Come on," she said and reached for Ines' hand. Ines' eyes a bright blue and regardless of her smallness, she seemed older than her years.

"She can't go until he comes back," she said to Michelle.

"Who can't go?" Michelle asked.

"Mammy."

"Oh honey, she's in heaven," Michelle said. She wanted to believe this and to forget about the paleness of Andre's face or the lack of questions.

Ines shook her head, but allowed Michelle to lead her downstairs. Ursula put her arms around her and asked what was wrong but Ines pulled free from the embrace to put her shoes on without answering. With her jacket on she stood at the door of the kitchen to say bye to Andre. Her nose was running and she had to snivel. He was sitting at the table with his dinner in front of him. It was probably cold. Michelle didn't know if he'd put it in the microwave. There was a soft curiosity in his eyes that may have been the reason for Ines's stillness at the door. Finally he said. "I'm not scared."

Martha said, "Scared of what?" she'd run out when she heard Ines coming down the stairs and refused to be shooed away. Ines said, "Nothing."

"Scared of what?" Martha repeated.

"That's enough," Michelle said. She noticed that Ines looked better, less tight around the mouth and sad around the eyes. She allowed Ursula to lead her out the door. Michelle watched them go to their car and fought the urge to run out and say sorry. She would think of Ursula throughout the night. Once or twice, she would feel close to phoning her, but embarrassment and pride kept her from dialing her brother's number.

The evening of the killing, Ursula would be the first person that would come to Michelle's mind and days after in her too-quiet house, she would call Ursula and sob on the phone.

****

"I'm not scared," Andre had said and he'd seen his sister's smile and felt the change in him. "I'm not scared," and his sister would have been thinking of his mother's ghost, that presence that he'd thought was his alone, but it wasn't. Where had Ines seen her? Had she gone into the shed for her bike and seen the same apparition? Had their mother come into her room and settled beside Ines? Had there been more than one visit? There must have been for Ines to be so sure of her ghost.

"It's okay for you, you don't see her," she'd said and that was true. He hadn't seen her since that first time. There'd been her scent and the feel of her, but she'd hidden herself from him and he didn't think her absence had to do with where he was. It was the same in his father's house.

He'd waited and waited and gotten nothing, so he felt betrayed by his dead mother. She had abandoned him too. Maybe she had not been waiting for him at all, but for Ines. If she was to speak, she might have said, "Oh no, Andre, not you."

He still remembered the days sitting outside her bedroom door when Ines was a baby. The hall had seemed so large and quiet and he'd felt lonely and on the verge of tears sitting on the floor with his legs pulled up while his mother and sister lay together in the room. "No, Andre," his mammy had said whenever he peeked in. "No, Andre, not you."

Ron went up to shower and Michelle was at the front door, seeing Ursula and Ines off, so it was easy for Andre to throw his dinner in the bin. The shower was running and a glance in the living room showed Martha watching Tom and Jerry cartoons with her legs falling over the top of the couch. Jamie sat perched on the couch beside her. It was Jamie's favorite video. Andre was going upstairs with the phonebook when Michelle came back into the house and told him to she wanted to talk to him.

She didn't respond when he said he had to do his homework, so he knew he had no choice but to follow. He left the phonebook on the hall table. She'd put the gas on under her Bolognese sauce and filled the kettle to heat up the pasta before asking him what was wrong with Ines. "What's she scared of?"

Andre shrugged and said he didn't know. He had stepped inside the door and felt uncomfortable under her probing gaze.

"Do you believe in ghosts?" she said and a burst of breath came from him, not quite a laugh but a guffaw that made him feel stupid. "No," he said.

She said, "You used to talk about it all the time. I remember how fascinated you were with Banshees."

"They're not ghosts."

"And you used to love the day of the dead, or whatever it was called," and waved away her confusion as if it was a bad smell, though he didn't trust her play of light-heartedness. She appeared stiff. Her brown eyes were pleading, though he had no idea what she wanted and when she tried to smile, she looked defeated by it.

"Día de Muertos," Andre said into the silence. He'd never liked the English translation. It sounded flat compared to his mother's tongue.

"Right, it's in November."

Andre didn't say anything. Michelle said she remembered Usao loved the idea because families welcomed the dead back instead of being afraid of them. And Andre felt something turn inside him, like a door closing and he was behind it watching Michelle from a distance, hardly listening to what she was saying now.

At one time he would have loved this conversation, but now it made him feel heavy and morose. Michelle was saying something about

118

bonfire night. It had been Usao's favorite celebration and Andre remembered that last bonfire night he had gone to the warehouse. He'd tried to build a small fire at the back for her, but it burnt out quickly and his mother never appeared.

"What do you think?" Michelle asked and he had no idea what she had said. "We could do one at the beach."

He was taken aback at first and Michelle might have seen his surprise as delight, because she managed a proper smile before he said no. She said why not.

"Because it's stupid." Because when he'd walked from the embers last year he'd promised not to do that again.

The kettle was starting to boil. Michelle went for it and Andre took advantage of her distraction to say he had to do his homework. He was gone before Michelle had a chance to ask if Ines had seen a ghost. It was on the tip of her tongue, but she didn't know how to say it without appearing foolish. It might have been different if he had been more open to the subject, though his reaction when Ines said. "It's okay for you, you don't see her," had been strange. He had asked no questions before the recoil, and then later in the kitchen he'd said, "I'm not scared," as if he'd known exactly what Ines had meant. It all sat with Michelle in a strange way, but she would choose to forget about it. Her unease would be easy to disregard as something she'd imagined. But when the sirens rang through the estate Andre would tell Michelle that he'd seen his mother's ghost and Michelle would believe him.

****

Michelle had just finished putting the kids to bed when the phone rang.

"Oh no, Mrs. Giles," she thought as she ran downstairs. She'd completely forgotten about the earlier phone call and her promise to phone back. "I'm so sorry," she said when Mrs. Giles gave a timid hello. Mrs. Giles said that was okay, but she didn't want to wait any longer in case she fell asleep. "It's too easy to nod off in front of the fire," she said and she might have continued on talking about the show on telly she was watching or how hard it was to get around with all the rain had Michelle not reminded the reason for her call.

"Did he tell you himself?" Mrs. Giles said. "I was thinking later that he might have told you and there was no need for me to pester you."

Michelle straightened. It was like having a knife in her back in the spot between the shoulder blades. She said no, he didn't tell me and hoped she didn't sound too cool, but the frivolousness had gone.

"He's a good boy," Mrs. Giles said, "He was trying to help the wee girl. The father was drunk as usual and he'd gotten out of the house. He was shouting about Josie Neary again. It's shocking what went on there. I can understand he is upset, but bothering Mrs. Neary won't help any. She's suffering too, I'm sure. He was right outside my front gate at teatime and I came out and saw the boy. He looks just like Eugene at that age. You'd know him anywhere, wouldn't you?"

"Mrs. Giles, what happened?"

"Oh nothing much, somehow they managed to calm Dan down and bring him home, but I thought the children might be a bit upset, I was shaking after, all that shouting, it's uncalled for you know."

"Yes."

"He wasn't always like that, was he? I remember him coming to help me that time the kitchen flooded and he used to help with the bins, though Johnny does it now. He doesn't mind anyway. He says there are certain things only family should do and maybe he's right."

"Yes maybe..."

"I, well, I'd just be careful sending the boy to the house. You never know what's happening these days."

Mrs. Giles would make a similar statement to the guards. "I knew it couldn't be good," she'd tell them.

****

There were three Mulligans in the phonebook and only one with an address near the bus station on John Street. Andre took that number down first. The other two were jotted down just in case. The house was quiet when he brought the phone book back to the hall table. Ron had gone to sleep an hour or so ago. Michelle usually went early too. "Ron gets up at five, which means I do too," she'd told Andre the first weeks of his living there, though he had the impression that she lay awake listening to the noises of the house for a long time after she went to bed. At least she used to slip from the room whenever he was on his way downstairs for something to eat. Tonight, she hadn't gone to bed and he'd waited for as long as he could before going downstairs to eat. He wished that he'd eaten his dinner earlier. In the restaurant with Erin, he'd felt uneasy with the thought of Colin and Manny and then the conversation had veered onto her mother so most of his fries had been uneaten.

There was a low hum from the radio on the kitchen. Andre noticed Jamie's door was ajar. It used to sadden Andre when he got to the house first, the simple sight of the door opened and darkness spilling out, the idea of the little body on the other side asleep. It made him think of Ines, the smallness of her, the need in her. After a while he banished the thought, but tonight it was hard not to think of Ines. Ines had come to him because she was scared, he knew that, and yet he had not been able to hold her and say it was going to be okay because he didn't know if that was true.

When they'd arrived in his room, she'd sat on the bed and he'd had no choice but to sit across from her.

Debris

"When are you coming home?" she'd asked and he'd shrugged and said he didn't know.

He was handing her the earphones. Eurythmics was playing when she'd said, "Dad said that it's up to you, that you can come home whenever you want."

"Dad's a liar," Andre had said and wished he hadn't when he saw the worry in her eyes and the fall of her mouth. Andre had felt sick with the idea that she might run down to Ursula or Michelle and ask why her dad lied, and then she might be told everything, but she'd remained on the bed, though distant and sad. Now he realized that she must have been wondering how to talk about their mother. The surprise from that disclosure still lingered in him, like a ball of ice on his chest and belly. The cold seemed to drift around him.

Michelle was sitting at the kitchen table. "Hungry?" she asked and he nodded.

He was getting the cornflakes down when she told him that Mrs. Giles had rung to tell her about the incident today. She pronounced it as if the word had left a bad taste in her mouth. She said she hadn't planned on bringing it up tonight since there had been enough excitement.

"But you're here now," she said and asked him what Dan was doing.

She'd risen while she spoke and brought her empty mug to the sink. Andre stood by the counter and had not gone for the bowl. He didn't want to turn his back to continue his pursuit now that Michelle had brought up Dan. He'd felt a surge of relief the moment she mentioned it because he realized she must know something of what happened to Erin's mother. He felt no guilt when he told her that Dan was going to Mrs. Neary's house.

Michelle didn't seem to think anything strange about this, or at least she showed nothing. She just turned off the tap and put her mug face down on the draining board, though later Andre would think that her actions were too deliberate, as if she wanted to waste time without looking at him and he would think that she must have been surprised with the news. In hindsight he would believe there was an element of disbelief when she finally stood with her back against the sink and said, "Why?"

Andre said, "He thinks she knows something about his wife."

"What does Erin think?" Michelle asked and the question surprised Andre. He felt an urge to flee the room. He didn't want to talk about Erin and what she thought, that was an act of betrayal. Yet there was an opening in Michelle's question, a comradery that made him feel like telling her everything. "Erin thinks something happened to her mother," he might have said, or "Her father did something."

Then he could ask Michelle if she'd gotten a strange feeling at the school. He had since he'd discovered the mother's visit. The thought of her walking along those corridors had brought a chill going down his spine, but he didn't say any of this to Michelle. He said Erin didn't know where her mother was.

"But Dan thought Mrs. Neary knew."

Andre nodded and wondered about Michelle's pensiveness. He asked if she remembered when Erin's mother left. He didn't remember hearing anything about it. She shrugged and said. "I don't like what happened today." She'd been avoiding looking at Andre until now. At least he had that feeling because she had spent a long time drying her hands on the tea towel. Now she looked at him and he saw the worry. "Dan didn't hit you or Erin when you tried to stop him, did he?"

Andre said no. Michelle nodded and said next time he needed to get an adult to help instead of dealing with Dan alone. "Okay," he said, though he doubted Dan would stand around while Andre ran to get adult help. Still he was glad he agreed when Michelle smiled. It seemed the first real one she'd given him in a while.

"I'm tired," she said, "I should have been in bed ages ago." She told him to go ahead and get something to eat, but he needed to be in bed in twenty minutes.

Michelle was leaving the room and Andre reaching for the milk when he realized she never told him if she remembered when Erin's mother disappeared. He was sure she knew something, but she was gone up the stairs before he'd reached the kitchen door.

Chapter Sixteen

Ronan's house was empty when Andre made it there the next day. The car was gone but Andre didn't think of it until he knocked several times. Sometimes Mrs. Neary would take her daughter to school or go to an appointment and Ronan would be left behind to wait for Andre. He had no doubt that Mrs. Neary was nervous with him after last night, but he hadn't expected this and his walk away from the house was slow and uncertain. He would have liked Ronan to be with him when he dialed the numbers he'd written on paper last night. Although he knew he wouldn't have thought of telling Ronan if he hadn't talked about the silent phone calls to his father.

There was a phone box near the entrance of the estate but Andre wanted to wait until he reached the one close to Daly's. He needed to change some pound notes in the shop, but even without that he wouldn't have wanted to step into the glass box outside the estate and be conspicuous to everyone. He could imagine Mrs. Neary coming back up the road and gaping at him or Michelle driving past. So he kept walking as clouds sped by, conscious of the paper in his pocket. He saw the curtains were closed in Erin's house.. There were a few students in Daly's. Andre bought some cigarettes and asked for change for the phone box. Inside the glass box, he started to sweat slightly and the moisture on his palms made the 20-pence piece slip. He smelled the metallic scent of his skin and a trace of cigarette smoke. A few butts lay on the ground by his feet. Mags loves John was written in black marker on the box, I hate Mondays was scribbled below it. He took out the paper from his pocket and lifted the receiver so the dial tone filled his ears. There was a temptation to hang up and walk out and forget all about Colin and Manny, but the forgetting would only last until lunch when he stepped out into the open air and started towards Erin. Then he would feel them as if they were breathing down his back. Every corner would hold a threat of them, and he couldn't go on like that. If they wanted to beat him up, let them get it over and done with. Still the thought scared him. The bruising had gone down, but it was easy to remember the heat on his cheek brought from Colin's hands and the pain on his cheekbone that made it feel like it might break any minute. This memory brought his heart into his ears and obscured the jingle of the coin falling into the body of the phone and the tap of the numbers dialed for the house on John Street, the closest one to the bus station.

The phone on the other side started to ring. Andre imagined Colin glaring at it before he pounced, so when eventually the ringing stopped and Andre heard the drowsy male "Yeah," Andre nearly lost his voice with the fright. The words came out choked and low when he asked if Colin was there.

"Who's asking?"

The question was unexpected and Andre's nervousness meant his name slipped out before he could think straight. He heard laughter and, "Little man, this better be good, you woke me up."

Andre's grip on the phone had tightened and the receiver was pressed against his ear and the discomfort made him hate the man on the other side of the phone. The weeks after the accident when he'd lashed out against David and any other classmate, who deemed to get in his way, it had been an instantaneous reaction. His body moved ahead of his brain, hitting and kicking and he felt a similar kind of detachment when he told Colin that he wasn't afraid of him.

"Oh yeah," Colin said.

Colin breathed out and Andre realized he must have lit a cigarette and the intimacy of listening to him taking a drag and exhaling made Andre's stomach turn. Colin said, "Is that it?"

Andre thought of Erin telling him to stay away from the fields and holding his arm to make him rush past the pub, but he didn't want to mention her name and it was hard to focus on what he wanted to say. All he could think of was, "I'm not hiding."

"Well you know where I live," Colin said.

That was why Andre called, to discover where Colin lived and go to him, but Colin seemed too happy about it. A lump had formed in Andre's throat and his mouth was so dry it was painful to swallow. Colin said, "It's too early now little man. I'll see you after school."

Colin exhaled into the phone and after a long moment said, "Okay?"

"Okay," Andre breathed.

****

It was a relief to get out of the phone box and away from the smells and confined space. Some students were still making their way towards school and their chatter rose and fell. Since he'd come to the school, Andre had gotten friendly with very few people. Ronan and Pete were the only ones he'd see outside school grounds. Now, after his conversation with Colin, he missed Erin and he thought of going to her and telling her what he had done, but he imagined the fall of her face and the disappointment and it was too easy to recall how drawn she'd been after the confrontation in the warehouse. He lit a cigarette and the taste was gross with his dry mouth, but he didn't put it out. He smoked while he walked to school and decided that he couldn't tell Erin about his visit. He had to do this alone. By the time he'd made it up the steep hill towards the school, he'd smoked two cigarettes and managed to forget how nervous he'd been talking to Colin. Andre had phoned just as he had planned, and so what if Colin was expecting him? At least this way, Andre knew Colin would be there when he went to see him. Besides what was the worst Colin could do in the middle of John Street?

The avenue to school was sheltered by a dozen trees. The hockey pitch surrounded by high wire fence was to the right and low buildings with galvanized roofs that were used for art was on the left. A few stragglers were ahead of Andre and a sudden image of Marie McEvoy's blonde figure walking amongst them made him uneasy. Above Andre, clouds were gathering and this with the shadow of the trees made him think of the Sluagh, spirits that came from the west. They flew in groups like flocks of birds and tried to enter a house where someone was dying to take away their soul. He'd read about them once and the thought of them had kept him awake at night, jumping with any shadow and now they made him quicken his pace. By the time he stood at the door of his class, Marie McEvoy had made rubbish of any concern about Colin.

Ronan was sitting in his desk at the back of the class. His chair was tipped backwards on two legs and he was talking to Pete, a lanky lad who talked about little other than soccer. When Ronan saw Andre at the door, he was up and off the chair before the front feet hit the ground.

"What did you say to Ma yesterday?" he asked.

Andre would have gone further into the class only Ronan had him by the arm and was pulling him out to the narrow hall. Outside the lines of the basketball court were faded, grass grew through the concrete, and the basketball hoop was stained with rust. He couldn't remember seeing anyone play on the court.

"She was raging," Ronan said, "and she was no better this morning either, wouldn't let me wait for you to walk to school. What did you say?"

Andre shrugged and before Ronan could argue with him, Andre remembered what Ronan had said about Marie and he stiffened. "Was she the one who told you about Erin's ma?" he asked.

Ronan frowned and Andre said, "That she was buried in the garden."

The frustration left Ronan's façade and he looked worried now. At the top of the hall, their math teacher Father Anthony, a small wiry priest with short grey hair and square glasses had appeared.

"What's that got to do with anything?" Ronan asked.

"Why did you say that?"

Students were filing in through the hall now. There were another two classrooms after theirs, a couple of girls were talking and they stepped around the boys without pausing in their walk. Ronan said, "He was out in the garden screaming one night."

"Who?"

L.M. Brown

Father Anthony was telling the stragglers to get into their classroom.

"Who do you think, Dan McEvoy!"

The priest was beside them. He was known for his halitosis. "Class is starting boys."

"Yes father," Andre said, wrinkling his nose. The priest went into the classroom and Ronan was about to follow when Andre stopped him with a hand on his arm.

"Quiet down," the priest said and the noise decreased, though there were one or two mumbles when Andre asked Ronan if he'd heard Dan McEvoy shouting.

Ronan said, "The whole bloody estate would have heard him and the next day she was gone."

"How do you know?"

To Ronan's frown, he said, "How do you know she was gone the next day?"

"I just do."

"Your Ma told you, didn't she?"

Ronan's face clouded over. Andre had no idea what he was thinking, but he knew that Mrs. Neary must have told him that Marie was gone, and because of the shouts Ronan had decided the woman had never left the garden. He might have told Pete or maybe not, maybe it was some macabre story for him to think of at home, some entertainment with his Da gone and his mother having no patience. Ronan pulled away and went to his seat at the back of the classroom. He ignored Pete's curious gaze and the subsequent thump on Ronan's arm made him glare at his friend.

"Whenever you feel fit to join us," the priest said to Andre and there were some giggles. Andre sat near the front window that looked out to the front of the school. He thought again of Erin's mother. She seemed held within the walls. He had flashes of her walking hurriedly down the avenue away from the school, and it got to Andre that he thought of her more here than he did in Erin's house or in the estate. The priest said something and there was the sound of flicking pages which made Andre look to the girl next to him and see page 89. He opened his book, though that's as far as the concentration went.

He tried to piece it together. There'd been the fights between Dan and the wife and then the wife decided to leave. She'd come to the school. Andre remembered Mrs. Neary following him when he'd left school early the other day. She'd seen him go to Erin's house and reported this to Michelle, so why couldn't she have said something to Dan. *She told me everything*, he'd said the other night. Andre sat up and he couldn't help glance at Ronan who was watching him with grave blue eyes. Mrs. Neary must have told Dan about the school, the pure bitch Andre thought, and something of this thought might have translated itself into his gaze because

126

Debris

Ronan straightened before Father Anthony asked Andre what was so interesting at the back of the class and if he had an answer to the problem yet.

"Nothing father," Andre said and he hunched up in the desk hoping the priest might get bored and pass him over which he did. Andre thought while Noel Donovan gave the answer, that there were the screams and shouts in the garden and the wife disappeared and Erin was left alone, and it had something to do with Mrs. Neary.

****

Michelle was nervous going towards the Neary house. She couldn't remember the last time her stomach felt so unsettled. It was impossible to know how to tackle Mrs. Neary about Marie's whereabouts. Michelle felt meddlesome and cruel, but she saw no way around it. She hadn't been able to sleep, thinking of Erin being left alone with her drunken father.

The day had started out nice, but the clouds were thickening, grey and large they blocked the sun. Jamie had gone to school nearly two hours ago and Michelle had pottered around the house until there was nothing more to be done. Her walk across the green was quick and she kept her arms crossed over her breasts, her shoulders back and she swore not to let Mrs. Neary's hard gaze wear her down.

Mrs. Neary's garden had been freshly mowed. Large plastic pots stood on either side of the door. They held red and yellow flowers and more than a few weeds. The garden had flowers around the borders, but it was not kept so well since the husband left. Michelle had often seen him outside and there was femininity in the way he would rise from some flower and flick his greying hair from his eyes and in the yellow rubber gloves he'd worn that went as far as his elbows. He was tall and skinny and of similar temperament to his wife. For years, they'd kept to themselves.

The car was outside the house and Michelle rang the doorbell. The door was covered with a net curtain, but it was possible to see movement behind it and there was nothing but a gloomy stillness that didn't sit well with Michelle. She rang the doorbell again and with her desire to flee came a tightening of her muscles and the decision to stay here all day if she had to.

Michelle had to ring the bell once more before she saw the kitchen door open, a spray of grey light, and Mrs. Neary's unsmiling face. She was dressed in dark pants and a long wool cardigan. Her blue eyes were tired and Michelle noticed the lines sprouting from them and pinching the corners of her mouth.

"I was asleep," she said. Michelle apologized for waking her.

Mrs. Neary nodded and wrapped the cardigan around her body. A horn blasted from a passing car and it made the houses seem too quiet and still. Michelle wished she'd worn a jacket. The day didn't seem so cold when she'd left the house, but now she felt vulnerable in her sweater and jeans.

"Can I come in for a second?" she asked.

"Why? What is this about?"

Michelle said it would only take a minute and forced a smile.

Mrs. Neary sighed and opened the door. The hall was painted a dark color and it made Michelle feel tight in the chest. A full length mirror was opposite the door and there were a couple of photos of the Neary children, but Michelle noticed some hooks stood unused and she wondered what photos had been taken down, wedding photos or the family together, and it made her steps awkward while she followed Mrs. Neary to the kitchen.

The kitchen was more untidy than unclean with a clothes horse behind the door filled with the children's clothes. The table was pulled out to the middle of the floor. Breakfast dishes were still in place, a couple of bowls and remnants of milk in two glasses. A mug sat at the edge of the range, and an armchair had been pulled up to the fire. The cushion was well worn and the arm tatty where Mrs. Neary's hands must have rested. She must have pulled the threads out in a restless habit and the nervousness this suggested made Michelle look at Mrs. Neary in a different, almost sympathetic manner.

Mrs. Neary asked if Michelle wanted tea. She said yes so the tension might ease in the time it took for Mrs. Neary to fill the kettle and put it on the range. Heat blasted from the fire inside so there was no wonder she'd fallen asleep in front of it. The room was stifling and Michelle would have liked to open a window. She stepped away from the source of the heat while Mrs. Neary got mugs and sugar. She seemed to think it pointless to ease her visitor with small talk. There was a deliberate quickness to her actions that shouted duty and no smile to go with them. There was an armchair near the range, but Michelle would have been too restless to sit even without the heat.

Day light was obscured by net curtains on the window and back door, so the room was highlighted in parts, the mugs on the table, the soft pudginess of Mrs. Neary's cheek, the black-bottomed kettle and the white t-towel thrown on to the table. Michelle strolled to the sink and was surprised by the dirt of the window, given that she'd seen Mrs.Neary washing her front windows every couple of months and with her clean car and haughty manner, she'd seemed fussy about the cleanliness of her house. Michelle stepped closer to the window and was conscious of the quiet and the new stillness behind her, but what she saw outside the window surprised her too much to care. The garden had been dug up. There were planks of wood thrown in broken piles and soil heaped in mounds here and there, leaving water logged holes. Even through the net curtain and grime on the window, the garden looked chaotic.

"Thomas had raised beds out there," Mrs. Neary said.

Michelle couldn't take her eyes of the mess. She felt a heavy sensation in her belly, a kind of sickening knowledge that was hard to process with the woman behind her, but she knew if she stepped sideways and stood at the back door, she'd be able to see the McEvoy's garden. She had never thought of this before and now there was something perverse and crude with the mess in back and the way the woman was so quiet watching her. Michelle sensed an element of amusement, but when she turned there was no hint of this on Mrs. Neary's face, rather her mouth had dropped slightly and she stood as if daring Michelle to make a comment. Did she expect some sympathy? Michelle wondered if she was waiting some comment like, 'it must have been terrible' and this was the cause of her defiance. Michelle doubted Mrs. Neary was the type to accept pity, and in any case Michelle felt none. Instead she was hit with a mild irritation that helped settle the unease in her stomach. She said, "Erin doesn't know where her mother is."

Mrs. Neary's shoulders came back and what might have been a dull shutting down in her eyes or a cloud passing. It took several uncomfortable moments before she asked, "What has that got to do with me?"

The kettle started to whistle and Michelle imagined Thomas getting to know Marie from across the garden wall and Mrs. Neary coming home early to see them together. She poured water into the mugs. Her face was unreadable. All night, Michelle had been kept awake thinking of Dan McEvoy coming to this house. Andre had said that Dan thought Mrs. Neary knew something and Michelle was sure it wouldn't have been the first time they'd spoken. She'd lain in bed and imagined Mrs. Neary storming over to McEvoy's house.

Michelle asked. "You told Dan, didn't you?"

"Sugar and milk," Mrs.Neary said.

"Did you think it would make them stop?" Michelle asked.

Mrs. Neary poured milk into one mug. Her hand trembled slightly when she lifted the spoon of sugar.

"It didn't work out like that, though did it? You told him and then Marie had to get away from Dan."

For a moment Michelle thought Mrs. Neary would sit on her armchair and put her back to her, but she pulled out a chair from the table and sat.

"Go on," Mrs.Neary said. "This is fascinating."

Michelle sighed. She couldn't move closer to the table. The garden behind her gave her strength because it told her there was something very wrong going on, not just for Erin, but in this house. How long had the garden been like that? It would have been hard for the children to step out into it and yet Mrs. Neary did nothing. Michelle said. "You can't just sit around and let Erin suffer."

"I have nothing to do with that."

"Yes you do, you know where her mother is. You can tell her."

Mrs. Neary said she had no idea where Marie McEvoy was, but Michelle saw the worry in her gaze and her unease. She gestured to the garden and asked, "Did Dan do that afterwards?"

Mrs. Neary said. "You haven't a clue."

"Then tell me," Michelle said.

"Why should I talk to you? There's nothing to say anyway. Thomas is gone and everything beyond else is beside the point."

"Erin is not beside the point."

Mrs. Neary said, "Erin McEvoy has nothing to do with me and it's not my fault her mother left her behind. She was the one who made that choice."

"But she didn't make that choice. I know she went to the school to transfer files only something happened."

"And you think *I* happened. You think *I* was the one who stopped her."

"Yes."

Mrs. Neary sipped her tea, the clock ticked and the room's light ebbed and flowed. Michelle felt lost here. She couldn't trust her senses, one second Mrs. Neary looked like a softened down version of herself and the next she was a rock of a woman.

Mrs. Neary said, "That doesn't make any sense."

"Can you give me his address?"

"No."

Mrs. Neary's smile was sharp and Michelle was sure she was amused now, and couldn't figure if it was from Michelle's discomfort or the thought of Erin McEvoy. Michelle asked if she had any conscience at all, "Think of your own children," she said, and Mrs. Neary's countenance changed immediately from the amusing interest to defense. She said, "Mary hasn't seen her father in a year."

"Do you think that's fair?" Michelle said.

"Who said anything about fair? I can't go into my own garden. Any time I do he comes out screaming and shouting nonsense." Michelle looked out the window and had a sudden urge to go outside and step around the mess of raised beds to the wall separating this house from the McEvoy's, so she could understand how everything had happened, but she stayed still.

Mrs. Neary rose from her seat. She'd drunk her tea in small regular sips. Michelle had ignored her mug. The light streaming through the curtain barely made it that far. Mrs. Neary went to the sink and rinsed

130

her cup. The silence dragged so when the water was turned off Michelle felt weighed down by it.

"You're not thinking of Erin," Mrs. Neary said when she'd placed her mug on the draining board. Her skin looked like dough in the light and Michelle was sickened by her words. They might have been half-true. Without Andre, Michelle wouldn't have thought of Erin, but he was there and Michelle couldn't just sit back.

"Where is Marie?" Michelle asked

Mrs. Neary said, "Do you know what Thomas said when I told him I was pregnant with Mary?"

Michelle didn't answer.

"Nothing," Mrs. Neary said. "He rose from the table and left the house and didn't' come back for two days and then it wasn't for long."

"I'm sorry about that, I really am, but that has nothing to do with this."

Mrs. Neary sighed and said that had everything to do with this. She said, "You still don't get it, do you?"

Michelle said, "I get that you've gone through a lot." Here she paused, the two women looked at each other and there was a small blast of light. The sun found its way through to pierce the stockier woman as she shrugged. She might have eased a little if Michelle didn't say, "You don't have to make Erin suffer. None of this is her fault."

Mrs. Neary showed not anger, or frustration, but hurt when she said, "I'm sorry you think that. Now if that's all…."

"Please," Michelle said, but Mrs. Neary was already walking away.

****

Ronan was one of the first out the door of the class with lanky Pete behind him. Andre caught up with them in the hall, a gaggle of kids went by, navy uniforms and voices that seemed distant to Andre. All he saw was the irritation on Ronan's face, the narrow blue eye and the tight mouth. "What happened to Marie McEvoy?" Andre asked after he'd blocked their way. Pete was watching them with curiosity, the freckles on his face made bright by the light coming through the window and his mouth dropped open with the name.

"She's Erin's ma."

Ronan told him to shut up and Pete said to feck off, he can talk if he wanted to.

He said, "She took off the same time as your da. Erin thought it made you best friends."

Pete laughed and Andre felt a terrible sinking in his gut. There was no mirth on Ronan's face. He was glaring at Pete when he told him to stop talking shite and there was no denying the threat in his gaze, though Pete didn't seem to notice.

He said, "It's true, remember she was waiting for you at Daly's every evening. She drove you mad."

The corridor was getting quieter and a stream of sound trickled to them from the stairs, a thudding and fading of steps. Ronan tried to walk away. Andre grabbed him again and was pushed back. Pete's chuckle got under Andre's skin, but he couldn't think of him now. He was too caught up in Ronan and the change in him. He seemed older with his shoulders bared and the narrow eyes and there was a tension coming off him that made Andre reluctant to grab hold of him again.

"Do you know where Marie is?" he asked.

"That's what Erin wanted to know," Pete said.

Chapter Seventeen

Ines lay in bed, listening to the sounds of her father rise. It was still early and the morning was starting to seep into the sky, ridding her of the blackness behind her window, which scared her sometimes, though she was getting better at dealing with this fear. She'd come to understand that it was her own reflection and the idea of being stuck in that place, not outside or inside, but in the space between them like a ghost was what scared her the most. Recently, she'd spent a long time staring at her reflection caught in the window and she was sure the face had changed into that of her mother. It had started off with the difference of the eyes, a broadening of space between them, and then the lengthening nose, a fullness of lips, and it had been like watching a drawing unfold. She had not run away, though if someone had tried to move Ines' hands that had gripped the windowsill they would have found her rigid from head to toe.

She had been just as tense the first time she'd seen her mother in the garden through the back door. It was after school and getting dark early when she saw the figure walking towards the low wall and facing the thunderous sea. Ines' body had turned into stone. She'd felt a need to cry and run, but the shock made it impossible to move or speak. Ursula had been concerned. She'd come from nowhere and gripped Ines arms, asking what was wrong. For a moment, Ines couldn't speak and when she did she said she'd seen a spider. Ursula hated spiders and though Ines had never shown fear of them before, the woman had become too frazzled looking behind her and exclaiming to worry about the girl's excuse. The next time Ines had run to open the back door and though the thought of her mother scared her, she had cried when she found the garden empty.

She'd said nothing of the visits to Ursula, who was asleep in what was once the guest room at the end of the corridor. Sometimes Ines wondered if Ursula had seen something too because Ines sometimes found the older woman staring out any window with a frown. When Ines asked what was wrong, Ursula would shake her head and say, "Nothing," in the way adults said 'nothing,' which meant 'everything.'

Ines' father said 'nothing' like that too, though he tended to smile and ruffle Ines' hair. She had begun to hate that.

He was in the kitchen now, waiting for the coffee to finish. He would eat standing up with his coat hung over the chair and his briefcase on the seat where he should be. Ines always saw his rush to get out of the house. It was in his eyes; the way they'd widen whenever Ines appeared. He'd say, "Morning," and she knew he was really saying, "I have to go."

She slipped out of bed and felt the morning press against her window. There was always the thought of her mother roaming and it had started to sadden her more than scare her.

At the kitchen door, she saw her father's broad back in his grey suit. His hair was clipped short and he was looking out the window, lost somewhere out there, so he didn't notice Ines's presence until she said, "Dad?"

When he turned, he looked sad. Recently he'd said, "You look just like her."

And she'd wanted to say sorry, though she didn't know why.

"What are you doing up so early?"

She shrugged.

He sipped his coffee. The distance was something she was used to, like holding your breath before going under water.

"Do you want some breakfast?" he said, "Are you hungry?"

She nodded, not because she was, but because she wanted him to stop looking at her, so that her voice might make its way upward. All night, she'd been thinking of what she wanted to say. By the time they'd made it home last night, Eugene's dinner plate was in the sink and he was ensconced in the study and even if Ines had known what she wanted to say, she'd felt incapable of approaching him. In bed the words had come to her.

Her father was pouring cornflakes in a bowl. Ines' fist clenched, the ball was tight in her chest. She didn't know if she could do it. She didn't talk much now. It always felt like too much effort, as if the words were part of her and she had to rip them off and throw them out. Ursula was used to this and she had a way of getting the girl to speak, mostly it was through questions, not 'how was your day' questions, but questions like the ones Ines used to ask, *where do thoughts come from?* or *Why do people die?*

When Ursula first came, Ines would sit on her knee and ask her these same questions. This was back when Andre was at home and the loneliness was not so engrained. It was like a lingering familiar smell, now his absence touched all her senses. Within the first months of losing him, she'd withdrawn and her questions about everything, other than why is Andre gone stopped. So Ursula began to ask her, "Ines, why is the ocean salty?" or "How many hairs do we have on our head?" "I've been wondering what exactly is night?"

No matter how she felt, Ines couldn't help wanting to know the answers for them and she loved Ursula for this.

Her father was going for the milk and Ines glanced at the clock over the door. She remembered in the days after her mother died when she'd asked her father, "Why have the clocks stopped?"

He said he didn't know.

Debris

She'd asked Andre then and he'd looked at her from across the kitchen table and said because they're sad, but he'd sounded more angry than sad.

The fridge door closed and she could feel the time slipping away and she closed her eyes, so the ball in her chest might unravel. She heard the milk on the cereal, and said.

"Mammy wants Andre to come home."

The sound stopped. There was nothing but her breathing and she wanted to hide behind her eyes. She couldn't tell if he was angry and that was what she was afraid of. Her father's temper was short-lived, but the burst of his raised voice always frightened her when it happened. There would be a blast of "For God sake," which was usually directed at Ursula, and, "Don't bother me with that now!" This was mostly about Andre, because Ursula had not given up arguing for his return and would broach the subject at least once a month.

"Don't worry, he's all bark," Ursula would whisper to Ines. But Ines didn't understand this, because she hated the bark and the way her father would bang his study table or kitchen table.

"Ines?"

He was before her now. She didn't remember hearing his approach. She'd been so caught up with the black behind her eyes, but she felt his hands on her arms. They were so large compared to her and she realized that her eyes were shut so hard, it hurt.

She refused to look at him because she needed to think of Andre and in front of her father she always lost the nerve to speak of her brother.

She said, "Mammy's looking for Andre and she's sad."

She heard a sound like a cry, a deep breath. His voice was low and didn't sound like him when he said, "Ines, can't you look at me?"

Her face was scrunched with the effort of hiding and she was starting to cry. She could feel it inside her and it was one of the reasons she didn't like talking so much because the loosening brought tears.

She said, "I'm scared."

He didn't ask what she was afraid of. He might have known it was him. There was no ruffle of hair and dismissal. He brought her to him and she realized he was kneeling on the ground before her. His arms wrapped around her and for once he was not leaving. Ursula was getting up, Ines was aware of the sounds in the periphery like a fly buzzing around the room, there and then forgotten. What was important was the warmth of her father, the feel of his breathing, and the quiet between them that held so much promise.

****

Andre stood outside Erin's house. The curtains were not closed fully in the living room. There was a slice of smoky light that showed an empty room. An ashtray was on the floor and a jacket thrown over the arm of the chair. The house had the feel of vacancy, but it always did. There was dull still gloom over it that spoke of desertion and it got to Andre now because he found no sympathy for it. Although he couldn't understand how he was feeling, there was a sense of betrayal, an idea that Erin had been laughing at him all the time with her stories about looking for blood in her house and talking about some accident that had befallen her mother, when in reality she'd been outside searching. At first he'd tried to understand Erin. Her mother had disappeared and she'd waited for her for days, maybe more, and then she'd decided to look for her. Was it then that she discovered that Ronan's father had disappeared too and from that decided that they must have gone together? Ronan would not talk of it again. Andre had tried.

"Did your Da know Marie?" he'd asked and Ronan told him to fuck off.

Andre was in French class when he remembered Erin's father in the kitchen, forcing him to look out the window, screaming about being hemmed in. Andre had seen the Neary house from their window.

A small concrete path led from the front of the living room window to the side of the house. They were separated from their neighbor by a low brick wall, and then ahead of Andre was a red shed with the door lopsided slightly so in order to close it one would have to lift it up. It stood ajar now, but Andre ignored it. The garden was small and square shaped. He walked on the wet muddy grass to the wall and had to step over an old clothes line with pegs still attached that lay on the ground. One side was attached to the roof of the shed and he didn't bother to see where the other side had hung. He felt a clammy heat in his chest with the knowledge that he was being watched, the moment he'd stepped onto the grass something changed. He couldn't explain it, a thickening to the stillness, a gaze settled, heavy on his back and it was tempting to turn and look—tempting to stop too because he would have preferred to ignore Erin's lies. The thought of her deception made him feel lost. Since he'd known her, he had felt some purpose and to go back to the endless roaming was impossible. The day was turning grey and cold. The grass was long enough to sway with the breeze but Andre hardly felt it as he stepped to the wall and looked across it. The Neary's garden was diagonal from him and close enough to make out two figures caught behind the net curtain of the kitchen window. On the other side of him, he sensed movement in the garden. He hated the thought of being seen and would have liked to hide, yet it was instinct to look at the woman hanging clothes on her line. She had a long black coat on that could have belonged to her husband and short hair. She smiled before bending down to what must have been a basket of clothes.

The back door opened and Andre turned again to the mess of the Neary's garden. He was sure it was Erin behind him and he knew she

Debris

wasn't angry, not like he supposed she would be if she found him here, looking over at something that must have driven her mad when her mother left.

The door closed and for a moment he was afraid that she had gone inside and locked the doors but he heard her come towards him. She stopped beside him in her jeans and a black hoody, her hair brushed back from her face and her arms crossed. Andre was afraid to speak. He hadn't realized how angry he was until she stood beside him. It was hard to look at her.

"How did you find out?" she asked.

Andre didn't answer and he didn't meet her gaze. "Andre?"

"You lied," Andre said.

"No, I didn't. I said something happened to Ma. Do you see her anywhere? Do you know where she is? Because if you do, you should tell me."

Her anger confused him and made it hard to hold onto his own. It was like holding wet soap.

"What about Ronan's Da?" He wished he didn't look at her because it was hard to stay angry when he saw her shoulders fall and how tired she looked. Her father was in the house somewhere, and Andre wondered if he was looking at them now or if he'd attempted to go to the Neary's since yesterday. Erin might have stayed up all night. She shuffled the wet grass with her feet. The laces of her sneakers were untied and her hands dug in her sweater pocket. A car started and there was a blast of a horn. Andre was beginning to think she wouldn't say anything.

"She told me about him," Erin said, and Andre grew aware of the space around them. Everything seemed too open. She glanced over the wall and was biting her lip. Andre knew she was trying not to cry and he resisted reaching for her because she seemed to be seeing something else, maybe remembering her mother and that man together, or just her mother's face when she first told her daughter about him.

"She was so excited when she told me. She sat on the edge of my bed and held my hand and said that she'd met someone who made her feel beautiful." Erin shrugged and the eyes that met Andre's were glistening and frightened. "I was scared. You get used to the way things are, even the fights and the days when she wouldn't get out of bed and I'd take care of her, it was what we did...you know."

He didn't know.

"She wouldn't tell me who it was at first. She said it didn't matter, that I would find out soon enough when the time came and I felt like I was losing her. Da saw a difference too. He watched her more. I'd see him in the evening when she was moving around the kitchen singing. She sang too much."

A breeze rustled her hair and she shivered.

137

"What are you doing out there?" her father was at the back door. His hair was tossed and he was wearing black pants and a white t-shirt. Even in the distance, Andre saw his fly was undone. "Nothing Da..."

"Get away from there."

"She doesn't care about us Da," Erin said and there was pleading in her voice. Her father said, "Get away from that fucking wall or I'll throw you over to the other side."

He laughed then, "Do you want that, eh? See if you can do some more damage."

Andre felt like a rock had landed on his head and the new weight made him feel it was impossible to move. He glanced at the mess in the Neary's garden and then at Erin, who was watching him with a look he couldn't decipher: regret, fear, a little pride.

Her father was out the door. His steps squelched in the mud and he shouted for her to get inside. "Da," she said and she avoided his grasp by stepping around him. The manoeuvre was so well done that Andre knew it must have been done before and he wondered how many times she had stood there and how much silence and absence she had taken before jumping the wall.

Erin was running to the door and Andre was so caught up in the Neary garden and the thought of Erin in there, creating havoc that he forgot about her father until his face was in his.

"What the fuck are you doing here?" Dan asked. There was a smell of drink of him already and his chin was greasy with what looked like butter. His red rimmed eyes were glaring at Andre, and still he didn't expect the slap that went across his head and made his head lower in defense and his arms come up around his head to guard him.

"Da," Erin screamed. Andre expected another slap that didn't come.

"Get inside," Dan said to his daughter. He was walking away, mumbling something about Erin having to do what she was told. She said, "Okay, I'm coming," and was beside Andre.

"I'm so sorry," she said. Because of the drink, the slap had lacked force, but it had been enough to shock Andre. Erin was holding his arm and the two children looked limp as they walked inside as if they'd walked miles. Erin said, "Imagine what he was like when he found out about Thomas."

****

Tracks of mud led from the kitchen to the living room, a waft of smoke and her father calling for her. "I'll be right there Da."

"Is your friend gone?" *Friend* was said in a mocking tone. Erin said yeah while she led Andre up the stairs. He avoided the third step and wished the television was on because the quiet scared him. He hadn't

Debris

thought of what he was going to do when he allowed Erin to pull him through the back door. She'd locked it after and said her Da was suspicious after last night. She'd smiled then and said her Da had found the ring in his room when she'd made him look again, but it wasn't in the envelope so he still thought someone broke in. She'd whispered while she'd talked in the kitchen and then had put a finger to her lips in a gesture of shush. Andre had nodded and let her guide him onwards.

In her bedroom, he saw her bed was tossed and a pile of clothes were thrown on the floor. She picked them up and threw them in the corner of the room. The air smelled of stale smoke and he imagined her sitting alone on the bed smoking a joint and wondered how she could have done it, to feel everything pile up in her head while her father roamed around the house.

"Did you know about the ring?" he asked. She was fixing the bed and she stood straight, but didn't look at him for a moment and he felt sad looking at the back of her head. When she finally turned her face looked pale and she seemed worried, so for the first time he felt the elder of the two and he didn't like the reversal. He needed her competency and wanted her to lead the way and tell him how things should be. It was how Ines must have viewed him, though he was incapable of that anymore. He didn't trust himself enough.

She said, "No, I didn't know." He wasn't sure if he believed her, but he wanted to. She sat on the bed. Her sneakers were still on and the laces fell soaked towards the floor. Her hands looked red and cold.

"I should have told you about Thomas Neary," Erin said. "But I didn't want you to think she just left." She managed a smile, "Ma thought I would like him. She said he knew so much about plants and flowers. That was how they got to talking, across the stone wall whenever she went out there, which was a lot because after her arguments with Da she liked to go out the back and most of the time she was crying. Thomas would have heard her." She paused.

Andre glanced at the photos of her mother staring out the back window and he wondered if she was thinking of Thomas then. He preferred to think she'd been watching Erin but he couldn't imagine her there anymore, not like he did the first time, playing in the garden as if she had nothing to worry about.

"She said he would take us away, me and her. She said it was like a fairy tale. I didn't know how Da found out until yesterday. I thought he might have followed her or something, I didn't know about Josie Neary, I promise."

Her father started calling her again and Andre felt an intense hatred for the man who did nothing, but drain his daughter. Erin hadn't moved and he realized she was waiting for him to say something. "Okay," he said, though nothing felt okay. He didn't want to imagine her father's rage after he'd discovered his wife's affair when he felt the sting of his slap on his head and he had done nothing to warrant it. The idea made the room gloomy and Andre's heart quicken. Erin rose from the bed and he wanted to grab her hands and tell her to stay, that he'd protect her, but he knew that was pointless, that there were no such things as hero's and people being saved and he understood why his mother had hated the Prince and Princess stories. She frowned whenever she'd seen Ines reading them and the books always mysteriously disappeared. "It's the fairies," she'd tell Ines and wink at Andre.

Erin smiled at him and her hand held his for a brief moment. Her skin was cold and dry and his fingers closed around them like she was a life line, and she was in a way. This girl who made him want to stay in the real world instead of joining the spirits and the ghosts and the banshees he had once read about. Before her, he'd wanted nothing more than to get away from everyone, and now he wanted nothing more than for her to stay in the room with him.

"You'll have to wait for a little while," she said, "before you go in for the letter. I'll try and give you a signal, listen for a cough or something,"

He'd forgotten about the letter in his rush to her house and now it scared him. There was noise from downstairs. Her father was in the hall, sending curses upwards and telling Erin to get down, and Andre thought of Erin's mother coming home to him after Mrs. Neary's visit. Did she find him in the hall like he is now, or was he waiting in the kitchen perched at the table and ready to pounce like Andre had seen him do to Erin? Had Marie known what was about to happen before the slap, or had she been distracted thinking of her escape? Erin must have seen something on his face, concern, a little fear because she squeezed his hand and she seemed on the verge of tears when she said, "Please, you need to find it. I can't stay here."

****

Mrs. Neary walked as far as the kitchen door. Michelle had not moved. Her 'please' had stuck to the walls and seemed to echo in the untidy room where the heat was starting to get to Mrs. Neary. It was okay when she was alone, to light the range and sit before it until her cheeks grew hot, but company made her breathing quicken. The heat settled into her skin and built up until the discomfort scared her. She hadn't always been this way, though it was getting harder to remember what she used to be like.

"I'll see you out," she said and hated the sound of her voice and the obnoxiousness in it. "I'll see you out. Where do you think you are?" Thomas would have said.

Debris

At one stage he would have laughed, but not towards the end, towards the end he'd felt the pressure of her company and any sound the children made irritated him. He hadn't needed the heat of the range to bring his pulse higher. There were days he'd spend hours in the garden, and days where he just disappeared. Mrs. Neary had known he was gone long before Marie.

Michelle glanced at the garden again. She said, "Why don't you clean it up?"

Mrs. Neary stood straighter. She wrapped her cardigan around her body and wanted Michelle gone so much it hurt her chest. She said, "To keep them away."

Michelle frowned and Mrs. Neary remembered what Mary had said when she was told the same thing.

"It's like a scare-crow," her seven year old daughter had said, "To keep the crows away."

Mrs. Neary had said yes, and Ronan had said, "If the McEvoy's are crows."

"They're not," Mary had said, and Ronan had avoided his mother's eyes. She'd known about Erin finding him before school, of the questions about his father and her mother and she'd seen the hurt and confusion on his face.

"I don't understand," Michelle said.

Mrs. Neary sighed and told her that Erin McEvoy did that to her garden weeks after Marie left. She saw Michelle's face fall. "Yes," she wanted to say, "This is the girl you're letting Andre hang around with," but there would be no pleasure in it now.

Mrs. Neary was tired of looking out the back and thinking of her husband and that woman. It was the woman she hated most, her and her small face and blonde hair and timid ways.

Michelle looked exhausted. Her steps were sluggish as she went to the front door. There was reluctance to her when she stepped outside, a question when she turned back to Mrs. Neary, but whatever it was, it was lost in the last instant and her face grew blank, though Mrs. Neary thought she recognized the hopelessness in it. She closed the door and watched Michelle walk away, and she thought of the letter upstairs that held her husband's address and phone number, the letter she knew had been taken out of her drawer and looked at, because it had been folded differently. She'd said nothing to Ronan about it. She thought maybe he'd given the information to Erin and that was why he'd looked since he'd stopped speaking about his father a long time ago. She didn't realize until she saw her visitor walk away and she turned back to the kitchen to sit and wait, though she had long forgotten what she was waiting for, that she had harbored a hope that he had given it to Erin because it would take the responsibility from her. She wasn't able to help Erin or her mother, not after Marie McEvoy coming to her and crying and pleading for help, as if Mrs. Neary was just a by-stander in this and not someone who had lost her husband, not after the humiliation of having Marie stand in her very own kitchen and tell her the plans she had made with Thomas and how scared she was for Erin when Mary was still so young.

"You know how I feel," Marie had said.

She had had no idea how Dan had found out about her affair and Mrs. Neary still felt cold with the thought, but she refused to feel guilty. When Marie McEvoy left that day, she left Mrs. Neary empty and when the phone number and address came in the post to give to Erin, Mrs. Neary copied it and wrote Thomas' name on the piece of paper. The letter she threw away because she had to forget the woman who believed that Thomas might love her daughter more than his own.

****

Andre couldn't leave with the letter this time. There was too much at risk. Her father could easily find it gone and there would be no stopping him from going to Mrs. Neary then. "She'd call the guards on us," Erin had said while her father's shouts had turned to a racking cough. Andre thought the guards couldn't do anything and then he remembered the garden.

Erin said, "Stay here and we'll read it and then put it back."

Her face was flushed and the worry he'd noticed earlier had disappeared with her excitement. He knew she was thinking of someone in England, a fairy Godmother who might save her from this house and her father's rages and madness and he was scared for her. When she ran down the stairs to her father and spoke to him in a jovial voice that seemed wrong in this environment. Andre took a long time before he could move from his spot in the middle of the floor. He sat on the edge of the bed, and after several minutes he took his school bag from his back. The weight had hardly been noticed but now that it was off he felt more comfortable. His shoes were next, they were a little muddy from the garden and he didn't want to dirty her bed. The sound of presses closing came from downstairs. He heard Erin's father shuffle into the kitchen after her. "I don't want egg, if I have another egg sandwich, I'll puke."

Erin must have said something to him because he cursed and, "I better have a drink than."

His laugh was grating and Andre felt a blast of rage well-up inside him and stay simmering. He wished he didn't have to listen to the sounds downstairs —the scrape of the table over the floor, the tap running, her father's mumbling and every now and again, something from Erin, a chirp that was too light and carefree.

Andre took off his jacket. He moved slowly and felt every inch of his body. The Walkman clattered when he threw the jacket on the ground and he was surprised that he'd forgotten about it. He'd put it into his jacket

Debris

pocket when he'd first arrived outside Erin's house, because he'd wanted the stillness and to be aware of everything. It was strange to remember how upset he'd been with Erin then. He'd felt betrayed and she had assuaged that, though it was hard to figure how when she'd told him things she should have shared from the first. Still he wouldn't dwell on it, as he wanted to be here more than anywhere else. So what if it meant letting some things go? He sat back, his legs dangling over the edge of the bed. He would have loved a cigarette but couldn't take the risk. Erin had left the door slightly ajar to let him hear what was going on downstairs and her father might have been drunk, but he was also paranoid.

Minutes passed and they didn't drag like he thought they might. He was suspended in them. He was sure he could hear plates knocking together as they were put in the sink and he remembered his own lunch though he didn't move to get it out of his bag until he heard Erin and her father coming from the kitchen and the television go on in the living room.

Andre ate and rested his head against the wall. He couldn't figure out what they were watching downstairs. Every now and again, he'd hear Erin go to the kitchen and move around and thought she was probably getting ice. Outside was cloudy and the sunlight came into the room in waves. Andre was sitting forward reaching for a stream of light when he heard the television go off and Erin cough.

Andre rose slowly. He felt sick and wished that he hadn't eaten his ham sandwich. The bread had settled on the bottom of his stomach and made him feel heavy. A glance at the top of the stairs showed no one there. Erin would have been on the couch keeping an eye on her father and what would she do if he woke and started for upstairs? What would her father do if he found Andre in his room? The thought made it difficult for him to move and it was worse than the last time he'd searched the room because then he'd gone in expecting nothing. Now it was like searching for treasure and he thought of Erin's father as the dragon, or something worse, Cerberus, the three-headed dog who protected the entrance of the Underworld and the idea of the letter scared him because he had no idea what would be on it. Erin wanted salvation, but what if she got something else entirely?

The room smelled of cigarettes and dirty socks, a dirty pair had been thrown on the bed. The bible was on the floor and on the bedside table there were loose pages of a newspaper, more was on the unmade bed. The ashtray was under the bed, some butts on the floor around it.

Andre opened the drawer and was reluctant to touch the papers from the memory of the old sodden tissue. Silence from downstairs, though it was hard to listen for anything with the thudding in his ears. The letter was three down in the pile and he pulled it out and felt as if heat was coming off it before placing the bills back and closing the door, and stepping over the bible lying face down on the ground.

L.M. Brown

In Erin's room he read the letter.

By the time she came up to see him, he felt as if he'd grown years older, the heaviness that had come when he thought of Erin in the Neary's garden was nothing to the weight he held now. It made it difficult to hold the sheet of paper and to look at her face, but he managed to meet her gaze when he gave the letter to her.

****

She was too excited to see the fall of his face and how slowly his hands had moved. She grabbed it. "That's Ma's handwriting," she said the moment she saw the untidy writing. She moved to the window. Light was there and then wasn't, so it gave Andre the impression of movement as if the house was spinning, though it may have been his head and the difficulty in understanding everything.

"It's addressed to me," she said and he heard her concern, and he might have thought of grabbing the page from her if he hadn't felt so lost.

Erin,

I'm so sorry.

Andre hadn't realized anything then, though Erin must have known something was wrong immediately.

I'm so sorry, please forgive me, but I have to leave.

Erin was so still. He thought she might have stopped breathing. There was no address or phone number on the letter. Andre knew this and knew Erin was looking for it when she turned it over. She hadn't read the letter yet. She still didn't know that Thomas Neary didn't want Marie to bring her daughter with them. Marie had never said she would. She'd led him to believe she was willing to go alone.

I went to the school in secret. He didn't know.

So it was Thomas she had been worried about.

I planned to take you. If you were there with me he couldn't say no, he couldn't turn you away, but everything's changed. Dan knows and I can't come back here and Thomas...

Andre thought Erin would have started to cry but she seemed to grow straighter and stiffer and he saw nothing but anger in the line of her mouth. Her mother had left that sentence unfinished, Thomas, and that was it, maybe she hadn't been able to understand it herself.

I don't know where we're going yet, Thomas won't say. I think he's afraid of Dan finding out. Once I get settled I will let you know, and you must come to me, or write.

Or write, Andre knew when she'd read those words. He heard the moan and intake of breathe but still she didn't cry.

I have nowhere else to go, Erin. I can't keep living like this. If I don't get in touch with you soon, go to Mrs. Neary for my address. I told her you would. His children need to know where he is. I will try to write.

144

Debris

I love you, Mom.

Erin's hand fell. When she looked at Andre he rose from the bed. There were no tears in her eyes. Andre went to her, but she stepped back. After a while, she said, "Da must have found this in my room the day she left. He came in and took it and never said a word when he saw me waiting for her."

Andre didn't know what to say. He'd expected her to break down with the knowledge of her mother's desertion, to be lost with it and instead she was raging. She held her head high and said, "It's his fault."

"Thomas Neary..."

"No, Andre, listen, if Da was gone Thomas would have no choice. He'd have to take me."

Andre couldn't say anything.

"It would be so easy," she said, "He's always so drunk, he's nearly fallen himself so many times."

Andre's stomach had started to turn and he had an urge to run and escape her face that held no surprise. She'd thought her ma was dead. She'd said her Ma was a ghost haunting the house, so how was she so calm when she'd just discovered her ma was alive? Erin was folding the letter and telling him he needed to put it back before her Da woke up. He didn't want to think that she'd known about the letter before this, which meant she'd also known about the ring. Had she realized the effect it would have on him because he believed in ghosts and his mother's spirit? It hurt to consider this, a piercing pain in the back of his eyes like looking at lights that were too bright, and it reminded him of how he'd felt when he'd sat with his father all night in silence. She was telling him that he had to go before her father woke and Andre remembered her at the fire the first night they met asking if he'd hurt anyone, the quiet when he'd said no.

"Andre," she said. "Will you help me? I can't do it alone."

She was waiting for him to say something when the phone rang. Her eyes widened. She cursed and started for the phone. The letter was in Andre's hand. She'd pushed it onto him before darting out of the room. The ringing was loud, but she got to it quickly and there was no sound from her father. Andre knew he should be in that filthy room already, sliding the letter back, but he stalled outside her bedroom door and heard her say, "Hello," and then, "Oh."

Andre thought it might be Michelle calling and that she was phoning because Mrs. Neary had seen him in the garden and he felt nothing about it. Numbness had spread through him as he heard her say, "Why would he?" in a worried voice, more high pitched than usual. Andre still imagined Michelle on the other end and couldn't wonder why Erin would stay on the phone with her. "No, don't," she said. Her "Please," made Andre feel something though it was short-lived and he couldn't remember what it was that had moved him by the time Erin said, "Okay," and hung up.

She didn't move for a long time after she hung up. At least he heard nothing while he stepped into her father's room and put the letter back. She was walking up the stairs slowly as he came out of the room. When she finally stood before him, she couldn't smile, though he saw the attempt in the corners of her mouth.

"Have you talked to Colin?" she said and he felt like she'd thumped him in the belly, but his guilt didn't last long, not with the memory of her with the letter and the way she'd stood rigid. Why feel guilty when everything she'd said was a lie?

He shook his head and asked, "Why, was that him?"

"Please stay away from him. He'll hurt you and I don't want him to."

She looked scared and there was clinginess in her grasp that he hadn't felt before, but she still hadn't answered his question and this kept him at a distance. She smiled and said, "I'll help you and you'll help me."

He didn't know what she meant or how she could sound so blasé, though he found nothing carefree in her gaze. He saw expectation and he couldn't meet it. He couldn't say yes or no because he was afraid of what he might agree to and just as afraid of pushing her away. He said he had to get back to school, otherwise Michelle might discover he was missing and then they'd be in trouble. Her hand dropped and a shy sadness seemed to come over her. And even with the strange feeling in his belly and the fear of not knowing what was going on, he didn't want to leave her and he knew he would have to come back, no matter what she had done.

****

Ines didn't go to school. She was too excited and could hardly sit still all day. Ursula had been shocked with the little girl bursting into her bedroom. Ursula had missed Eugene holding his daughter and saying, "I don't feel Usao anywhere, why don't I feel her?"

Ines said she didn't know. She said again, "Andre needs to come home."

And it was agreed, though it took longer than that. There were the minutes of her father wandering around the kitchen while Ines stayed by the door, still feeling where her father had held her. She listened to him talk about not knowing anything anymore and having to start from scratch. Ines didn't understand what he was saying, though she was sure he was scared too and that was the crux of it.

Then he'd thrown out her cereal and given her a fresh bowl and sat while she'd eaten and said, "He might not want to come."

She was not an eight-year-old who liked to squeal or jump around. She froze and couldn't eat anymore and asked if that meant Andre could come home. Her father's nod was short and he looked worried, and Ines didn't like when he turned away from her to look out the window because she had a feeling that he was hiding. She kept still and waited for him to look back and smile at her, before she asked if she could wake Ursula and let her know.

"It will have to be later," her father said. "Andre is at school now and I have some meetings I can't cancel. You'll have to wait."

She shrugged and slipped off her chair to run to Ursula, who she could show her excitement to easier. With her father it was like treading water. Five o' clock he would get home and they would go to Andre together.

Chapter Eighteen

Andre Nolan was seen leaving the McEvoy's house at two in the afternoon. Mrs. Giles, three doors down from the McEvoy's, saw him pass by and went out to see if everything was okay. She told the guards that he was very polite. He paused in his walk, unlike many young ones and he said, yes, everything is okay, in such a polite manner when she inquired about the McEvoy's.

Another neighbor told the guards of the beating Andre received.

"I was hanging out my clothes when Dan McEvoy came storming out and hit the boy. I was so shocked I couldn't move. The sound, you have to understand, I wasn't prepared for it. Anyway that poor girl had him by the arm and before I knew it they were gone. I didn't think there was anything I could do. My husband said to keep out of it when I phoned him. I feel terrible. I should have done something. It wasn't the first time I saw something unpleasant in that garden. We all should have done something instead of sitting back and letting that girl suffer. It's hard to go into the garden now."

Later Andre was seen in the bus station in town. The woman working behind the ticket counter said he came in just after 2:20 p.m. She said he looked like he had been crying, though that might have been her eyes. They got tired at that stage from working since eight.

"There was something terribly sad about him. The bus station isn't the best place to hang around. It's drafty and the seats aren't comfortable. Kids usually hang around the Four Lanterns because management let them sit around cokes for hours, but he was alone and he was jumpy too. He kept looking at the clock. He'd sit for a minute and his legs would be going non-stop and then he would step to the door to look out. He'd stand there for quite a while before finally closing the door and walking back to the seat. More than once I was just about to ask him to please stand inside or outside because he was letting the heat out, but he'd move back and close the door at exactly that moment.

"I didn't realize he was listening to music until I approached to ask if he wanted some help. I thought maybe he was waiting for some-one and the bus from Dublin wasn't due until after four. There was something about him that made me want to help him. I think he reminded me of my granddaughter. I know he's a boy, but he had the long hair and her shy way about him. My granddaughter would never ask for help so I called out to him. I said 'hello, excuse me' a few times from the desk and I thought he might be deaf. He was staring at his feet so I went to him and stood right in front of him and then I saw the earphones in his ears. He pulled them out and appeared scared when he looked at me. I don't know what that boy has

Debris

gone through, but he said he was sorry when I hadn't said anything at all. I told him he had nothing to be sorry for and asked if he could use any help. He said no thanks and I asked if he was waiting for someone. He said no, then yes, as if he didn't know himself. He was flustered when he said he was waiting to go to a friend's house but they were at school. Any other child, I would have said. 'You should be at school too.' Half of these children don't appreciate the importance of education, but I couldn't say it to him. I just said that's okay. Shortly after that, close to four, I know because one or two people had started to trickle in, he was starting for the door again and he stopped suddenly. He was looking out the window and his face had turned pale as if he'd seen a ghost. He stood still for a few seconds. I couldn't take my eyes off him. One minute he was still as a rock and the next he was going so fast he nearly tripped over his feet. I ran out from behind the counter and saw him running towards Forester Street. I saw no-one on the street that I can remember and I don't know where he went after he reached Forester. A customer had come in and there were tickets to be sold, but I couldn't stop thinking of him and I can tell you that poor boy was sweet and scared and there's no way I believe he meant any harm."

****

Erin had appeared on Forester Street in her jeans and black hoody. She looked cold with her hands dug deep in her pockets and her shoulders folding forward. It was hard to make out her face. The bus station was at the back from the road. Between the depot and Forester Street was a wide carpark. Directly across from bus station and at a right angle to Forester Street was John Street.

Andre watched as Erin crossed the road towards the street with rows of attached white town houses that had no gardens, and still he couldn't believe it, still he waited for her to turn around or walk past number 12, the fourth house on the right that he had walked by before going to the bus station. The curtains had been closed and it suddenly hit him that Colin and Manny were in that house, and he'd felt stupid for thinking of walking into that hornet's nest. He hadn't been able to go in and had gone to wait in the bus station where he'd been overcome by fear.

Now, watching Erin, his body had become one huge organ, his beating heart filled every pore. He was vibrating, and when Erin stopped walking, the beating stopped and he thought he might fall, and the blood had turned cold underneath him. His fist closed and the sting of his nails scraping his palms helped him to move. He grew aware of the woman staring at him and the couple sitting on the chairs behind him giggling. He fumbled to get the door open and ran towards Erin who had already disappeared and everything he had felt leaving the house, the sorrow that had descended on him, the hopelessness from not knowing what was true anymore, from doubting the one person he had come to trust was nothing compared to the notion of her laughing at him now. He wouldn't have cared if a car had come thundering towards him on the street. He didn't look before he ran across and he no longer cared about Colin. The pain of being slapped again and again would be nothing compared to Erin's betrayal.

Number 12 was a narrow two-story with a sorry patch of green behind an iron fence. The garden would barely hold one person. The front door was opened, but this didn't make Andre pause. He burst through and stumbled on the carpeted hall. He could smell a sweet scent of cleaner. Coats hung on a coat rack by the door. The kitchen was in front of him. No dishes in the sink, a sweeping brush leaned against it and the touch of domesticity confused him. For a second he didn't see Manny. In Andre's hurry, he'd stumbled ahead of Manny who stood in front of a door to the right. Manny was wearing jeans and t-shirt and he was barefoot. His hair was standing up at the back as if he'd just woken and a glimmer in his eyes that made Andre feel cold, even before he heard Erin from the room behind Manny. She wasn't laughing. There was no mirth in her voice. She was talking quickly, apologizing and saying he wouldn't do it again. *He*, Andre knew she was talking about him, his stupid phone call and need to go out in the open, when he should have known that it wasn't as simple as that. Andre went towards the voice but Manny blocked him from entering the room. There was a couch inside the door, brown with a red throw and eighteen-hole doc martens stood before them and something about the boots, their careful positioning and the white socks tucked in top scared Andre in a way he couldn't understand. He shouted for Erin. Even then he thought he could give himself for her, lay himself down for her, but the hope started to disintegrate the moment she came to the door. She was so pale and drawn just like after the warehouse and Colin was behind her. Andre bristled with the sight of Colin's hand on Erin's arm. "Told you," Colin said and Andre didn't know who he was talking to, but Erin nodded. There was no anger or remorse, no judgment, just sorrow. The fierceness of her when she'd stood by her bedroom window with her mother's letter was nowhere in sight.

What Andre would remember was how she seemed to disappear. Her gaze fell within itself and then dropped away from Andre as Colin grabbed her. Andre started to scream with the first touch of Colin's hand on her jeans. With Andre's first inkling of what was going to happen, he felt as if the world had stopped and that there was no one but Erin. All he wanted was to reach her and to stop the touches, which must have burnt Erin, leaving its mark, because they seared Andre and he would never get rid of the feeling under his skin from having to watch Colin tug on her jeans. The front door was open. Air came in from the street. Did people pass? He couldn't tell at the time. He was fighting to get through Manny.

Debris

His voice wet with tears and his body was a well of helplessness. "Erin, stop, please, no!" He didn't understand her detachment as a need to survive until later. Manny laughed while Andre fought. With the first bearing of Erin's thighs, she flinched and pulled back and Colin slapped her face hard, and Manny's fist knocked the wind out of Andre. He fell forward and was kicked in the stomach, a hot searing pain that made him fall on his knees. Still he tried to stand, the pain nothing compared to the sight of Erin crying. Manny hit him again. The thumps he would hardly remember. Everything else would come back to him in pieces, the pale skin of her belly, the way Colin pushed her on to the couch and fell on her, the bony thin strength of Manny, his laughter, and the sharp knee that made contact with Andre's balls, so he was on the ground trying to breathe, pulling air in deep hungry gasps, while Colin's white thighs were in view and his breathing grew more rapid. Andre clung to the walls in an attempt to stand and Manny thumped him in the stomach each time he had nearly made it. Manny never hit him on the face. There were no slaps to make his eyes water or his head spin so Andre was always able to see Erin.

Andre was on his knees crying when Colin rose from the couch and told Erin to hurry up and get decent because his ma would be back soon. His ma was told to come back at 4:30 and she always did what she was told. Colin buttoned his pants, then turned to Andre and said. "Are you scared of me now?"

****

"I didn't mean to," Andre would say to the guards and he would believe it when he remembered stumbling outside of number 12 John Street. It was hard to walk. His urine would have traces of blood from being hit in the kidney. At the hospital the nurses would find extensive bruising on his abdomen and back. The air felt dirty. He didn't want to look around him, to see other people walking here and there, oblivious and stupid and to think they might have passed the house without wondering about the noises because he'd screamed. He was sure he'd screamed and shouted her name, though it might have died quickly. How long had Manny waited before kicking him in the crotch? It was hard to know, seconds had become years, and then there'd been nothing but silence. Erin was beside him. She held onto his arm and leaned slightly towards him and he had to hold back his tears, though with every step the grief from the memory of her on that couch hardened a little more and the self-consciousness he'd first felt when he'd stumbled out of that house and the utter shame and disbelief turned inside him and he stood a little straighter, held Erin a little closer and stared a little harder at the people passing by.

He would never know when it came to him. It might have been at the house in John Street when he first saw Erin's face and he understood what she had meant by saying, *You help me, I'll help you.* Or it might have been from the first moment he met her and he was already afraid of losing her and every other meeting from then only pummeled the nail further into the ground, though it was on their walk to the estate that he understood he had no choice. As he neared the estate, he knew he didn't want Erin there. *You help me*, she'd said, but this he could spare her. She deserved at least this after what he had made happen.

They had not spoken one word in their near thirty minute walk. Neither had they let each other go. Her arms were around his and he held her hand so they resembled an old couple. When the houses were in view, he pulled away and the breath that came from her was a small dying cry. "It's okay," he said.

She'd stopped in her tracks and he thought of her that other day not long ago, though that seemed like decades now, when she'd opened the door in her tracksuit and walked slowly up the stairs. She had the same far away distant look and he could see her attempts to come back, like a tide moving in and out.

"No Andre," she said, when he told her he'd see her in her house.

"He'll be drunk," Andre said.

"No," she was starting to cry and her hands were clinging to him and he had to push her away. He hated himself for the gesture, and he hated Colin and Manny, and her father, and fucking Mrs. Neary and her nosiness, and Ronan and the whole lot of them. He was running now, but not as fast as he would have liked. His body was tender and he seemed to move up rather than forward. His body hated the contact on the ground. Each step made him cringe with the sharp pain in his back, but he was in the estate and moving down the row of houses towards Dan McEvoy's house. No one saw him that time. Mrs. Giles, like most residents, was getting her tea.

"It's a pity he went back," Mrs. Giles said. "That man really hurt him by all accounts."

Erin had started to run too. She wasn't far away when he reached the front door of the house and started to bang on the door, once, twice, he imagined her father on the armchair shouting fuck off and Andre went to the living room window and banged. He saw a flash of her father's body rising from the armchair and Andre prayed he was drunk. The smell when Dan opened the door left no doubt, but Andre didn't pause. He pushed past the man who stumbled backwards and asked, "What the fuck are you doing?"

His voice was slurred. A cigarette burned in his hands and Andre was up the stairs, the father shouted at him. Andre didn't want to stop because if he did he might think of what he was about to do and then it would be the end of everything. He felt he was running towards a wall at high speed, like the ads he'd seen for wearing seatbelts when the dummies crashed through the windows, and the cars became tiny things after driving into walls. He was on the top of the stairs now, thirteen steps, and then the

Debris

glass glinting at the bottom. Her father was still shouting. He'd thrown the cigarette out the front door and was coming up the stairs, but he could hardly walk. He gripped the banister and for a moment Andre thought he'd give up and go back to his seat and his drink. "You're a bollix," he said and the father's laughter surprised him, though the face was hard when the laughter stopped.

"In my own house," he said. He was nearly half way up the stairs when Erin appeared breathless. She could have called him then, could have said. "Don't," but she didn't. She watched and she seemed more fully present than she had since leaving the house on John Street and Andre understood that she'd survive that house because she had no choice. It was then he got the scent of violets, and it was like having an itch where he couldn't scratch. He couldn't take his eyes of Dan who was so close and so drunk. Each step brought a wobble and his mother was there, a witness, and Andre felt a tarnishing inside that might never turn bright again. He almost stepped back, and he might have if Erin was not there watching with a dire need. A shadow was on the landing, her long hair and a flash of pale skin, and he wouldn't look at his mother who he'd searched years for.

"You're not real," he said and he'd always think of this as the moment he grew up, not while fists had landed on his stomach and back, or when Dan McEvoy said, you want to see how fucking real I am, or when Erin called for her Da, so he looked behind at her, and he might have stumbled and fallen himself but not so hard and forceful, not so his head would crash against the bannister and he would continue to tumble until he smashed against the glass at the bottom. No Andre grew up when he let his mother go.

****

Erin ran screaming from her house and banged on Mrs. Giles's door. She was breathless and crying and could hardly make any sense. "He nearly killed him, please, please."

Mrs. Giles ran back to the house where Andre had not moved from the top of the stairs. He was sitting and staring in shock at the still body by the door and the trickle of blood that ran down Dan's head. Mrs. Giles was the one who called the police and an ambulance. She phoned Michelle then. Michelle was hardly there five minutes before half the estate in the middle of the chaos, and Andre's father came soon after and cried and held his son when he saw the beating Dan McEvoy had given him. Erin told the guards that he'd been running up the stairs after Andre when Andre pushed him away. Nobody could figure anything but self-defense. Erin and Andre were sitting in in the back of an ambulance with a blanket around their shoulders when Erin saw Ronan run towards them. So often, she had pleaded with him to tell her where her mother was and now she stared at his figure until he slowed from the force of it. They said nothing to each other. A crowd had gathered. Mrs. Giles told Ronan, "One of those children could have been killed," and she noticed Ronan's face grow pale and was sorry she'd spoken so openly to him. She wasn't surprised when he went running back to his house.

"What's going on?" his mother asked when he came bursting in. She'd stayed with Mary because she would not allow her to see anything unpleasant. "Ronan," she shouted, when he ran into his room, but she didn't persist. She might have known what he was going for, or she might have seen in his feverish wide-eyes and the quick darting movements the guilt that he needed to assuage. He dialed the number in London, and afterwards he would wonder on his mother's lack of reaction and questions, the way she stood loose by the kitchen door, but then he thought of nothing but the ringing phone. "Come on, come on," he said. He'd hated Marie and he'd hated the thought of Erin McEvoy having his father when he could not.

"Hello," his father said.

Ronan closed his eyes and said, "Is Marie there?"

Epilogue

The young man walking the London Street had black hair to his shoulders and a looseness in his walk that didn't deter from his nervous edge. He'd stop every so often to scan the crowd and his face would open with the thought of glimpsing her on the street. She would be listening to music and hardly aware of anyone she passed. She'd said once that the Walkman was her most prized possession, but that was years ago when she'd first gone to London with her mother. There had been many letters since. She'd written about Thomas and his strange quietness, how it made her feel tiny and then about the day he left. Her mother had locked herself in her bedroom for hours. When she'd come out, she'd taken Erin to McDonalds and told her never to mention Thomas again.

Erin wrote that she'd tried to go back to school, but it was impossible to concentrate and besides she needed to help her mother pay rent. She described her jobs, while Andre told her that he was the opposite. With Erin gone, he had little interest in anything other than books. He didn't go back to his old school. He'd written that he'd tried but didn't get past the gate, so he went to a school fifteen miles away. Ursula drove him every day.

He didn't write that he was coming to visit. Even in their letters, he detected a distance with her. He knew too much and Erin had started to become someone else in this large city where no one knew about her father or who she used to be. So Andre had stayed away while he was at school and for his first year at college. All that time, he'd forced himself to be happy with the letters sent from across the water, but he never forgot the feel of her leaning on him, her hands in his, and the way they'd hugged at the airport until Marie had to tell her it was time to go.

Coffee Republic was the name of the café Erin worked in. He had the address written on a piece of paper, though he'd known that by heart for weeks now. The crowd jostled around him, horns blared, buses weaved towards bus stops, passengers got on and off, and he noticed none of it. The café was ahead of him.

My hairs long now, she'd written once. *I wonder if you'd know me.* He had thought that a silly thing to write, but now he was afraid they wouldn't recognize each other, that he'd walk into the café and they would nod as if they were strangers. She might bring him a menu and smile and there would be no way to speak.

There were a few customers sitting by the window, a couple talking, a young woman sitting quietly stirring her coffee. She stopped stirring when she saw him. Her hair was long and tied back, but he would

155

have known her anywhere. For a moment they didn't move, but merely watched each other through the window of a café.

Author Acknowledgements

The journey to 'Debris' would have been a lot more difficult without support from my family and friends. Thank you to my mother, who reads everything I write, but is still trying to get me to write a romance, and to my three wonderful sisters, Rachel, Susan and Elizabeth, who are all artists in their own way. Thank you to my very first writing group in Galway and my first readers Bernie and Sonya, for being my sounding boards. To Sharon, my rock, and Jackie for holding me up whenever I needed it and always knowing how to make me laugh even from across the Atlantic.

I am eternally grateful to my family in Boston, Gloria, Davor and Noelia whose generosity of spirit knows no bounds. For Kate, who saw me doing a Masters at Emerson College and wouldn't let me give up, you're amazing. For Sarah and your years of friendship and providing my second home in Maine, to Anthony for reading all the books I've sent you, even though the first ones were terrible. Jen for our dinners, readings and advice, Christy for always asking the right questions and making me really think of what I want to say, Ryan for taking the time to give me feedback even when you're moving States and organizing your wedding, Araceli and Giovanna for your continuous support and friendship, and of course Kim for the late night talks and wine. I'm also grateful to Corinne Anderson and all at Ink Smith Publishing for saying yes, and being so great to work with.

And a special everlasting thanks to my husband and three daughters, Leyla, Amelie and Cameron, for always being there.

L.M. Brown

CPSIA information can be obtained
at www.ICGtesting.com
Printed in the USA
FSHW04n2145230418
47185FS